Praise for Cherrie Lynn's *Rock Me*

"Rock Me by Cherrie Lynn is one hot read...a great story that touches on the prejudices of family and the constraints they place upon their members...I loved this story and would recommend it as a priority read."

~ *Two Lips Reviews*

"You want a story that's hot from the word go? Then you very much so need to read Rock Me... This is one for my keeper shelf."

~ *Long and Short Reviews*

"Stories that suck us in and make us have emotional reactions to the characters and their decisions are my favorite kinds. Cherrie Lynn's style and her expert use of voice draw you in and her great story keeps you there."

~ *Happily Ever After Reviews*

Look for these titles by

Cherrie Lynn

Now Available:

Unleashed

Sweet Disgrace

Far From Heaven

Rock Me

Cherrie Lynn

Samhain Publishing, Ltd.
577 Mulberry Street, Suite 1520
Macon, GA 31201
www.samhainpublishing.com

Rock Me

Print ISBN: 978-1-60928-080-2
Digital ISBN: 978-1-60504-955-7

Editing by Linda Ingmanson
Cover by Natalie Winters

First Samhain Publishing, Ltd. electronic publication: May 2010
First Samhain Publishing, Ltd. print publication: April 2011

Dedication

To my own bad boy hero and our awesome offspring. You guys rock! Special thanks to the Romance Divas for all the support during JulNoWriMo.

Chapter One

It was only a tattoo. A cute, colorful little design that would be on her skin, oh, forever, and no one would see it unless she wanted them to. Yet Candace Andrews sat in her car staring up at the neon sign of the tattoo parlor as if it were some harbinger of doom.

It's not that big a deal, she told herself. *Everyone I know has at least one.*

"I think you're insane."

Well, almost everyone. Candace's best friend sat beside her, her features washed in the orangey hues of early twilight. Even that didn't soften Macy's disdainful expression.

"Why?"

"You've absolutely gone mental."

Candace waved her to silence and popped open her car door. Macy's anxiety always seemed to give her a firmer sense of control. "You're the one who said I need to celebrate."

"Yeah, celebrate, not take complete leave of your senses. Your parents will *kill* you. Hell, your parents will kill *me.*"

"They won't see it."

Macy grabbed her arm before Candace could make a move to exit her car into the mild, late April evening air. "Where do you plan on getting it? Don't tattoo your butt, Candace."

"I won't! And it's not as if I'm going to run off and join a biker gang because of one patch of ink on my skin. I swear, sometimes I think you're on Daddy's payroll." Wrenching her arm from her friend's grasp, she got out and bent down to peer at Macy's stricken face. "Now, are you coming, or are you going to sit out here and pout?"

Trying to suppress her trembling as Macy grumbled her way out of the car, Candace let her gaze crawl over the ultra-modern exterior of Dermamania. She'd never been here before, even though she knew the owner. He was her cousin's ex-boyfriend, and he was working tonight. His truck was parked in the shadows around the side of the building, its color a blue so dark it was a shade away from black. If he hadn't been here, then her birthday wish would've been put off for another day. Brian was *the* guy to go to in town if you wanted ink.

God, she couldn't stop shaking. But she was here and she couldn't back out now. She wasn't a huge fan of needles, especially if they were going anywhere near her skin. Whether it was the thought of pain that had her pulse fluttering or the thought of seeing Brian, she didn't know. When he was dating Michelle, Candace's heart had hit the pit of her stomach on more than one occasion under the cool appraisal of those dark blue eyes. He was the very definition of off-limits, but that didn't dampen the effect he had on her.

"I'm not watching," Macy informed her as they approached the entrance.

"I'm not asking you to."

"You have *one half* of a wine cooler on your birthday and this is what happens?"

"Oh, shut up. That was hours ago."

Inside, it seemed someone had cranked the air conditioning up to levels more appropriate for the dead of summer rather than mid-spring. Three tattooists glanced up from the clients they were working on without interrupting their stream of chatter. Candace naturally zoned in on the one girl who appeared to be in a bit of distress while getting a butterfly colored on her inner ankle. Her face looked pained, her teeth gnawing her bottom lip.

Candace swallowed thickly, trying to buoy her flagging courage. She'd been prepared to run straight to Brian's side, but he wasn't anywhere in sight.

"What can I do for you ladies?" the guy tattooing the butterfly asked, barely looking up from his work. He was bald with a pointy goatee and a large plug in the earlobe Candace could see from her angle.

"Is Brian here?"

"He is, but he's not, know what I'm sayin'?"

"Um, no?"

The guy still didn't look up from filling in the butterfly wing with hot pink. It was going to be really pretty when he was done, and she felt a jolt of excitement despite her jitters.

"He's not seeing clients tonight."

And just like that, her heart sank. It had taken every ounce of courage she'd mustered to walk in here, and there wouldn't be any left to work with later on. This was a one-shot deal. "Oh. Well, I know him, I mean, do you think I could talk to him for a second?"

Mr. Goatee shrugged and turned his head toward the rear of the building. "Hey, B! Some people here to see you." He went back to coloring without giving Candace or Macy—who had stood frozen during their exchange, her eyes darting around fearfully—any further notice.

She could say one thing for Brian's employees: they were intent upon their work. As she took a seat in the waiting area near the door with Macy following her every move, she was impressed with the neat, shiny appearance of the place. The walls weren't papered with flash like in some of the places she'd seen, but with abstract art and posters of rock bands and Kat Von D. A music video played on a couple of plasma screens, one at each end of the room. Because some of Brian's taste for the darker stuff had rubbed off on her while he was dating Michelle, she recognized it as Nine Inch Nails' "Deep".

"This is...different," Macy muttered, her gaze on one of the screens. She was more accustomed to Toby Keith.

"Yeah, this is a good one."

"Didn't realize you were into them."

"I got into a lot of different bands because of Brian. He would let me borrow CDs."

"Well. Learn something new every day."

Candace shrugged. "If I broadcast the fact that I like rock music, even some heavy metal, you and my family would be convinced I was worshiping the devil or something."

"Oh, I would not." Macy's voice pitched lower. "Michelle dated the guy. No one said anything about her."

"Are you kidding?" Candace whispered as loud as she dared. She was pretty sure the sultry beat of the music, the buzzing needles and the jokes flying fast and furious drowned out their conversation. "It drove her parents insane. And mine, even. She liked Brian a lot, but she never really got into his scene."

All the parental units would have been ecstatic over Michelle dating someone from Brian's family if she'd only chosen the right brother. Candace had always thought it a cruel trick of fate on all of them that Brian had been stuck in the middle of an affluent family who expected the children to become doctors or lawyers. Among his siblings—his brother Evan the lawyer and his sister Gabby, who would soon start med school—he stuck out like a zebra among sheep, and by all accounts, he seemed to like it that way.

"Somebody better be dead or dying..."

She'd been so caught up in her thoughts that she missed his emergence from the door behind the counter, but that deep voice slid down her spine like caressing hands. Whether it was gentle or teasing or harsh, it always seemed to flow over her skin, manifesting itself in skitters of gooseflesh.

He froze mid-step when he saw her. It might have been wishful thinking, but she could've sworn his face lit up. "Or just sitting there looking pretty," he finished with a heart-stopping grin.

She lost her breath. It had been months. Six, to be exact. Much too long to go without feasting her eyes on the only real object of desire she'd ever had. But she wasn't here for that. At least, that's what she had to keep telling herself.

Given that smile, she could sympathize with Michelle's heartbreak over losing him soon after their trip to Hawaii for Evan's wedding. The details of their demise were fuzzy, but it didn't matter. Candace would weep oceans to lose a guy with a smile like that. It was infectious, and she was on her feet and crossing the room toward him almost before she realized it.

Brian folded his arms on the countertop as she approached. "Hey, sunshine. What brings you out?"

Whatever the reason he often called her that, it made her giggly as a teenager. "Guess."

Brian's gaze flickered over to Macy, who had somehow mustered the courage to follow her to the counter. His smile intensified. "Bringing your friend in for a tongue ring."

Candace laughed as Macy blanched and stepped back in horror. She grabbed the other girl's arm before she could bolt for the door. "God, no. She's a weenie." *And so am I, truth be known.* Why in the world was she acting so tough? One touch of the needle might cause her to dissolve in hysterics.

"And you?" Brian asked, one dark eyebrow raised.

"I was kind of hoping for a tattoo."

"There's no 'kind of' to it, girl. You get it or you don't."

"I know that." She tried to keep her gaze from straying to his arms resting on the counter. He was wearing a form-fitting black shirt with sleeves so long they almost covered his hands, but she knew that underneath it, the flesh of both his arms was a riot of color from his shoulders to his wrists.

Pity that it was all hidden from her sight now. She thought his sleeves were beautiful, and always struggled not to stare...actually, on second thought, maybe it was best he was covered. After going so long without seeing him, she might have very well embarrassed herself. How often had she fantasized about running her fingertips along all those lines and patterns and hues, deciphering all the meandering shapes, exploring the statements he'd found profound enough to mark on his skin for all time...?

Plenty of times. She'd felt horribly guilty about every single one. But now Michelle was out of the picture, and in a happy relationship. Besides, it didn't hurt to simply admire the scenery, did it?

Tonight, from head to toe, Brian looked quite subdued. For him, anyway. She was tempted to ask him what was going on. His hair was its natural lustrous black—she'd seen it every vivid color in the rainbow—worn a little long so that it fell into his face. Not shaggy or messy like she so hated to see on guys, but silky and gorgeous and touchable... *Okay, down, girl, stop right there.*

Even his eyebrow rings were MIA. Normally he had two side-by-side in his right eyebrow. Something was definitely up in his world.

Maybe he had a date later. Some ultra-gorgeous conservative type he desperately wanted to impress. Maybe she wouldn't appreciate his body art. The very thought, speculative as it was, made Candace seethe. Brian was Brian. If he had to change for someone, anyone, he didn't need them.

She cleared her throat, trying to chase the images away. "I do want a tattoo. It's my birthday and I'm feeling rebellious."

His perfect lips quirked at one corner. "You want me to do it, don't you?"

She nodded and tried her best not to pout. "But they said you weren't seeing clients tonight."

He tugged up one shirtsleeve and checked his watch. She caught a flash of his vibrant skin and felt her heart plummet to her toes. "I have an hour or so." *So he does have some place to be.* "I can get it done unless you want something massive."

Candace laughed and held up her hands. "Oh, no. Nothing like that." Now, *where* she wanted it was another matter.

"What did you have in mind?"

"I have an idea, but can I look through some of your designs?" She tilted her head toward the poster displays.

"Yeah. There's plenty of flash here, too, especially smaller stuff like you're probably looking for." He leaned down behind the counter and produced a couple of black, bursting-at-the-seams photo albums, sliding them toward her. "But don't just settle for anything. If you don't see something here that grabs you, I can draw up anything you want. You might not be able to get it tonight, since I don't have a lot of time, but it would be worth it in the end."

"Now you're making me feel I'm being way too hasty," she said, flipping open one of the books. To her amazement, Macy leaned over to study the pictures, as well. Some of them were color drawings, but others were live shots of fresh tattoos, the bearer's skin still reddened. Candace's stomach flipped over on itself. *Please God, don't let me faint when this all goes down.*

"Some people are too hasty about it," Brian said, and she could practically feel the warmth of his scrutiny on the top of her head, like some freakish kind of osmosis. Or maybe she was imagining it. Her thoughts tended to run rampant when she was near him, all sorts of crazy images flashing through her head.

"I can't see wanting something that bad," Macy interjected. "On my body. Forever." Candace fought the urge to elbow her in the ribs.

"No?" Brian asked.

"Absolutely not."

Candace glanced up as he moved away from them and pushed open the half-door at the end of the counter. "Come here and let me show you what I've been working on. It'll just take a second."

He led them through the door he'd exited earlier, down a short hallway and into a sparse room with ample lighting and little else except a slanted drawing board. She found it hard to pull her gaze away from his dark-clad figure in front of her, the way the breadth of his shoulders stretched the fabric of his shirt, the way his black cargo pants hugged the curves of his butt. It was one she could imagine sinking her fingernails into. No question about it, he was magnificent eye candy. Why was she surprised to be so vividly reminded of that fact?

"Check this out," he said, and her gaze followed his to the drawing he'd been laboring over. Next to it was tacked a picture of a beautiful little girl, dark-haired and smiling with her chin resting on her small fists. He'd transferred it to paper perfectly, only he'd managed to make her look somehow ethereal, like an angel. On a banner beneath her likeness, in beautiful, flowing script, were the words "Too Beautiful for Earth".

"Oh," Candace breathed. There was nothing else to say—and she feared she would burst into tears if she tried to conjure words.

"Doing this on a guy's back next week. Starting it, anyway. It'll take several sessions. She's his five-year-old daughter who died in a car accident." Brian's eyes were intense as he scrutinized his work. "I think it's coming along pretty well. I hope he likes how I've done it."

"It's…amazing," Macy said softly. Candace cut a glance at her and saw her friend was transfixed by the graceful lines and angelic beauty of the drawing. She couldn't suppress a grin. Brian's talent could astound the most hardened critic.

"Thanks." He actually looked sheepish, shoving his hands into his pockets. "I just wanted to show you how it's possible to want something on your body forever. How could he ever regret this, even when he's eighty years old?"

"That's the big argument, isn't it?" Macy asked. "People always say 'You'll be sorry you did that when you're old and wrinkled and it looks like crap'."

"I hear it all the time. But I'd rather look back and regret something I did when I was young and crazy, than look back and regret something I never had the courage to do, and realize it's too late."

"Excellent point," Candace murmured, and if her mind hadn't been completely made up before, it was now. She wanted to get started. "But I don't want to make you late, Brian. Are you sure we have time?"

"Absolutely." He reached over and rumpled her hair, and she wanted to groan. It was such a you're-like-my-kid-sister thing to do. "Let's go find you something."

The books were still out on the counter and there were more people in the waiting area when they emerged from the back. Candace resumed her search for the perfect tattoo as Brian surveyed the shop, which had every chair filled. "We'll have to go in one of the back rooms," he said.

"I was going to ask if we could, anyway." She tried to keep her voice even and nonchalant as she said it, but she saw his gaze dart toward her out of the corner of her eye. Her heart kicked up to a frantic pace. It was finally out there.

"Yeah? Why?"

"Because of, um...where I want it."

She sensed his grin rather than saw it. "Where is that?"

"I'll show you when we get there."

"I could have one of the girls do it if you'd rather—"

"No. You." She struggled to keep her hands steady as she flipped a page. Macy, thumbing through the other book, took that moment to let out a startled yelp. Candace looked over to see that she'd stumbled upon the pictures of body piercings. Of the genital variety, to be more exact. Oh, hell. Macy was flushing crimson to her hair roots. On the page beneath her stricken face was the *male* genital piercing section.

Candace choked on an embarrassed laugh, feeling her own blood pool hotly in her cheeks. Brian snickered.

"Okay, I can't deal with that," Macy was babbling. "That's too much for me. Why anyone would want to—"

"It enhances sex," he said, as if the answer should be obvious.

"The sex I've had was just fine; I don't see the need to torture oneself to make it better."

"That sounds like a problem," Brian told her, and Candace felt like she was watching a tennis match as the two went back and forth.

Macy's eyebrows were in her hair. "What problem?"

"The sex you've had was just 'fine'. Sounds like a problem to me." He sent Candace a slow wink that turned her knees to mush.

"What, are you saying you've got a...doohickey like that in your...?"

Brian's smile was long suffering. "That 'doohickey' is a Prince Albert. I only started out with one of those. Eventually I went to an apadravya. Gotta think of the ladies." He tapped the page, his grin as wicked as sin on Sunday. "In fact, you never know, one of them might be me."

Macy pushed away from the counter, having reached the limits of mortification she was willing to endure. Candace tried not to glance down at any of the pictures in question but couldn't help herself. She had to sneak a peek. Some of them were...well, really impressive, and she wondered if—

"So are we gonna do this, honey?" he asked, and she looked up into his eyes. They were a beautiful, mysterious shade of dark blue she didn't think she'd ever seen before. He must wear contacts. Her breath seared through her lungs.

"I've decided. Let's do it."

Chapter Two

"I have to apologize for my friend." Candace settled herself on the padded table in one of the small back rooms. "I love her dearly, but not the giant stick up her ass."

Brian laughed. "Sorry if I embarrassed you, but I couldn't resist squicking her out."

"So…you were joking, then?" Inquiring minds had to know.

"About the apa or about putting it on display out there?"

"Both, I guess."

"I'll never tell." He winked at her before going back to fiddling with his equipment. She hadn't a clue what any of it was, but it looked scary, and she admired the confidence and efficiency with which he handled it. He'd already gone over all their sanitation techniques as if she were any other customer and he'd selected the colors he would need, which were only red and black. The inks sat in two tiny cups on a table beside her.

She'd chosen a small blood-red heart design with black tribal art extending out from both sides. Brian had already transferred the purplish outline to her skin…so low on her belly that even the flimsiest bikini bottoms in existence would probably cover most of it up. She often went swimming in her parents' pool and there was *no freaking way* they could ever see it, so unless she wanted it smack on her butt or her boob—which she didn't—it was the only place she could think of.

Shedding her jeans to mid-thigh and pulling her underwear down until it only covered her most private area had almost been the deal-breaker. When she'd planned out her act of rebellion, she hadn't really let herself think that far ahead. If she had, she might never have gotten through the front door.

He'd made her stand while he got down on his knees and rubbed the transfer onto her skin. Thank God she'd waxed. She could only hope he hadn't noticed how her legs quaked and her nipples beaded at the feel of his fingertips gently smoothing the stencil on. He hadn't so much as blinked at her dishabille, and she had to keep in mind that he'd probably had hundreds of girls drop their pants in here to get him to do far more risqué body mod than her little tattoo.

Now, lying on the table with her design perfectly centered and ready to be inked, she stared at the ceiling and tried to concentrate on keeping her breathing steady.

"Nervous?" he asked, and she looked over to find his steady gaze on her. "You have a certain deer-in-headlights look I'm quite familiar with."

"Yeah. Really no use in denying it."

"It'll be all right. Most people compare it to a bee sting."

"Which isn't very fun."

"Not fun, but nothing you can't take, right?"

"If you say so."

He chuckled. "If you need a break, tell me, but I'm betting you won't. Do you want me to do a dry pass so you can get an idea of what it's like?"

Candace considered. "Better not. I might chicken out, but if you go ahead and start, I'm kind of stuck going through with it, right?" Her eyes widened as his black-Latex- covered hands tore open a package containing a needle. "Holy..."

"Now settle down. It's not a shot at the doctor's office. You just get the very tip." He wheeled the stool he was sitting on closer to her. At that moment she *was* reminded of being in her doctor's office, a dreaded event that always made her panic.

Oh, Jesus. There was no way. She couldn't get through this. Closing her eyes, she tried to concentrate on the music filtering through the speaker system. It was Killswitch Engage, one of Brian's favorite bands, if she remembered correctly. The singer had an incredible voice. She focused on that rather than the sounds of him getting his machine assembled—*machine*, he'd told her, not *gun*—and testing it out. But that whirring buzz whisked her straight from her doctor's office to the dentist's chair, and nothing on earth caused her more anxiety than that. Being helpless, immobile, at the mercy of someone wielding an instrument capable of causing her great, agonizing pain...

What in the hell had ever made her think she could do this?

"Have you ever had anyone start to get the tattoo, freak out and not be able to finish?"

"Don't worry about that. Everyone's experience is unique, and yours is the only one that matters."

Great. A whimper escaped her lips before she could stop it even though he had yet to lay the first hand on her.

She must have caught his attention. "Breathe," he said calmly, and only then did she realize she wasn't doing so. "Slowly. In through your nose, out through your mouth." She filled her lungs to capacity and exhaled as he instructed, but she was still too frightened to open her eyes and see how close she was to feeling that needle in her skin. "Keep it up. You're gonna be fine."

"I'm glad you're so sure of that."

"How old are you today, sunshine?"

She smiled, and suddenly wanted to cry. Yeah, that would be utterly cool of her. But he was trying to put her at ease, and maybe she was a fool of the worst sort, but it made her feel cherished somehow. "Twenty-three."

Daring a glance at his profile through her lashes, she saw one corner of his mouth tug up. "Twenty-three," he echoed wistfully. "That was a good year."

"Oh, yeah? What was so good about it?"

He paused before answering. "Hell, I couldn't really tell you. Just the mere fact that I was younger than I am now, I guess."

"You talk like twenty-seven is old."

"Twenty-eight. My birthday was in January."

"Oh, right. I haven't seen you in so long. Happy belated birthday, since I didn't get to tell you then." She studied him while she had the opportunity. He'd slapped a black baseball cap on his head and twisted it around backwards to keep his hair out of his eyes. Dressed all in black from head to toe now, down to the gloves he wore, he looked ready to pull off a burglary later tonight.

His olive skin was maddeningly without blemish. Exquisite lips, full and defined, were framed by a goatee that looked so sleek and soft... How would it feel against her skin if he ever kissed her? Rough or silken? Would it tickle or scratch? She would never find out, but a girl could dream.

Yeah, a dream some other lucky wench would probably experience for real tonight. What the hell was an apadra-whatever, anyway? She'd have to hit Google as soon as she got home just to figure out what he might have going on down there. She had a feeling he'd only been teasing about the picture, but with the piercing? She would bet good money he had it.

"Thanks." He smiled at her. There was a hint of wickedness behind it, a wickedness she'd love to see fully unleashed. On her.

Maybe it had been a mistake coming here. She didn't want to spend the rest of her birthday depressed and pining over something she didn't need and would never have. For so long, Brian had been labeled Michelle's Boyfriend, pretty to look at, but nothing else. She'd been unprepared for the intensified effect he would have on her now that he'd shaken off that relationship.

"Are you ready to do this?" he asked.

One more deep breath... "Yes." She closed her eyes again, unwilling to give him any more reason to think she was a total wimp.

"Get through the first few minutes, then your endorphins will kick in and give you a thrill ride."

"Riiight."

His chuckle turned into an outright laugh when the first touch of his gloved fingers on her lower tummy nearly jolted her off the table. So much for not appearing wimpy. "Candace, you can't do that when the needle hits," he scolded.

"Darn it," she grumbled, opening her eyes and drawing another breath. "Okay. Just do it. I'm ready. Oh, God."

"Here we go."

She forced her gaze downward, when it suddenly seemed far more ominous to not see what was going on down there. Even more striking than the sight of the needle hovering over her skin was Brian's presence there, leaning so close to that part of her. She could smell the mint of his gum. Her heart was racing like a frightened rabbit fleeing a predator.

With a firm touch he pulled her skin gently taut, and she sank her teeth into her bottom lip as the very tip of the needle nudged her. She could imagine those fingers, so close to the lacy edge of her panties, slipping lower to do far more pleasurable things... his touch would be at once gentle and confident in his abilities, as it was now.

Her eyes closed again. She bet he would know just how to stroke her, just how much pressure to exert to leave her moaning and gasping for more...

"How does that feel?"

"Hmmm?" she asked dreamily. Did he even have to ask? It would feel magnificent.

"Not so bad, is it?"

Oh, but she *wanted* it to be bad, bad in the very best way. Just as the outrageous thought flashed through her mind, she realized that the needle tip had been dragging through her skin for the past few seconds and she'd hardly noticed. "Um...that's *it*?"

"That's it. All that freaking out for nothing."

The buzzing went on, the needle leaving a sting in its wake. He paused often to wipe excess ink off her skin with a towel, and she found that the hardest part was lying still under his hands. She wanted to writhe and arch against them. Force them lower. Being trapped and helpless under his control was turning something on inside her, a burning need that had her stomach flipping slow somersaults. An aching throb built between her thighs, inches away from where his left hand rested on her skin.

She licked her lips, watching his intense expression, his unrelenting focus, and wondered what he would think if he knew what was going on in her head, her body. What he was making her feel.

When the pleasure-tempered pain of the needle caused her to break out in a fine sheen of sweat, she was wholly grateful they kept it rather cool in here. She began to watch the slow, easy rise and fall of his shoulders as he breathed. Her own rhythm was growing far too ragged and needy, threatening to dissolve into full-on panting.

Think about that Probability and Statistics final you have coming up. That should do it.

"Still with me?" he asked.

Oh, didn't he see what he was doing to her? She glanced down before answering. Roughly half the outline was done. Still a while to go. Thank goodness. She wasn't ready for this to be over yet, because she couldn't imagine ever finding this agonized bliss again. Unless she came back to him for more. If she did that, she'd end up covered in ink from head to toe.

"Um, I think so." *And please don't notice how my voice is quivering.*

No such luck. For the first time since he started, he drew away and faced her fully. She was certain her cheeks were flushed and her forehead was glistening. "Do you need anything? A drink?" he asked.

That sounded heavenly, but she was probably already making him late for whatever he was doing later. On the other hand, if she was keeping him from some female undeserving of his attentions, that was okay by her. "I'm fine."

"We'll keep going, then. It's gonna look tight, girl."

"Okay." She supposed that was a good thing.

He gave a single nod and got back to work. "So what else have you done for your birthday?"

Now she was actually going to have to carry on a normal conversation with him when she was on the verge of orgasm. Never in her life had she imagined she would ever pray *not* to have one. But how embarrassing would that be?

Her earlier question rephrased in her mind. She shouldn't have asked him whether anyone had ever freaked out and been unable to finish. She should've inquired about how many of them lost control and begged him to take them right here. "N-not much. Macy and I have been hanging out for most of the day."

"That's it?"

She flinched as he passed over a particularly sensitive spot, clenching her teeth when he wiped it with the towel. It was growing more and more difficult to resist rubbing her thighs together. "Pretty much."

"I figured some lucky guy would be in the picture by now."

Her short bark of laughter was immediately regrettable, and this time, her wince had nothing to do with the burning scrape of the needle tip. "No, no guys, lucky or otherwise. Oh, God, that's starting to get to me."

"The needle, or the lack of guys?"

Both. "I meant the needle."

"You're doing great."

"Where are you going later?" she blurted, and was momentarily aghast at her impulsiveness. Chalk it up to desperately needing a distraction from the towering need pulsing at her core.

"Family function. My brother's birthday is next weekend, but we're all getting together tonight. I don't know why now and not next weekend." He shrugged. "I was just informed my presence was required. Hey, did you hear I'm an uncle now?"

Ah, no date. So much sweet relief swooped through her that she momentarily forgot everything else...until she realized that didn't mean he wasn't seeing someone already. What if he had a girlfriend? "Yes, I'd heard. Congratulations. I bet he's so cute. You must be excited."

"It's pretty cool."

"No wonder you're...um, dressed up a bit. Or down. Or whatever." It was hard to resist the urge to touch his eyebrow, where the two rings usually resided. Heck, who was she kidding. It was hard to resist grabbing him and pulling him on top of her.

Especially when he grinned like he did then. "My mom will be there, and my body art drives her nuts."

Candace could sympathize, but it drove her nuts in an entirely different way.

"I try to accommodate her," he went on. "Sometimes. Most days I just don't give a damn."

"How long has it taken you to get all your tattoos?"

"I started when I was eighteen. It's been a couple of years since I got a new one, and to tell you the truth, I think I'm done. And I never was about the really extreme shit. I'm actually pretty fucking tame, by some standards." He shook his head, his gaze still intent upon his work.

She repressed a sigh. Nothing about him was tame, at least, not to her. She'd been brought up in such strict surroundings and her friends monitored so carefully, she hadn't been around people like him growing up. Homeschooling had kept her sheltered from the world most of her life. It wasn't that her parents were religious freaks or anything like that, they just thought most things were...beneath them.

College, needless to say, had been an utter, almost incapacitating shock. It had taken some begging, fast talking, and several tears to get her parents to allow her to attend the neighboring university. They had only given in on the condition that she live here in town under their watchful eye, and commute forty-five minutes every day, which was the only plus they could see in not sending her off somewhere smaller and way more prestigious. She'd accepted those terms grudgingly.

As much as the thought of having her own life away from

here had appealed, in the end she'd balked, so she really had no one to blame but herself that she was twenty-three and still living a life dictated by her mom and dad.

Not for long. Her new tattoo was only the first in a series of changes she wanted to make. Soon. There was no reason she and her parents couldn't coexist in the town she grew up in and loved without having them run every aspect of her life.

The coloring part of the process wasn't nearly as intense, and it even tickled, wringing a giggle from her every so often. If she did it on purpose a couple of times just to watch Brian's lips curl up and his eyes crinkle at the corners, well, he didn't have to know that.

When he sat up straight and announced it was done, she didn't think she had ever felt such a rush of excitement or pride in herself. She'd done it. Without utter embarrassment. The little black-and-blood-red design was perfect, with remarkable shading. And it was all hers, something her parents couldn't take away even if they did find out.

"It's beautiful!" she exclaimed. "Thank you so much."

"You're most welcome." He lightly smeared it with some kind of ointment, and she bit her lip on a sigh. That touch of his was driving her out of her mind.

"Did that hurt?" he asked, and she glanced up to see him looking at her with his brow creased.

"No, it's fine." It did hurt, actually, but nowhere near the way he thought.

He put a bandage over it, then reached in a nearby drawer to pull out a sheet of paper with aftercare instructions. "Quick overview. Wait at least two hours before you take the bandage off, then wash it with antibacterial soap. Generic is fine. No Neosporin, but coat it with Bacitracin. Keep it thin. No baths or swimming or hot tubs for two weeks at least. And, I'm just saying, if the lucky guy happens to come along in that time, be creative. You don't want any persistent rubbing and you damn sure don't want anyone else's sweat on it until it's healed."

She blushed fast and furious, stopping short of blurting out that that *definitely* wouldn't be a problem. "Got it." She took the paper from him and folded it in half, hoping he didn't notice if her cheeks were as red as they felt. But he had busied himself with cleaning up. She slid off the table and buttoned her jeans as fast as she could while his back was turned. All the while three little words kept playing in her head: *I did it! I did it!*

Man, she could see how this could become addictive.

"So what do you want next?" Brian asked with a grin. He closed the last cabinet and turned to face her, crossing his arms and leaning against the counter. At that moment, with his dark eyes twinkling at her, she wanted to maul him. She'd never really noticed before that he had dimples. They took the edge off what ordinarily was a fairly intimidating appearance. How could a guy who smiled like that be in any way bad for you?

But she bet even a guy with dimples would have no qualms about planting her back hard against the wall and...

"Are you reading my mind?" she asked. Oh, wow. That had sounded way too flirty for her own ears. "I was just thinking it could be addictive."

"No need to read minds, you've got the look. And I know how it feels. How do you think I ended up like this?" He tugged up one sleeve, flashing a precious glimpse at his artwork.

"I love your tattoos," she said, a moment of boldness sweeping her away. "And your piercings too. It's a shame you took them out."

Was that a darkening in his expression? Suddenly, there seemed to be a shift in the air between them, and chill bumps skittered up her spine. She promptly hugged herself.

"Oh, they'll be back ASAFP, I promise you that." His voice was warm and smooth as a caress, refueling the mini-fantasy she'd indulged as she'd been lying on that table. If her blush had receded at all, it resurged full force. He'd stripped off his black gloves and she couldn't resist staring at his long, tapered fingers resting on his arm. Now if he touched her, it would be nothing but flesh against flesh...hers soft and yielding, his hard and demanding...

She had to stop this. Now. Taking a breath, she reached for

her purse and withdrew her wallet. "Um, how much do I owe you?"

He shook his head. "Happy birthday, sunshine."

"Brian, no. I came barging in here and dragged you out and probably made you late, so there's no way I'm not—"

He held a finger in front of his lips. "Shhh. No arguing. Would you throw a gift back in my face? Nope. So there you go."

"But..." She fumbled around with logic and finally gave up. "Oh, all right. I guess if you insist."

"I do."

She put her wallet back in her purse. They were silent for a moment, awkwardness like a third party in the room. She wanted to hug him, ask him if she could do anything for him. Maybe make him dinner one night or...*something.* Would that be too much like asking him out? Crap. It would.

"So, um...thanks again."

He pushed himself away from the counter, blinking as if some spell over him had been broken. "Hey, sure thing. Let me walk you out."

They emerged to a roomful of laughter, where Brian's employees and their clients were fully engaged in a very loud, very boisterous conversation about funny names for sexual positions. Incredibly, Macy was laughing along with them from her spot in the waiting area as she fiddled with her iPhone.

"...then there's the Dutch Rudder, like the dude was talking about in *Zack and Miri Make a Porno.*"

"That movie was friggin' hilarious."

"Haven't seen it. What's the Dutch Rudder?"

"Aw, man, it's when someone else holds your arm and moves it for you while you're—"

"Hey," Brian interrupted. "Ladies on the floor. Last thing I need is fucking sexual harassment issues."

"Nobody's getting harassed in here, boss." The bald, goateed guy, who was now in such a jovial mood, looked at Candace. "Are you harassed?"

She laughed. “Not me.”

He looked at a cute girl with a blue pixie cut Candace hadn’t seen before. She was perched at the computer behind the counter. “Are you harassed, Janelle?”

“Disgustedly intrigued, maybe, but not harassed,” she said with a grin, not taking her eyes off the flat screen monitor.

“Yeah, well, *offended* is enough to get my ass in hot water, and my brother’s a lawyer, so don’t argue with that. You guys save it for the bedroom.” Brian gave Candace’s shoulder a squeeze as he moved out from behind her, and she swore the warmth of his touch lingered as surely as the burning low down on her abdomen from her new tattoo. She missed his presence immediately.

“Or *not*,” Janelle said in horror as he joined her behind the counter. “You should have heard some of the stuff they were saying.”

“I can imagine.” He glanced at Candace and motioned her over. She couldn’t shake the feeling that Janelle was sizing her up a bit as she approached. Brian plucked a business card from the holder and scribbled something on the back of it before sliding it across the countertop to her. “That’s my cell number. I’m sure you won’t have any problems, but if you do, hit me up if I’m not here.”

“Oh, thanks.” She’d guard that little rectangle with her life. Giving in to a wild impulse, she picked up the pen he’d just laid down and scribbled her own number on the flap of an open envelope lying between them. Hopefully it wasn’t anything important. “And, um, there’s mine, just…um, just ’cause.”

Without daring to look at him, she dropped the pen on the table and all but ran over to the waiting area. Crap. What had she *done*?

Macy stood, shouldering the strap of her purse. “So? How was it?” she murmured.

“It was…*awesome*.”

A frown marred her friend’s features as she seemed to study Candace from her hairline to her toes. “You did only get a tattoo, right? Nothing else you need to share with me?"

"Oh, please. Come on."

The argument over what constituted "offensive" continued to rage as Candace glanced over at Brian again, finding that his gaze was following her despite whatever he was currently saying. Her heart took a swan dive into the pit of her stomach. It decided to stay there and rattle around weakly at the sight of him holding a white slip of paper in his hand, torn from the envelope she'd scribbled her number on in a fit of insanity. He smiled at her as he pulled out his wallet and stuck it in there.

No shoving it in his pocket to be lost in the wash, she thought. *He's protecting it.*

Along with a dozen others, probably. Stupid girl.

Mr. Goatee wouldn't give it up. "I'm just sayin', man. 'Offensive' is a relative term. For instance, I get more offended watching Skinemax than I do watching a porn star get plowed. That softcore shit is utterly offensive to me."

As they were stepping out the door, she heard Brian's deep, rich voice one last time, speaking to his employee. "Shut up before I make you perform the Angry Cobra." The door swung shut on the howls of laughter that followed.

"Those guys are sick," Macy observed.

"I think they're hilarious."

"Then you're sick too."

Chapter Three

Brian needed a cigarette in the worst way.

It was habit: he walked out of the parlor after work, he reached in his pocket, he pulled out his smokes, and he lit up on the way to his truck. That's the way it was supposed to go when all was right with the world. Now all his questing fingers found in his pocket was a flattened pack of Doublemint.

"Fuck me," he muttered, confronted with the thought of facing the family unit with no nicotine. He unwrapped a piece and popped it in his mouth, chomping in aggravation. Normally he chewed gum only when he was slinging ink. Mellowed him out, helped him concentrate, because he was usually fiendin' for his next smoke. But now he needed it all the damn time. He could break down and go for the Nicorette, but if he couldn't lay down the nicotine by sheer power of will alone, then to hell with it. He would smoke.

This time, though, he was determined. Thirty would be knocking on his door soon. He didn't want to meet fifty on a respirator.

Waving goodnight to another one of his artists who was leaving, he hopped in his truck and plucked his cell phone from the cup holder. It wasn't much of a surprise to see he had six missed calls, but he grumbled all the same. One number he didn't recognize, and his heart gave a little kick. *Candace? Already?* He pushed himself up so he could dig his wallet out of his back pocket and check the number. Nope. Damn. He took a minute to enter her into his contacts.

Until that moment, he hadn't fully realized how eager he was to hear from her. It made him feel a bit like a dirty bastard. But it also set his blood racing, especially after having his hands all over her flawless, tan flesh just a half-hour ago...giving her something she would carry with her for the rest of her life.

Ordinarily, he wasn't one to get revved up by his clients. He was all business. But his cock apparently wasn't privy to that fact. He was still sporting a semi, and the tugging weight of his barbell was not helping matters in that area.

He could still visualize her big blue eyes staring anxiously up at him. Sweet, beautiful *Candace*, trusting him for her first experience under the needle. Damn, but for a minute there, he could've sworn she was turned on, all bright-eyed and flushed cherry red. Some people did find the experience highly sensual. He was used to girls slipping him their numbers after he worked on them, but she was the only one to whom he'd slipped his first.

Being "all business" hadn't stopped him from wanting to strip off his gloves to determine whether her skin was as smooth as it looked.

He sighed when he checked his other missed calls, the fog of euphoria receding as if a gust of wind chased it out. Two were from his brother. Three were from his sister-in-law. Both Evan and Kelsey were no doubt ready to ride his ass because he was late. Jesus, he was only running fifteen or so minutes behind. It was probably a personal record. Since Kelsey was definitely the lesser of two evils, he called her as he cranked up and sped out of the parking lot.

"Brian, are you coming?" was her greeting. But at least she didn't sound pissed, only worried.

"Yeah, I got tied up at work. I'm on my way."

"Whew. I tried to call you there, but they said you were busy. You don't take your phone in?"

"Nope. Too distracting."

She laughed. "I guess so. Okay. Don't worry, no one else has made it yet, either. You'll probably be the first one here."

"For real? That's a first. I'm becoming more responsible all the time."

"They're all on their way. Gabby hit traffic and it threw her off about a half-hour. Not sure what's holding up your mom and dad."

"With those two, you probably don't want to know."

"Um, yeah. You're probably right. Anyway, I'm glad you're on your way. Evan is grumbling. He's feeling unappreciated."

"Aw, well, tell him welcome to my world."

"I appreciate you! I need to come in and have my belly button re-pierced."

Kelsey had let the original piercing he'd given her grow up while she was pregnant. "I can't believe you didn't use retainers. I gave them to you so I wouldn't have to torture you again."

"Oh, it's not so bad. I didn't think I'd care about having it anymore, but I miss it. Now my stomach looks...plain."

"You don't have to tell me." He felt like a freak without his brow rings. Damn conservative family.

That was something else about Candace, he thought as he hung up with Kelsey. She'd had her streak of "rebellion" tonight, but at her core? She really would fit right in with his relatives. Regardless, he didn't feel the need to be all uptight around her, or hide who he was. Michelle had tried to turn him into her fucking pet project, tried to mold him into Mr. Nice Boyfriend. Candace had always looked at him and seen *him*, not what she wished he would be. He could zero in on that quality in a person within the first five minutes of knowing them.

Damn. It had been good to see her. He was definitely glad he'd gotten her number. Now, if only he had a legitimate excuse to call her. His fascinated gonads weren't enough.

Kelsey cracked open the front door ten minutes later with her index finger pressed to her lips, presumably so he wouldn't stomp in and start banging on pots to wake the baby. He stepped in past her and spied his brother kicked back in the recliner, sound asleep with three-month-old Alex snoozing in the crook of his arm.

"Isn't that sweet?" Kelsey whispered, positively glowing as she eased the door shut behind him.

"That's just...precious."

She smacked his arm. "Oh, you. I've waited a long time to see that sight."

Poor girl should've seen it long ago. It'd taken them ten years to get their shit together. Which only proved Evan, smart as he was, could be an absolute moron sometimes.

Brian was happy for them, even if it meant he had to watch them moon all over each other every time he came around. His nephew was a really cute kid, though. He looked forward to imparting all sorts of useless knowledge to him as the years passed.

"I can't wait for the right girl to get her hands on you, Bri. It's going to be so much fun to watch."

He scoffed and followed Kelsey into the kitchen, where some heavenly aromas were drifting from the oven and the stove. "If you think you'll ever see me domesticated, think again. And tell me that's shrimp manicotti I smell. Holy crap."

"It is. Evan's favorite."

"Mine too."

"Great!" Kelsey grabbed a Monster out of the fridge and slid it toward him. It was something else he needed to cut back on, but what the hell. He could only deal with exorcising one vice at a time. "I swiped your mom's recipe, but I bet it won't be as good as hers. And don't change the subject. I'll see you domesticated." She flashed him a maddening grin. "It's only a matter of time. I'm totally going to say 'I told you so'. Get ready."

He perched on a barstool and popped the tab, fidgeting because her words were hitting too close to home given the thoughts he'd been entertaining about a certain blonde. Thoughts he had no business allowing to take hold. It actually occurred to him that maybe he should have invited her. The whole evening would've been far less excruciating.

But how weird would that have been?

Their voices must've roused Evan, who ambled into the

kitchen with Alex still sleeping in his arms.

"Look at that old bastard," Brian exclaimed. "Can't even stay awake for his own birthday party."

As was becoming more commonplace of late, Evan ignored him. "You shouldn't have let me fall asleep," he said to his wife, planting a kiss on her forehead as she took the baby from him. Alex's tuft of black hair was sticking straight up. It was friggin' adorable. He lifted his head from his mom's shoulder and looked around with big, dark eyes, then gave a drowsy yawn.

"But you two looked so comfortable," Kelsey said. "And we didn't get much sleep last night."

"Spare me, please," Brian muttered.

Kelsey rolled her eyes toward him. "Because of the *baby*."

"Whatever. Hey, Ev, you wrecked our plan," he said, trying again. "We were all going to gather around you and marvel at the rampant cuteness all night."

Evan laughed in the middle of a yawn and stretch. "Sorry to spoil the fun. Should've taken a picture."

Kelsey winked at Brian and grabbed the digital camera off the kitchen island with her free hand, brandishing it at Evan. "Oh, I did. Several in fact."

He shook his head at the ceiling. "Of course you did. You're deadly with that thing."

"I can't help myself."

Evan looked at Brian. "I think Alex's every living moment since birth has been recorded or documented in some capacity. Poor kid, we'll have plenty to torture him with when he's sixteen."

"As if having you for a dad won't be torture enough."

Evan sent him a withering look as Kelsey gasped and spoke to Alex in mock indignation. "Did you hear Uncle Brian? He's saying mean things about your daddy." She smothered the baby's face with kisses.

Oh, sweet Jesus. Here comes the baby talk. It was on the tip of Brian's tongue to say he was going to step out for a smoke. And then he remembered. Fuck.

You could still use it as an excuse, he thought. He hadn't told anyone he'd quit so he wouldn't have anyone except himself to answer to in case he failed.

"Brian, you look great," Kelsey said suddenly. That brought his head up. "Really."

"Hey," Evan chimed in. "You could almost pass for normal."

"Don't get used to it," Brian grumbled, tugging at his long sleeves. Goddamn, but he needed a cigarette. He shouldn't have let himself think about it a minute ago. He could practically feel the shape of the cylinder on his tongue. He could taste it. Could feel his lungs expanding with sweet, soothing, blissful...

Carcinogenic smut! Stop it, dammit!

"Are you okay?" Kelsey asked.

"No," he snapped, giving up and shoving the sleeves up his forearms. "It's too fucking hot for this shit."

Kelsey covered Alex's ear and drew his head to her shoulder. "Don't cuss around the baby!"

"Jesus Christ. He doesn't understand what the hell I'm saying."

"You have a date later or something?" Evan asked.

"No, man. I just thought, since it's almost your birthday and all, that for one night I would appear to be everything you ever wanted me to be."

The indifferent expression Evan had been wearing turned icy cold in an instant. "Why do you have to be such an asshole all the time?"

Brian stopped fidgeting long enough to bat his eyes. "Because I only ever wanted to be like you."

Kelsey muttered something about needing to change Alex and scurried out, knowing full well what was coming. Brian didn't know why it always came to this...well, yes he did, and it didn't have anything to do with nicotine withdrawals, though he supposed that could exacerbate any heated situation.

The fact was, no matter what he did, being in his brother's presence lately never failed to make him feel like something that had crawled out from under a rock in a scum swamp, and the "normal" comment had only driven the dagger deeper.

He wasn't stupid. He knew he was the black mark on the family, the monkey wrench in Evan's political endeavors...and he had them, whether he admitted to it or not. The guy's dream since high school had been to be a U.S. Supreme Court justice. Yet he was stuck deep in the heart of fucking Texas pretending to be content slaving away as an assistant DA.

Maybe it was Brian's own fault for taking so long to get his shit together. But he had it as together now as it was ever going to get. Everyone might as well face that fact.

"You said I looked almost normal? Dude, it's relative. To me, you're the freak. Keep that in mind and get off my ass." Brian swigged his energy drink, wishing it were a beer. Or hard liquor.

"I never called you a freak. What's your deal? You can dish it out, but you can't take it?"

"The difference? Is that I'm joking around, and you're not."

"That's bullshit, and you know it. Why are you always so pissed at me, Brian?"

"Whatever. Happy fucking birthday." He slid off his stool. Evan crossed his arms and blocked his way.

"You're not leaving."

"You think you're stopping me?"

"I am. If I have to throw you in the pool like last year."

"I seem to remember you making that trip with me."

"Guys." Kelsey reentered the kitchen without Alex and insinuated herself between them. She put her hands on Evan's chest. "Come on. For one night, let's not do this, okay?"

Brian held his brother's cold stare, and it was Evan who finally blinked and looked down, focusing on his wife's face. "All right, but only because you put so much work into this." His green eyes flickered up to Brian again. "Not because he doesn't deserve a beat down."

"Try it, you motherfu—"

"Brian!" Kelsey turned to him. "Please stop. You're both acting like kids. Call a truce for tonight."

"I'm hearing enough from him right now, and that shit is about to be magnified fucking tenfold when the others get here. I'm done listening to it."

Kelsey looked practically on the verge of tears. "Look, I'm sorry. If I knew some way to get you to get along, I would do it. I just—"

"Stop worrying about it, baby. It's been like this since he was twelve years old. It's not going to change now." Evan put his arm around her shoulders and glared at Brian over her head, as if to say *See what you've done now, you asshole?*

His fault, again. As if he needed to feel crappier. Lack of nicotine was short-circuiting his brain. He was never a paragon of virtue, but lately he felt he was teetering on the knife's edge of sanity, about to fall off on the wrong side. "I'm sorry, K. I'll be good. Seriously, you'd probably have to beat me away from shrimp manicotti with a stick, anyway."

"Thank you." She reached up to give him a quick hug, and there was a knock at the door.

What followed was a blur of relatives *ooh*ing and *ahh*ing over Alex. Then they all did the same over Kelsey and how *great* she looked and how no one would *ever* think she'd had a baby only three months ago.

Brian maintained his safe perch on the kitchen barstool and knew it was only a matter of time before he would be forced to interact, but put it off as long as he could all the same.

His older sister, Gabriella, came in to give him the obligatory hug, still wearing her SpongeBob scrubs and her brown hair pinned up from her shift at the pediatric ward in a Dallas hospital. Then she went straight back to dishing out baby advice Kelsey hadn't asked for.

His dad naturally questioned him about how the business was faring. Then dished out advice he hadn't asked for.

His mom looked him up and down and beamed, making him bristle to the point that he began considering that Mohawk again.

Evan generally ignored him.

All in all it was a typical Ross family get-together.

And they wondered why he never brought any girlfriends around? Jesus. His earlier thought about inviting Candace had been ridiculous, he'd known that, but it would hold true with anyone he was ever interested in. What would the poor creature have witnessed so far? Him being an asshole and almost coming to blows with his brother over nothing. Damn near making his sister-in-law—who championed him way more than any of the rest of them—cry. The look of relief from his mom to see nary an inch of anything inked or pierced. His sister treating him like a casual acquaintance rather than someone she'd grown up with.

He told himself it didn't matter. Until something his mother was saying in the living room drifted through the other various conversations and perked his ears up.

"...can't believe I finally have a grandbaby and now you might be taking him away."

Taking Alex away? Where?

Curiosity piqued, he slid off his stool and wandered into the room where Evan and Kelsey were talking to his parents. His mom held Alex, stroking his hair as he lay against her chest.

"It won't be anytime soon," Evan was saying. "And even then it'll only be temporary."

"Where are you going?" Brian blurted, garnering surprised looks from everyone.

Evan, standing with his arm loosely around Kelsey's shoulders, massaged her arm. "Kelsey's going to start applying to law schools for next year. We're hoping she'll get in at UT, or Ole Miss near her parents. We'll move wherever we have to."

"We'll come visit as often as we can," Kelsey said reassuringly to her visibly distressed mother-in-law.

"Yeah, you think that now." Evan laughed. "Just wait until you're reading two hundred pages every night."

"You're going to have your hands full," Gabby agreed, shaking her head. "Taking care of the baby on top of all that. I remember Evan being a zombie whenever he would come home from school."

"I'll be there to help her," Evan said. "With all of it."

"Yeah, how lucky are you, to be married to someone who's done it already? I need to hurry up and marry a doctor before I start school." Gabby laughed and sipped her drink.

His mom snuggled Alex closer and rained kisses on his dark little head. "I hate the thought of you moving, but I'm so proud of all of you..."

And blah, blah, blah. Brian turned around and headed into the kitchen, this time for a beer for sure, digesting what he'd heard.

Well, damn, without Evan around to take the brunt of the back-patting, how in the hell would Brian make it?

Yeah, even his thoughts were turning sarcastic.

He managed to get through dinner without insulting anyone or starting another fight, so he supposed it could be considered a successful evening. And Kelsey had been wrong; her shrimp manicotti rivaled his mom's in every way. He told her as much as quietly as he could when she hugged him goodnight, and she practically beamed.

Knowing he'd be the first to leave, he'd parked a bit down the driveway. The gravel crunched under his feet as he hitched up his itchy shirtsleeves and breathed deep the muggy night air with its tinge of floral sweetness from Kelsey's rose bushes. He felt like a caged animal that had finally been given its freedom. Now to get home, jump into a T-shirt, watch a movie, whatever the fuck he wanted.

Only he'd be by himself, and despite how penned up he'd felt in that houseful of people, he didn't really care for that idea too much.

It really would be nice to have someone who didn't drive him nuts. Someone to laugh with over what a miserable ordeal that had been, someone to curl up with and enjoy the hell out of a good slasher flick. His ideal woman, right there.

As he popped open the door of his truck, Candace's face swam through his mind. He wondered if she liked horror movies. As much as they'd hung out together, he still had no idea.

"Are you all right?"

The delicate features and clear blue eyes dissipated, and Brian turned around from staring blankly into the dark depths of his truck to find his brother standing behind him.

"Why wouldn't I be?"

Evan shrugged and walked closer. "All that talk about us moving away…I was thinking back. You had a pretty rough time of it when I left for college."

"It didn't have anything to do with you."

"Really?"

"Nope. Don't flatter yourself. Plus I'm not fourteen anymore, don't forget."

Evan didn't look convinced. "Like it or not, I'm always going to see you as my kid brother."

"Well. I don't like it."

"You know you're going to miss me."

"Dude, if you're trying to get me to squeeze out a tear for you, you can—"

"Have you ever thought about getting out of here?"

"What?"

Evan shoved his hands deep into the pockets of his jeans. "I've always thought you'd do well to get away from here, from some of the people you know."

"What's wrong with my people?"

"Come on, Brian, I've been on the other side of the courtroom from half the guys you associate with. It's only a matter of time before you're in their spot."

"No, man, I don't run with those guys anymore. I finally got my place off the ground; I work and I go home. That's my life right now."

"Really?" Evan asked, one eyebrow raised. The skeptical look on his face pissed Brian off even more.

"I'm not quite the fuck-up I once was. I don't go out and get trashed anymore. I don't do drugs and I never have, no matter how hard a time you have believing me." It was probably the hundredth time he'd gone down the laundry list.

"I've always believed you. I've seen enough that I would know if you were lying about that." Evan was silent for a moment, and the only sounds surrounding them were the crickets and some distant chatter. The party must've moved around back to the pool. "But if you wanted to come with us, wherever we end up... I mean, you'd be welcome. Kelsey says so too."

"I appreciate that, but things are finally working out for me. You have a family now, and you don't need me tagging along. It would be lame."

"I'll worry about you."

"I'll worry about me too. Without you here, I might finally go commit that armed robbery I've been dreaming about." He grinned to show he was joking, and Evan laughed.

Truthfully, he didn't know how he felt about his brother moving away. He could certainly deal with it without going ass-out wild again, but he'd been lying when he said his transgressions as a rebellious fourteen-year-old had had nothing to do with Evan leaving for college. He'd been lost. He'd let himself fall in with the wrong crowd, which resulted in him being brought home by the cops to his father's wrath more times than he cared to admit. Not to mention a fairly impressive juvy record. He'd damn near been shipped off to boot camp, but instead, his parents had sent him to Italy to live with his grandparents. Change of scenery, removal of bad influences and all that. But after a few months' worth of running wild in Florence corrupting his cousins, he'd been shipped right back.

All his own fault...there was no one to blame for his bad behavior but himself. And it had been half his lifetime ago, but he still felt the echoes of those actions today, in the way his family dealt with him, in his reactions to that treatment. It was a vicious cycle, and no one made any effort to break it. Certainly not him, even though he knew that as the orchestrator of all that pain and grief, the responsibility should fall on his shoulders.

What they didn't realize, as they sometimes looked at him in horror, was that the very things they detested about his appearance were the very things that had saved him. If he'd never walked into Marco's parlor in Dallas for that first tattoo at eighteen, he might be in prison right now. That night he'd found a purpose. He'd found what he wanted to do with his life; he just hadn't wanted to do it for anyone else. Now that his dream of having his own parlor was finally realized, he'd be damned if he was going to do anything to fuck it up.

Evan talked for a few more minutes and finally headed inside. Brian shut himself in his truck and watched his brother disappear into the bright cheerfulness of the house. Back to a wife he adored, a baby he was crazy about, a family who loved him.

It would be so, so easy to feel resentful for his older brother's good fortune, but Evan deserved everything he had and then some. He'd worked hard for it, and he still did. Brian might give him a lot of shit, but the truth was...he was damn lucky to have him as his brother. Because there was no way in hell a guy like that would give him the time of day if they didn't happen to share parents.

As he cranked his truck, he told himself he would do well to remember it.

Sighing, he sifted through the CDs littered across the bench seat and popped in Pantera, something brutal to fit his mood. The growling guitars hammered his eardrums and, as habit dictated, he plunged his hand into his pocket to pull out a desperately needed...stick of gum.

"*Fuck* me."

Chapter Four

"It's been a week. Call him already."

"Don't you dare."

Candace had to laugh. Her two best friends, each currently situated on either side of her, were like a gleeful devil perched on one shoulder and a disapproving, morally outraged angel on the other. There were moments when she wanted to strangle both of them—and vice versa, she was sure—but she loved them dearly.

Samantha, the devil, was investigating Brian's business card and his scribbled number on the back, turning it over with her graceful French-tipped fingers. "His handwriting is sexy."

Macy rolled her eyes. Candace swallowed her gulp of iced cappuccino and laughed. "His *handwriting*?"

"Sure. Look. It's confident. Decisive. Dark. Strong slant. No timid, flimsy marks from him, oh no. He wants that number ingrained in your memory. Burned into your brain."

"Since when have you taken up handwriting analysis?" Macy asked.

Sam handed the card to Candace, her brown eyes lit up with amusement. "What can I say? I've always had a thing about guys' handwriting. Michael writes as if he's trying to murder the page or something. It's so hot."

Candace stared at Brian's number, seeing what the other girl meant. What Sam hadn't mentioned was that there was also an unexpected elegance to it. Sighing, she pulled her wallet out of her purse to tuck it safely away. She'd already programmed the number into her phone, even though she was sure it would never be used, no matter how much Sam begged.

Macy stirred her shake with a straw, pulled it out and licked off the ice cream. “Forget the writing. I'm more interested in their *hands.*”

“I bet Brian has great hands,” Samantha said enthusiastically. “Artists usually do. So what are his hands like, Daisy?” Sam sometimes called her “Daisy” as a play on the last syllable of her name. She knew Candace hated “Candy” with a passion. It was what her mother called her.

What the hell was up with her nicknames anyway? Sunshine. Daisy. Candy. All bright, sweet things. She should insist on being called Spider or something. Darken her image a bit.

Sam snapped her fingers in front of her face. “Hey, over here. Are they that good?”

“His hands? They're—” *Beautiful.* “Heck, I don't know. They're hands.”

Sam wiggled her eyebrows. “Big?”

Candace felt a flush beginning to creep up her neck. “Yes.”

“Stop it already,” Macy said. “You're going to drive the girl crazy, and she needs to forget all about that guy.”

“But why?” Sam asked, sounding like a petulant three-year-old.

“Because he isn't right for her.”

“For her, or for you?”

“What have I got to do with it?”

“*You* seem to be the only one who has a problem with him.”

“Her parents would have a hell of a problem with him.”

“Oh, to hell with her parents.”

Candace sighed and sat back as her friends went at it as if she wasn't even sitting there. “Stop, stop,” she said wearily, making the time out gesture with her hands when it appeared either girl was preparing to draw blood. “I'm afraid Macy wins, Sam. I can't just call him. I mean... I can't. He gave me his number in case I had any trouble. I'll be bugging him."

"When a guy slips you his cell number, honey, he wants you to call it. Trust me. Do you think he does that to all of his clientele?"

"Probably not, but we know each other already. He did it being friendly."

"Then call him being *friendly*. Be *friendly* as you mention that it was great seeing him and you'd like to hang out with him more."

"We're not that friendly. It would be totally weird if I did that."

Sam looked at Macy and sighed. "We've got to teach this girl how to land a man. She's hopeless."

"Hopeless is good right now."

"No, it's not."

"The guy allows a picture of his junk to be on display in his tattoo parlor. Hopeless is damn good in this case."

Sam burst out laughing as Candace gave Macy's shoulder a shove. "He was messing with you, Mace. I'm telling you."

"And lighten up. Jesus," Sam interjected. "I think it's hot that he's pierced downstairs. I've always wondered what it would be like."

"To get *pierced* down there?" Macy asked.

"No. Well, yeah, that too. But mainly to have sex with someone who is. I've heard it's amazing. You know Candace is wondering too." Sam winked at her.

"She's wondering what it's like to have sex at all." The two of them burst into another fit of giggles as Candace's mouth dropped open and she swept a glance around the coffee shop, wanting to melt through the floor.

"Could you maybe, um, not announce it to the whole room?"

"Aw, she's blushing. Stop it, Sam, you're embarrassing her."

"Me? You're the one who trumpeted it. Poor girl is going to

give it up just so we'll stop harassing her about it."

It had occurred to her once or twice. But their ribbing was good-natured, so she tolerated it fairly well, even if she thought her friends—Macy especially, although Sam had her moments—were a little too overprotective of her whenever a guy came sniffing around. As if her hymen was a handicap. She was actually surprised that Sam was so gung-ho for her to initiate anything with Brian.

"So why are you so happy about this?" she asked her friend, when curiosity got the better of her.

"Honey, I just think it's time."

"And she should pick someone off the street because it's *time*?" Macy asked in horror.

"No, you idiot, she should pick someone she likes. And she likes him a lot. You can tell from that dopey look she's had on her face ever since we started talking about him. She stares at that card as if she wants to frame it."

Candace tossed her straw wrapper at Sam. "Leave me alone. I might have always liked him, but I doubt I'll hear from him again. As far as sleeping with him..." She trailed off, unable to complete the sentence. Oh well, it didn't matter. It was so impossible it didn't even bear thinking about. But then why was she nearly breathless?

"There's no telling what kind of freaky stuff he's into," Macy said seriously, all joking aside. "Really. You don't want your first time to be with someone who scares the hell out of you."

Candace dropped her gaze and took a long pull on her drink, uncomfortable under her friends' scrutiny. If Macy only knew some of the fantasies she'd entertained about him, she might roll out of her chair in a dead faint.

"I'm sure he'll forgo the freaking ball gag her first time out, Macy," Sam said sardonically.

"He might. He might even be considerate of where he stabs her as he sacrifices her virgin body to his demon gods."

Okay, Candace had to laugh out loud at that.

"Do you have a mental disorder?" Sam asked. "I mean

seriously. You've gone completely off the reservation."

"Will you stop encouraging her!"

"Will you stop *dis*couraging her? You're the one trying to scare her."

"Okay, if you guys don't stop it, I'm seriously leaving. I officially declare the matter closed." Candace downed the last of her icy slush and leaned over to pick up her purse, holding it in her lap like a shield. Both her friends looked crestfallen. "Now, are we going to get a movie or what?"

"So you are in fact not calling him, right? I win?" Macy asked, collecting her own bag from the one empty seat at the table.

"No, you don't win—"

Candace raised her voice to talk over Sam's outrage. "You did *not* win, because I made that decision the second he gave me his number. That's why I gave him mine, and as you know, I haven't heard from him. You two have been going on and on for nothing."

"Dammit, Candace," Sam muttered, shaking her head. Candace blinked innocently at her just as the cell phone deep in her purse rang.

Tired of the wild jolting of her heart every time her ringtone blared for the past week, she'd assigned Brian his own ringer ID. That way there were no more instants of sheer panic when she heard the thing. Now there was only the moment of mild annoyance when the external display showed it was her mother calling.

"Great," she muttered. There'd be an inquisition later if she didn't answer, so she flipped it open and greeted her mom as she and her friends stood to leave the shop.

Not one for small talk or beating around the bush, Sylvia cut right to the chase. "Candy, have you spoken with Deanne?"

Deanne was her cousin, and Michelle's older sister. Despite being close as sisters to Michelle, Candace rarely spoke to Deanne unless forced to at family functions. "Um, no. Should I have?"

"I got off the phone with her a little while ago. She's in a tizzy. One of her bridesmaids has been dismissed and she's desperate for a replacement. I told her you'd be glad to stand in for her."

Dismissed. Wow. Two weeks before the wedding. And how nice of her mother to volunteer her services. "Does she even want me?"

"She was all for it. I think she'd take anyone at this point."

Anyone? Sometimes, Candace swore someone had left her abandoned on Sylvia and Phillip Andrews's doorstep when she was an infant. "I'm bowled over," she muttered.

"Don't be cute. Tomorrow you'll go to the dress shop with her and see what alterations need to be made, so they'll have plenty of time to get them done."

"Okay, yeah, fine. Can she call me up and ask me to do this? Since I'm *her* bridesmaid and all?"

"She has a million things to worry about right now. We don't have time for you to get all in a snit. I'm sure she'll get in contact with you and tell you what time." Her mother paused for a moment. "Where are you?"

Great. She glanced up at the back of her friends' heads as they walked down the sidewalk of the shopping center toward the video store. Falling behind a few more steps, she pitched her voice lower and mumbled her answer, knowing full well how her mother felt about Samantha. "I'm out with Macy."

She could hear the relief in her mom's voice. "Oh, good. What are you girls up to tonight?"

"We're going to rent a movie and go to her place."

"Well, have fun, dear. If Deanne doesn't call you, then call her. She's likely to forget all about it, she's in such a state."

Right. Candace flipped her phone closed and shoved it in its pocket in her purse, jogging to catch up with her friends.

Samantha smiled at her, and she felt like throwing herself under the car that was easing by out in the parking lot. Was she such a coward that she couldn't stand up for someone who'd been such a good friend? It wasn't fair. Sylvia's disapproval didn't even have anything to do with Sam as a person, but the girl's mother was an alcoholic who'd been in and out of jail and rehab. So naturally, in Sylvia's eyes, Sam must be one too, or either on the brink.

"I have to be a bridesmaid in Deanne's wedding," she told them.

"Oh, you *have* to, huh? Fun," Sam said.

"Hey, maybe you'll meet someone at the wedding. Fall madly in love and not give another second's thought to what's his name."

Not likely. Not even possible. Candace sighed. "No, Macy, I will not meet someone there. I can say this with absolute certainty."

Macy wouldn't be dissuaded. She pulled open the door of the video store and they all filed in. "How?"

"Because Brian's the *one*," Sam said happily. "Now we have to reel him in."

Yeah, this was pretty much one of those moments when she felt like strangling both of them. "Did you guys trip over the dead horse? Please, stop beating it."

It was at that moment something happened that almost caused her knees to give out. For a split second she thought someone else's cell phone was ringing, but when Sam and Mace looked at her in puzzled expectancy, she realized it was her own. Playing a ringtone she'd heard only once...when she'd set Brian's number to it.

"Oh...oh, God." Her fingers were shaking as she plunged her hand into her purse and scrabbled to get it out of its pocket. She fumbled and dropped it into the depths of the bag, uttered a word she rarely used, and followed the little square of light to retrieve it again.

Sam was practically standing on top of her. "Is it him? Is it?"

"Damn it," Macy muttered.

"Oh, crap, it's him." Candace was almost stuttering.

"Answer it, fool!"

Licking lips that were suddenly dry as the Sahara, she flipped it open and almost dropped it again before she got it to her ear. "Hello?"

Sam beamed at her. Macy glowered.

"Hey," came the casual reply in her ear, toe-curlingly deep and with that easy male confidence that could drive a girl right out of her mind. Her heart was beating so crazily she wondered if her friends could hear it. "A phone number is like the combination to a safe, isn't it? I figured you gave me yours because you wanted me to crack it open, and it would be a shame to let it go to waste."

As his voice purred into her ear, the breath left her lungs in a rush. It was a struggle to fill them again before she could speak. "Of course, I wanted you to use it."

"I'm not interrupting anything, am I?"

"Oh, no, not at all."

Sam was bouncing on her toes. The three girls were practically blocking traffic flowing into and out of the store, so Macy grabbed them both by their shirt sleeves and tugged them out of the way before they could get cussed out.

"Hmm, doesn't look like it."

That was an odd thing for him to say. "So...what are you up to?" she asked.

"I'm looking at a pretty girl."

Huh? If this were texting, that would definitely earn a WTF reply. "Okaay..."

"She's blonde, wearing blue and standing with two friends. She's talking on her phone, probably to some unworthy jerk, but damn, I wish I were him."

Her head came up as the light bulb went on, and she scanned the aisles in the video store, searching...and she'd only thought the breath had fled her before. At the sight of him grinning at her from one of the far corners, it was knocked out completely.

"He's here," she said to her friends, then realized she still had the phone to her ear. Their heads cranked around faster than Linda Blair's to follow her stare. "You're here," she said stupidly.

"That I am." She saw him clip his phone closed and beckon her over with slow sweeps of his index finger. Swallowing hard, she put her own phone away.

"Oh. My. God." Samantha leaned in close. "That was one sexy move right there. Macy, you're insane. Candace, get your ass over there *now*. Don't mind us." For good measure, Sam planted the flat of her palm on Candace's back and practically shoved her away. Macy was obviously not amused, but held her tongue, recognizing her sound defeat.

Rows of movies passed her in a blur as she tried to maintain a casual stroll without tripping over her own feet or sprinting toward him. He was wearing jeans that hugged his thighs and ass like a dream and a black Affliction tee with splotchy white chaotic patterns. Those tattoos flowed down his forearms with an almost liquid fluidity. Greens and blues and... She was staring. Crap. She didn't need to do that. But she wanted to lick him like there was candy in his skin; there was really no use denying it.

She almost plowed over two little boys who ran in front of her. Lifting her gaze to Brian's face as her legs ate up the last distance between them, she saw light glint on the two hoops through his right eyebrow. His hair was just long enough to brush the collar of his shirt, and it fell over his face as he looked down at whatever movie he was holding in his hand. He was in the horror section.

It occurred to her that he'd probably seen her fumbling freak-out and Sam's happy dance when he'd called. That was *wonderful*. She wasn't safe anywhere.

"Hey, you," he said, closing one eye in a wink. "How's the tat?"

That was probably all he wanted to ask. "Oh! It looks great. Hasn't given me any problems at all."

"Cool."

Why had she never really noticed that he was oh-my-God tall? When she stood next to him, the top of her head came no higher than his shoulder. He'd have to bend to kiss her, and she'd gladly rock up on her tiptoes to meet him halfway...

He cleared his throat. "I've been wanting to call you." Candace wondered if she should confess the same thing to him. It hadn't seemed— "It didn't seem right, for some reason," he finished.

"I know what you mean." Her gaze was focused resolutely on the cover of *The Evil Dead* sitting on the shelf in front of her. She hated how small her voice sounded.

"But I saw you there just now and...it seems ridiculous that we can't still be friends, doesn't it?"

Well. Ouch. She thought only girls were supposed to run the "let's be friends" line. Of all the bad ideas in the world, this had been the granddaddy. As much as it wounded her, she should accept his casual friendship and stop obsessing. Quit setting her fool self up for heartbreak. Because that's all she was doing.

But she *missed* him. Seeing him in his tattoo parlor last week and thinking about him all day every day since then had shown her how much. His breakup with Michelle had devastated her more than her cousin, if only because if Michelle wasn't seeing him, then Candace couldn't see him, either.

"It seems really ridiculous," she said, not intending for the sad note to enter her voice. "I always liked hanging out with you."

She had the bad feeling that he wanted to reach over and rumple her hair, and she didn't think she could bear the kid-sister gesture right now. "Likewise, sunshine."

This wasn't going nearly how she'd planned when she first looked up and saw him standing over here. That excitement was in ashes now, incinerated by one little "f" word that under normal circumstances was not considered dirty.

Sam was going to be so disappointed. Somehow, the thought of watching her face fall when she heard they'd decided to be friends in the horror section at the video store was the most devastating thing of all.

But she supposed having him in her life in that capacity was better than not having him at all.

"I didn't mean to abandon you when Michelle and I stopped seeing each other. I figured you were mad at me, or you didn't care."

"Oh, no. Don't ever think that. Whatever happened with you guys, it wasn't my business."

"I know how close you two are."

"We're close, but she never told me why you ended things. It's cool. I totally understand why you didn't keep in touch. It's the same reason I didn't."

He put the movie he'd been looking at back on the shelf and turned to face her. "How is she?"

This kept getting worse. "She's great. She's still working on getting her Master's degree, happily seeing some guy I don't like at all."

He laughed. "That makes me feel better."

"How so?"

"I'd hate the thought of you liking her new guy better than me."

"That would never, *ever* happen." She couldn't look at him as she said it, and he didn't reply. Maybe she'd shocked him. Maybe that had been too suggestive. But it was the truth, and she wanted him to know it. "So, um...what are you looking for here?"

"Anything. I was bored and couldn't find anything to stream, so I was hoping to grab something here. Not much luck so far."

"Why? Seen everything?" she asked teasingly, reaching over to give his arm a pinch. She really just wanted to touch him.

"Pretty much, yeah."

Wow. She'd known he liked scary movies because Michelle had always whined about it. Candace wanted to roll her eyes at the thought. They didn't bother her in the slightest, and given the opportunity to snuggle up and grab onto him during the jumpy parts...no, she wouldn't have any problems with that whatsoever.

"Have any recommendations for me?" she asked.

"What are you into?"

"Um...what do you mean?"

"Well, do you like slashers, or gory torture porn, or psychological? Or what?"

"I have no idea."

He laughed. It was a deep rumble that melted her very bones. "Most of the drivel Hollywood churns out lately is crap. You have to look to other countries to get the good stuff. France is awesome. Very extreme."

"I've never seen a French horror movie."

"They're definitely not for the faint of heart." He strolled away a few steps, scanning the shelves. "Let's see... Hey, there's a good one. Have you ever seen *The Descent*?"

"No, I wanted to, but..."

"But?"

"Well, honestly? I love scary movies but my friends hate them, and I don't like watching them by myself. It seems every little creak or bump freaks me out afterward. I know it's stupid."

"Aw, getting spooked out is the most fun," he drawled, flashing her that grin she really wished he'd stop flashing before she ended up hanging onto his leg. He bent to snatch a movie from the shelf. "You're watching *Descent*, I insist. It's one of the best to come out in recent years, in my humble opinion, but if I have to come over and babysit you through it, then so be it."

"Hey, now. I don't need a *babysitter*."

"You totally do. What are you doing now?"

"Now? Um..." She glanced over the shelves to where Sam and Macy were strolling through the new releases a few aisles away, occasionally sending her a glance and a thumbs up. She hated to skip out on her friends, but Sam had told her not to mind them... "The girls and I were going to watch something tonight, but it wasn't set in stone or anything."

"Oh. Well, I was going to say we should hang out, but I hate to drag you away from—"

"It's totally fine!" Sam bellowed, waving at them as Macy shook her head. Candace face-palmed as Brian burst out laughing.

"I don't think they really wanted to hang out with you all that much," he observed.

That wasn't it at all, and he knew it. But God bless him, he seemed to be trying to save her from the embarrassment of having this raging, out-of-control crush on him. She would be forever grateful. "Sounds like you're right about that."

Chapter Five

If only Mom knew what I was doing now.

Candace tossed a popcorn bag into her microwave and set the timer, unable to repress a smirk.

It was hard to believe Brian was in her living room. Brian. Was in. *Her* living room. Feeding the DVD into her player right now. Moments before, he'd been fiddling with the color on her TV, after proclaiming it "crap". Before that, he'd been in the kitchen with her, casting such a dark shadow around her cheerful white-and-yellow décor that she'd hardly been able to breathe.

His very presence here overwhelmed and unnerved her. Not that she didn't like it, or want it. The unfamiliarity of having a man in her living space was manifesting itself in a thrum beneath her skin, a slight tremble in her fingers, and perpetual dryness of the mouth. She'd nearly dropped everything she tried to pick up and she'd probably choke on the popcorn if she tried to eat it right now. Heck, she needed one of the beers he'd stowed in her fridge. And she hardly ever drank.

Her cell phone bleeped at her from the counter and she picked it up to find a text message from Sam: *Have u handed in ur V-card yet?* Even as the question made her want to dive under her bed and hide, she had to snicker at the idea that she and Brian had a captive audience across town.

We just got here! Call u later, she tapped back, and hoped that would be that for the night. Knowing her friends, they were going to harass her all night, demanding updates. What did they expect her to do, hop on Twitter during the act and give them a play-by-play?

She gave a half-hysterical giggle at the thought as the microwave chimed.

"What's so funny in there?" Brian asked.

"Oh...oh, um, texting with Samantha." She shoved the phone in her pocket, peeking over the bar that separated her kitchen from the living room. Brian was perched on the edge of her sofa, thumbing the remote control. Once the movie was queued up and ready to go, he sat back, his long legs sprawled in front of him.

Candace swallowed hard around the fast-forming lump in her throat. Images flickered through her mind. Sauntering naked into that room and straddling him. Her fingers deft and confident as she freed his erection from his jeans and guided it inside her. Riding it to ecstasy with his mouth all over her breasts. All week long she'd been having fantasies like that. But now, with his presence, they were so much more vivid. So much more...within reach.

Ridiculous. Just because she had him in her apartment didn't mean she was any closer to *having* him than she'd ever been. Sighing, she retrieved the popcorn bag from the microwave, dumped its fluffy, fragrant contents into a big bowl, and joined him on the couch.

The movie kept her riveted from the start, but she was always aware of him. They were seated far enough apart that another person could have fit between them, and she ended up setting the popcorn bowl there so they could both have easy access. When he wasn't digging into it, he would stretch his arm across the back of the couch, but the action only brought his hand close to her left shoulder. Nowhere near as close as she would've liked.

It was hard for her throughout the course of a film to remain quiet and not make comments or jokes, and he was the same way. Michelle had always been hissing and bitching at them whenever they had all watched one together, because it never failed she and Brian struck up a constant stream of witticisms. It was no different now, except for this interminable tension that had her stuttering over most of her words. And sometimes he'd say something that ordinarily would have her in hysterics, but she could hardly even dredge up a chuckle.

He wasn't going to put the moves on *her*. She'd accepted that. If she wanted him—and did she ever—then it was all on her to get him.

That thought terrified her.

"Hey, what's up with you tonight?" he finally asked, giving her shoulder a playful nudge that nearly made her leap off the couch. His expression fell. "It's not scaring you, is it?"

"Oh, no way. I'm enjoying it." She resisted all urges to place her hand over the spot where he'd touched her. Her flesh was still tingling there.

"Are you all right? Nothing's got you down?"

She fidgeted. "No. Just...um, preoccupied, I guess. I'm sorry if I'm not good company."

He waved a hand dismissively. "You're great. But I imagine you're really busy with school and stuff." She could have hugged him for the out he gave her.

"Yeah, that's it exactly. I think I'm overloading myself sometimes, trying to hurry up and get done with it."

"What's the rush? It can't be good for you to kill yourself like this."

Getting the hell out from under my mom and dad's dictatorship, that's what. "The sooner I finish, the sooner I can start working, and the sooner I'll be my own person." Frustrated at the admission, she shoved her hand in the popcorn bowl only to brush it against his as he was reaching for another handful, and that thrill shot up her arm again, frazzling her thoughts.

"So how is it that you're not your own person already?"

She shrugged. "Don't mind me, I'm rattling on. It was kind of a stressful day."

"If there's something you should be working on right now, we can do this some other—"

"No, no, I'm glad you came over. I'm really...um, really glad you're here."

He grinned, and she could've sunk five inches into the couch for the way she melted. His teeth were perfectly straight, even and dazzling against his olive complexion. "I couldn't believe it when you walked into my parlor the other day. It was damn sure the most pleasant surprise I've gotten in a while."

That warmed her all over, rendered her momentarily speechless. "Well, good. I'd have gone in to see you sooner if I'd known you...I mean, that you..."

"Missed you?" he asked, giving her shoulder a few teasing taps.

She shivered. "Well..."

"I did. More than I wanted to admit to myself."

What did that mean? Apparently, he wasn't going to elaborate. Tearing his gaze away from her suddenly, he took a drink from his beer and focused on the movie again. On her flat screen, the cave-dwelling monsters were launching their attack upon the hapless spelunkers. Candace shoved the wad of popcorn she was holding into her mouth and tried to concentrate. Her phone buzzed in her jeans pocket...probably Samantha requesting another update. They would have to wait.

"Can I ask you a question?" she blurted.

"Shoot."

"I know I said it's not my business, so feel free to shut me down. But...why did you and Michelle break up?"

"Honey, we were just totally wrong for each other. Two more wrong-for-each-other people never existed."

She had the feeling he was patronizing her, as if she was a naïve little girl and he was trying to protect her from all the ugliness in the world. "But what finally made you decide that?"

"I always knew that. But I was willing to let it ride." He shrugged. "I liked her."

Hmm. She had the feeling "liked her" equated to "she was dynamite in the sack". Michelle was a self-proclaimed nymphomaniac. "Did she do something?"

"Not one thing. If you want me to pinpoint some catalyst for you, I can't. The longer it went on, the more serious it started to get, and it wasn't happening for me. Or for her. We were both two entirely different people, heading in different directions."

"You don't want a commitment," she supplied, sounding too glum to her own ears.

"Actually, I'm not opposed to a commitment, Candace." His use of her name right then sent a funny jolt through her stomach. He didn't look at her. "It's a matter of finding someone who doesn't drive me up the fucking wall."

"Is that all you need? Someone you can tolerate? What about finding someone you love?"

"Never known it."

"But surely you know it's out there."

"I guess. My brother's in love. My parents have always been disgustingly in love. I can't see myself ever having that."

"Why not?"

"Damn, girl, you are inquisitive."

She straightened, certain she was blushing. "I'm sorry. Never mind."

"It's all right. But let's put you on the hot seat. Ever been in love?"

I'm at least ninety-nine percent certain I am right now. Ohhh, that was a dangerous thought to entertain. And her mind returned it way too easily. So easily it could have rolled right off her tongue. "No. I mean, I've loved someone, but, um...I don't think there can be true, unequivocal love unless that person loves you in return. If they don't, it's just...unfulfilled. Don't you think?"

He was watching her now. "Any man you're in love with who doesn't love you back is a damn fool."

She wanted to laugh out loud. If he only knew... "That's sweet of you to say."

"It's the truth," he said, his gaze lingering on her face. Something in that dark look stirred a longing between her legs that had her shifting positions. It brought back everything she'd felt lying on that table in his back room.

"So you're saying...I'm lovable to you?"

He shook himself suddenly, emitting a laugh that made her jump. "Oh, hell. I've talked myself into a corner, haven't I? Yes, sunshine, I think you are undeniably, exquisitely...lovable."

But could you *love me?*

The question hung in the air, unspoken. She had the feeling he sensed it as well as she. His gaze still searched her face as if he pondered the answer.

Filling her lungs with adequate amounts of oxygen was proving to be more of a chore as this night wore on. For probably the millionth time, she wondered how it would feel to kiss him. Amazing, that for all her inexperience, in that one particular moment she was most concerned with something as simple as a kiss. Although with him, she would lay bets it would be anything but *simple*.

He was staring at her lips now as if he was wondering the same thing. Reflexively, she wet them with a tiny flick of her tongue. His mouth was so sensuous, it drove her crazy. The fullness of it, the beautiful definition. There was no question that it would be strong enough to make her weak, should she ever get lucky enough to feel it touch hers.

It wasn't to be. Blinking as if coming out of a trance, Brian turned back to the bloodbath on the screen and took a breath. Candace pulled her poor, denied lips between her teeth to repress a sigh of frustration.

Damn, damn, damn. If she didn't have the nerve to make a move tonight, she never would. He was here, they were alone, he was drinking. Not drinking a lot, but still. Maybe she really did need a beer. It might loosen her up a bit. Too bad she couldn't stomach the stuff.

What the hell did she need to get his attention...and keep it? Bigger boobs? Fuller lips? Ass, she had in spades. It wasn't *big*, but if she did put on a few pounds, it went straight in the trunk. And she had a few she was grappling with, truth be known.

Maybe you need to act out that fantasy you had in the kitchen. Could any man really resist a naked female straddling him?

"What are you thinking about so hard over there?"

She didn't realize she was staring at him until he spoke. Tearing her gaze away, she shook her head and grabbed another handful of butter-drenched popcorn. Something else to go straight to her butt. "Nothing."

"Doesn't look like it."

"I have a major headache," she mumbled. At this point, it wasn't a lie.

He laughed. "Well, with the way you were looking at me, I'm led to believe it's me. You want to call it a night?"

"No, Brian, I really don't. Seriously, tonight would probably suck so much more if you weren't here."

She watched in stunned silence as he grabbed one of her throw pillows and laid it on his lap, then patted it invitingly. "Come here."

She couldn't get the bowl out of her way fast enough, but for the sake of dignity, she managed to not sling popcorn all over the room. Settling her head on the pillow, she almost groaned in ecstasy when his fingers sank into her hair and kneaded her scalp. A moment later, the sound slipped out despite all her desperate restraint. He chuckled, his massaging fingers draining the last of her strength. "Better already?"

"Ohhh, yes." She'd seen him do this so many times with Michelle. The girl was like a cat; she loved to be petted. And he was very good at it. From her head down to her toes, Candace felt the tension slowly ease its grip on her muscles.

The gentle tugging sensations at her hair roots were activating all the right pleasure centers in her brain. The TV screen blurred in her vision just before her eyes fell closed. Brian's fingertips circled her temple and moved down to explore the crease behind her ear, giving her a little shiver. She turned her face into the pillow a bit more and he was able to reach her nape, digging firmly into the column of her neck. She hadn't realized how achy and stressed she'd been until all those wretched feelings dissolved into the sheer bliss of his touch. It was almost enough to make tears prick the back of her eyes.

"That...is...awwwesome," she moaned. The man had magic in his hands. To feel them in other places... "Can you do this for me every day?"

He exhaled a soft laugh. "Anytime. Maybe now you'll have a reason to call me."

"Mmm. You might have to change your number after this."

"Never."

She smiled dreamily into the pillow. The last thing on earth she wanted was to fall asleep and miss any moment of this. But the weight of her eyelids was becoming too much for her to bear. Before long, she lost the battle. Her thoughts muddled, drifted...and finally darkened.

Brian leaned over to see that Candace's eyes were closed, her breathing deep and steady. She practically looked boneless, and he had to smile. That was exactly what he'd been going for.

She had some incredible tension in her muscles, and he had to wonder what was stressing her out so. She had so much going for her. Parents who catered to her every need, from what he could tell. Friends who loved her. College work was probably draining, but he couldn't imagine that was the only thing that had her drawn so tightly. He'd always envisioned it as one big party, and for him, it probably would have been.

Candace was different. She probably had a 4.0 average. Overachiever. Too damn good to even call her a friend of his.

She was...exquisite. Her hair was a silken slide between his fingers, and he couldn't keep his hands out of it. The smooth skin of her neck had been just as enticing, not to mention the throaty moans that had made him glad he'd put the pillow on his lap. Everything, everything about her enthralled him, from the relaxed curl of her fingers beside her face to the tiny gold earring glinting in her earlobe to the mouth-watering curve of her hip.

He could imagine those fingers curled somewhere else. That little gold ball was inviting his tongue to circle it. Those hips...Jesus Christ, it didn't bear thinking about. All the same, his cock pulsed, pressing against his zipper as his hand ached to slide down her body and travel that delectable curve.

He'd never wanted to let his mind *go there*, but Candace was undeniably one of those girls a man took one look at and knew she would eat him alive and lick her fingers clean afterward. Strong and curvaceous and devastatingly feminine. He didn't know why she played it down so much, but more often than not she hid that incredible body beneath baggy clothes, and stuffed that shimmering blond hair up in a cap. It had always driven Michelle nuts, too.

One thing was for certain: he was stuck. The movie was ending but there was no way in hell he was disturbing her. Careful not to make any big movements, he toed off one Nike and then the other, getting as comfortable as possible. If she slept in his lap until the sun came up, that was fine with him.

Chapter Six

She awoke to him shifting under her. Turning her head back toward him, she saw that he was asleep, but he had to be uncomfortable with his head rolled over on his shoulder like that.

"Brian?" she whispered, sitting up and rubbing his arm. He winced and straightened, his brows drawing together as his eyelids lifted. Those incredible eyes focused on her. "Sorry I fell asleep on you."

"S'all right. I should get going," he said, and the drowsy cadence of his voice started a delicious melting in her lower belly.

The clock on her bookshelf revealed in glowing green numbers that it was after three a.m. "It's so late..."

He stood and stretched his tall, lean physique in a way that reminded her of a sleek black panther. "I shouldn't have crashed on you. You should go on to bed."

She scrambled up next to him. "No, I mean...it's so late, and you're sleepy, so, um...you don't have to go." She became lost in the flickering light from the TV reflected in his dark eyes. "I hate to think of you out driving right now. I would worry about you."

"Trust me, I've been out later than this."

He must think she was a naïve little kid. Maybe she was. She felt she was operating on auto-pilot here. "I'm sure you have, but...I'd like for you to stay."

"I really shouldn't."

"Why not?"

He just looked at her, a puzzled line appearing between his eyebrows.

"I'm not asking for anything," she said in a rush. "I—"

Her voice gave out. How in the hell could she think she was ready for this, any of this, when she didn't even have the guts to tell him out loud what she wanted?

She was a colossal failure at playing the seductress, and the humiliation bit into her hard and deep. If she struck out now, she would never be able to face him again, the only guy she'd ever felt...*this*...for.

Maybe it was twisted that she was contemplating exploring territory her cousin had treaded well, but that had become nothing more than an unhappy circumstance in her mind. Michelle had only seen him first. Michelle would probably do the same thing, were their positions reversed. Michelle would certainly know what to do in this situation, with a man she desperately wanted standing in her living room in the middle of a lonely night. She'd take him, make him hers, make him crazy with desire for her.

"You're not?" he asked darkly, and her heart kicked against her rib cage. The look in his eyes then terrified her far more than any movie ever could have, but it was a thrilling, exciting fear. Like the last heart-stopping second before the roller coaster plunged down a straight-down track.

"I...well, y-yes, I am, actually."

He took a step closer, and another, until he was only inches away. So close she could've reached out and slipped her hand under his shirt. Or put her arms around his waist to pull him closer. Or...

She couldn't look up at him after her confession, focusing instead on the splotchy patterns on his shirt, on trying to keep her breath steady and even. It was a losing battle.

When his hand came up and his fingers brushed her cheek, she couldn't help closing her eyes at the exquisitely gentle touch and leaning into its warmth.

"Candace," he said softly. "You're incredibly beautiful, and I—" He gave up with a sigh. She opened her eyes to see him lean his head back in despair for a moment. "I would be a fool to leave."

He thinks I'm beautiful. She trembled, searching his face for any emotions that might cross it. All she saw was that his jaw was visibly clenched and his own gaze was now locked on where his hand lay against her cheek. He gave her skin a light stroke with his thumb, sending tingles down her spine. "But this isn't what I had planned when I came here. I promise you that," he said.

"That's okay. I didn't have it planned, either."

"But I don't think you were opposed to the idea, were you?"

"Were *you*?"

"I've told myself it's not going to happen with you, yes."

Her heart withered. "Why not?"

"Because you're you. I can't explain it any better than that. I think about you all the time, but whenever I do, I feel like a scumbag."

"What do you think about?"

His sensual lips twisted. "Are you really going to make me answer that?"

"Oh." She forced her lungs to expand with air. "It's okay. I...think about you too. A lot. And I always wonder what Michelle would think, which makes me feel guilty, but I can't stop myself. She's with someone else now and seems really happy, so I don't feel so bad anymore." Another deep breath. "I've missed you. I don't want to go back to missing you so much."

"Sweetheart," he murmured. Then he did what she had been fantasizing about from the moment he'd touched her: he slid his hand farther along her cheek, into her hair. Past her ear. Until his fingers threaded deep and tight into her locks and he palmed the back of her head, bringing her closer until their lips hovered a breath away from each other.

She made a whimpering sound she hated herself for, and

his other hand came up to smooth her hair away from her face. Trapped against him like this, she was powerless. Consumed by him. His breath on her lips, his scent filling her nostrils. The warmth of his hands and his lean body against her. But it was the hard column of his erection pressing into her abdomen that left her in ashes.

He wanted her. It was all the evidence she needed, all the encouragement. She transferred all her weight to her tiptoes, the subtle movement all it took to fit her lips against his. Her heart leapt for joy with the simple, soft contact, and she reveled in the silky scratch of his goatee. The brush of his warm, dry lips opening against hers. But it felt too tentative, too cautious. It wasn't what she wanted. She wanted to-hell-with-the-world passion. She wanted him to feel all the things she was feeling, the delight and the terror. How could she break the dam?

She meant to lift her arms to put them around his neck, but where they went was under his shirt, to the hot, hard flesh beneath. His muscles tensed beneath her touch and, taking that as a good sign, she didn't retreat but explored further. Tracing the ridges of a six-pack and well-defined pecs. He stiffened and moaned as her fingers passed delicately over the circlets of his nipple rings, and that was all it took.

The hand at the back of her head fisted in her hair and she had the crazy thought that this was a Jekyll and Hyde kiss. Demure and passive one minute. Monstrous the next. His mouth claimed hers in a burning rush, and she bent back beneath the onslaught, buffeted by sensations that had her gasping against him every time she could come up for air. His tongue invaded her mouth and coaxed hers into a sinuous dance behind her teeth.

She pulled her hands away to clutch fistfuls of his T-shirt and wrenched it upward, desperate to finally bare his flesh to her sight. "Take this off," she pleaded against his mouth. He broke the kiss to peel off his shirt in one fluid motion, tossing it on the couch as she marveled at the TV-lit expanse of skin he revealed. It would take hours to lie down and inspect the detailed markings on his arms. She would love to have that kind of time with him.

Smoothing her hands over his skin, she wondered if he noticed how they trembled. When she dared a glance at his face, his eyes were closed, his head tilted back. The star on his left pectoral was a beacon for her lips, and she leaned forward and brushed it delicately.

His hand clenched again in her hair and the hard line of his jaw rubbed over the top of her head. She flickered her tongue across his skin, savoring his answering groan. The rush of power was heady and intoxicating, and she gasped when he pulled her head back by her hair to brand her lips again with his.

*Oh...*Jesus. She'd been kissed before, but never like this. There had been the guy who tried to swab her tonsils and the guy who seemed to be trying to draw blood with his teeth and the guy who did it just right, but didn't make her feel...this. Brian's taste invaded her mouth, sensuous and dark and everything she had ever imagined. No, it was more. His tongue touched and teased hers until she melted away and leaned her knees into his in an effort to remain standing. The liquid ache between her thighs had drained all strength from the waist down. She needed him to catch her before she fell. She was sliding...

His arms swept down around her waist, strong and solid. "I got you," he murmured, one hand sweeping down to cup her ass and lift her against him. She took the welcome opportunity to wrap her legs around him, grinding her crotch against his erection. It felt huge. Oh, holy hell.

"Where?" he whispered, still sliding his lips over hers, scrambling her thoughts, and her trembling redoubled.

She managed to nod toward her bedroom door. He carried her through it, and she wanted to cringe because it was such a mess in there: bed unmade, clothes flung over chairs, books stacked precariously on her nightstand. At least it was dark, the only light filtering in from the living room. Why in the hell hadn't she had the foresight to tidy up?

Because she hadn't expected this. Still, surely it had

always been *somewhat* within the realm of possibility. Here he was now, about to make love to her.

Her heart twisted up as she realized she was romanticizing this. Brian wasn't a "make love" kind of guy. Brian was going to fuck her, and then he would be gone. It was evident in the way he flung her down, causing her waterbed to slosh, evident in the almost feral glint the distant light cast in his eyes.

She couldn't keep her breath steady. It was as erratic as her thundering heart rate. Desperate to match him, she swept her shirt off over her head and reached for him, craving the feel of his bare flesh against hers. He dropped to the bed and went into her arms, pausing only to grab her battered old teddy bear from underneath him and give it a fling across the room. She could imagine him doing the same thing to her heart.

Sliding her arms around his back, she arched against him as his lips trailed down her throat to her breast. She wanted his mouth there, where she felt so hot and heavy, straining against her white cotton bra. Dammit, couldn't she have at least worn something sexy? Something silky and lacy? She was no freaking good at this. She could've taken the damn thing off after her shirt, but she hadn't had the courage.

Brian hooked one finger under the fabric and tugged it slowly down, her nipple slipping free and immediately into his mouth. A moan ripped itself from her throat at the shocking sensation, warm and wet and drawing contractions from between her legs. His knee slid between hers, and she gripped it tight with her thighs.

"Oh, God," she whispered shakily as he sucked her, gently tugging her nipple between his teeth. The weight of her breast trapped the fabric of her bra beneath it and he moved his hand, caressing her bare belly with the back of his knuckles. Her muscles pulled so tight they trembled beneath the feather-light brush.

His dark head lifted, and his gaze roamed her face. "Okay?" he asked, and she nodded and tilted her hips toward him, wanting those fingers to go where she needed them, where she'd wanted them ever since she was stretched out on that table under his needle. Down, down...

She sank her teeth into her bottom lip as he unbuttoned and unzipped her jeans, resuming those delectable ministrations at her breast until she was ready to shed bra, jeans, panties, wrap herself around him and not let go. The tips of his fingers slid over the silk of her panties, and her legs fell apart, allowing him, needing him, to go wherever he wanted.

The sound he made then, a slow hiss of air through his teeth, was off-the-freaking-charts erotic. Her cheeks flamed. Along with other, more needy parts of her body. His hand cupped her, his wrist caught between her belly and the denim she wore. His fingers pressed into her cleft, barred from her flesh only by a damp scrap of fabric. She squirmed, needing more, aching for him to slide it aside and plunge into her. "Hold on, baby," he murmured.

Oh, but she couldn't. She was in flames, undulating against his hand, frustrated when he eluded her. "Please, Brian. *Please.*"

"That's what I wanted to hear."

Damn him for making her beg, for—

All those thoughts fled when he moved aside the thin panel of fabric between her legs and explored her wetness, caressing her sensitive folds with unbearable gentleness.

The sensations he had evoked were too acute; she couldn't think straight. She was wound too tight, clinging to him and panting into his shoulder while he took his dear, sweet time winding her even tighter.

When he finally pushed deeper, parting her labia and seeking her entrance, she struggled to spread wider for him. His fingertip sought and breached her, and she gasped as it burned through her passage. A whimper escaped her before she could suppress it, and Brian growled low in his throat. "So tight."

She winced and adjusted as he pushed deeper. She wanted to struggle out of her jeans, but at the same time there was a delicious wantonness in lying here with his hand shoved down her pants and her panties pushed aside while he stroked her depths.

"Up here, baby," he murmured, and she tilted her face up for his kiss, tasting his heat, his lust, as he teased her lips apart with his and then devastated her with the mastery of his tongue as it plundered deep. He dragged his finger out of her, swirled it over her too-sensitive clitoris in the exact same pattern his tongue danced in her mouth. She tensed and shuddered and tried to wriggle away, but only half-heartedly. Brian smiled wickedly against her lips. "What's the matter?"

"Feels...*oh*. It feels too good."

"Then you'd better stay right here," he murmured, lips skimming over hers. Two blunt fingertips trailed down and pressed into her opening. Her mouth fell open against his, but when he tried to penetrate, she couldn't control her reaction. She gasped and dug her heels into the bed to fight against the shocking pressure, but her jeans kept his hand trapped there.

"Shh, shh," he said, immediately withdrawing once he realized she had gone from agonized pleasure into real distress. "Jesus, Candace. Please tell me you've done this before."

Tears pricked behind her eyes as he looked down at her. The words gathered behind her mouth, she just couldn't force them out.

Her silence must have been answer enough. Brian smoothed the hair away from her forehead, brushing her brow with his lips. "Oh, baby. Never?"

"I think I'd remember." Her voice sounded tiny even to her own ears.

"I know that, but..." He exhaled shakily. "Damn."

"Does it really matter that much?"

"Hell yes, it matters. Obviously. Were you not going to tell me? I could've really hurt you."

She swallowed thickly. "Are you mad at me?"

"Not at all." He shook his head, his face close enough to hers that the tip of his nose almost brushed her own. Then he laughed, a little self-deprecatingly. "I just don't know what to do with you now."

"What do you mean? Do what you would ordinarily do."

His thumb continued stroking her hairline. “I can’t be the one you want to give it up to your first time.”

What the hell? “I’m only lying here with my legs open for you.” There. That was better, that icy, steely tinge in her voice. His questioning her judgment this way was not cool in the least. “What you did…I wasn’t prepared for what it would feel like, but I don’t want you to stop now.”

He shook his head again. She wished he would quit doing that. “Honey, it’s not that I don’t want you, because I’m about to explode here. I want to bury myself so deep inside you, you’ll think you won’t ever get me out.”

Ohhh.

“But I can’t let myself do that to you. I can’t.”

Given the determination he managed to inject into those last two words, she knew no amount of arguing would change his mind. But she’d come this far and she couldn’t let go of him without some answers.

“Not tonight, or not ever?”

His voice was tight. “Candace.”

“You said you want me. I want you too. Is that not enough?”

“You make me feel too…” He trailed off, staring at her. She lifted her hand and stroked his cheek.

“Feel too what?”

“I don’t deserve this.”

Her heart broke. She’d never taken Brian for a guy who suffered from lack of confidence. He’d always been so vibrant and sure of himself. Why would he begin to have doubts about his self-worth here in her arms? Surely nothing she’d ever said or done led him to believe she didn’t think he was good enough for her.

“It’s not about deserving,” she said softly.

“You’re probably right, but it’s the easiest way I can sum up the situation. I can’t be who you need me to be.”

“I only need you to be you.”

"No. You need more, you need better than me. You're everything that's beautiful and innocent, and just looking at you this way makes me feel like a filthy, debauching bastard." She opened her mouth to protest there was no reason he should feel that way, but he laid a silencing finger on her lips. "At the same time, it makes me want you more than anything else in my life."

She kissed his fingertip, opened her mouth to let it slip between her lips, her teeth. He shuddered against her, groaning when she sucked gently on it, drawing it deeper. His erection ground against her thigh, sending a thrill through her stomach. Until he abruptly pulled away from her. "Christ, Candace."

Damn him. What did she have to do? Who did she have to be?

"You know," she said, "I'll never be able to get filthy and debauched with you until you let me get a little bit dirty." She hated herself for the way her voice broke at the end, and for the tear that slipped from the corner of her eye. Maybe he couldn't see it.

No such luck. He wiped it away, staring down at her with an appraisal that made her feel stripped way more naked than she was.

"We could take it slow," she said, thinking it incredible and maybe slightly pathetic that she was having to talk him into this. Wasn't it supposed to be the other way around? "I liked it when you touched me. A lot. I wanted more. I think I just needed you to take more time."

"The things I'd like to do to you," he murmured darkly, lowering his lips to the hollow of her throat.

"Do some of them," she whispered, shivering. "Or just one. Do one thing. Please?"

When he lifted his head, she could hardly see his expression in the near darkness, but she had the sense he was debating whether staying was a good idea. She was debating it herself. If he didn't want her, why torture herself by making these memories? At least before, he'd only been a fantasy. Now she knew what he tasted like. What he felt like. She knew the scent and warmth of his skin and the feel of him touching her more intimately than she'd ever allowed anyone else. But the words were out there, and she wouldn't take them back. She couldn't have let go of him if the building caught on fire.

"Take this off," he murmured, urging her up and reaching behind her. A brush of his fingers against her back, a momentary tightening of her bra, and then it loosened, undone. She bit her lip as the straps fell down her arms, and then the cups when he tugged them away. He'd just seen her moments ago. Still, she wanted to cover herself, afraid he would find some flaw that would turn him off. She forced herself to lie back and not give in to such a virginal impulse. He was being skittish enough about this and she was actually afraid of scaring *him* away.

His gaze moved over her as gently as the fingertip that stroked the side swell of her breast. Her nipples tightened agonizingly for that touch, so close and yet too far away. She closed her eyes when he moved his hand away, traveling down, farther and farther, until he grasped the gaping waistband of her jeans.

"And let's lose these." She lifted her hips from the bed to help him, feeling the rough denim slide down her buttocks, her thighs. In a moment of heart-stopping shock, she realized her panties had gone with it. The air from the ceiling fan swirled over her naked thighs, then her shins, and finally her feet as he flung the garments to the floor. She shivered though she was burning up inside.

Brian surveyed every square inch of her in the near-dark, as if committing it all to memory. His hand closed on her ankle and moved up her leg inch by inch. Thank God she'd shaved. "You're so beautiful, sunshine."

He shouldn't do that. Not now. She didn't want to lose it completely. "You can't see me well enough."

"I can." His hand roamed higher, to the crook of her knee. His fingertips skimmed behind it, and she drew in a breath as he grazed that soft skin that was so seldom touched. "And I can feel you."

A whimper escaped her. “I want to see you, too,” she said.

“You will.”

Finally, he lowered himself over her and grazed her lips with his. She couldn’t help herself, her arms went around him and she cradled him between her legs. He was hard everywhere she touched him, from his hips holding her thighs apart to his smooth, firm back muscles beneath her hands to his chest pressing against her breasts. The thick ridge beneath his jeans rubbing against her clitoris with every one of his movements...oh, Lord help her, that was the hardest part of all. How would that feel thrusting into her? She thought of the way his fingers had singed her. That feeling magnified? She wouldn’t survive it.

He kissed her gently, teasingly. His entire demeanor had changed since her revelation. It was all the more heartbreaking for her. Their tongues danced around each other, and it was so sweet she wanted to cry. Not just these stray tears, but really let the dam burst. It was everything she’d ever dreamed of since she first decided boys were something that might be of interest to her, and she couldn’t have it, not like she wanted.

Brian’s hands found hers, his fingers intertwining with her own. “I could lie here and kiss you all night,” he murmured against her lips. That sounded nice to her. She realized that their bodies had involuntarily begun to move with each other in a semblance of lovemaking, spurred on by the natural motions of the water mattress beneath them. She thought the easy, fluid rocking alone was going to make her climax. Heat permeated her lower belly, spreading languorously throughout the rest of her.

This wasn’t enough. She needed his hands on her. His mouth. As if reading her mind, he eased down her body, still keeping her hands pinned in place, to tease first one nipple and then the other with his tongue. His hair fell forward, long enough to tickle her skin, and she writhed on the bed helplessly, bringing her knee up to press her groin tighter to his. That mouth of his would be the death of her. Hot as fire and unspeakably skillful. When it began to travel down her stomach, kissing a slow, damp trail, panic flared through her even as she wanted to purr in ecstasy. Oh, yes yes yes...

He let her hands go, moving his own down to keep her legs splayed wide. She was near sobbing now, especially when he stopped and lifted his head, apparently admiring his handiwork as he stared at her tattoo. "When I told you to be creative if the lucky guy came along, I never in a million years thought it would be me."

"Me either," she whispered. "But I wanted it to be." When he lowered his head and nuzzled between her thighs, she reached frantically to grab his hair—not wanting to stop him, but what else was she supposed to do? "Brian!"

"Shhhh." Warm wetness slicked over her clit. She nearly came undone, clenching up all over, gasping in shock. He chuckled softly and she felt the breath of it on her enflamed flesh. "Never?"

"Never."

He groaned, the vibrations of it soaking into her, causing her legs to jerk in his hands. "Hang in there, I'm nowhere near done yet. And just a warning: when you come, I'm giving you two fingers. You'll need them."

Unable to form words, she merely gave a soft cry.

"I won't hurt you." Beneath the gentle kisses and licks he was bestowing on her pussy, she felt his fingers stroke her entrance. Not penetrating, but letting her know they were there. Ready and waiting.

Oh, but he didn't play fair. He built her to orgasm so hard and fast she didn't have time to prepare. Or maybe she'd been on the cusp already. She only knew everything that had been accumulating inside of her over the past week all converged at once, and flew out of her as soon as he closed his lips on her clit and sucked. There was no resisting it. She went into a million pieces and every one of them screamed his name.

So many nights she'd lain here and listened to the couple next door bang the walls and raise the roof getting it on; now they could probably hear her. Brian took the moment a contraction wrenched her so hard she arched off the bed to slide his fingers in, and she sucked them in greedily. The stretch dismayed her, but he'd been right, she wanted it. Her body was in a place beyond pain. All the stress, all the anger, all the love, seemed to explode out of her and at one point in the madness, she thought she laughed.

The only thing she could think as she slowly floated back down to earth was that this was *nothing* like the orgasms she gave herself, and she could get used to it.

Brian raised his head, planting a kiss and then a gentle nibble on her inner thigh. "Mmm. Seems you needed that," he murmured.

"Oh God, oh God... I'm s-sorry." Her mind scrambled to right itself as her face flamed. Every bone in her body had melted, but she was shivering uncontrollably.

"Don't apologize. Come here, sweetheart." He prowled up the length of her body and lay beside her, pulling her tight against him. She absorbed his strength, his steadiness. Tried to sync her breathing with his just as she'd done in his parlor. His shoulder was pressed against her lips, and she sank her teeth into it without conscious thought, holding on for dear life.

Silent minutes passed and finally she trusted herself enough to speak to him without bursting into tears. "I had no idea."

"That it would be so good?"

"Yeah."

"Or you might've done it a long time ago, huh?" he teased.

"I'd still want to wait for you." She hoped she was wrong, but she thought she could feel the unease creeping into him at the implication that she'd been saving it for him all this time. She hadn't been, really, but only because she'd never thought there was a chance in hell she would end up here. If she had, she might not have allowed another guy to get close enough to even put his arm around her.

"You're sweet," he said, trailing his fingertips up and down her spine. "I can't believe there hasn't been anyone. I know you've dated."

"That's not the equivalent of putting out."

"It's not?" He laughed, and she smacked him on the arm.

"*No,* it's not. I've dated a few guys. None of them did anything for me. Then there was an incident..." She trailed off, not sure she really wanted to tell him about that. She should have known he would pick up on it. Suddenly his voice wasn't low and seductively rough, but sharp and like the crack of a whip.

"What incident?"

The memory was still as vivid in her mind as it had been the day after it happened, but she no longer felt the crushing panic in her chest she'd felt then. Surely it would be safe to share it with him without freaking out. "It was something that happened at Deanne's graduation party. This guy was drunk and wouldn't leave me alone, and he ended up trapping me in a corner, pulling a forced seduction bit. I'd let him kiss me at first, but when his hands started wandering, I tried to push him away and he wouldn't stop. He got his hands under my shirt and was saying really nasty things in my ear. I guess to everyone else we looked like another couple making out in the corner, and it seemed to go on forever before anyone intervened. Deanne's fiancé finally dragged him away, but he was Tyler's friend so they were all playing it off like it was so funny. Saying, 'Oh, don't mind him, baby, he's just drunk'. But for a minute there, I was scared to death. I couldn't stop shaking afterward."

"Who was it?"

"No one you know. He doesn't live here." Fortunately for him, because Brian's tone held the promise of murder.

"Fucking bastard," he growled. "Tyler's a bastard, too, for not yanking his boy in line. I can't stand that little frat-rat douche bag, and if I knew the son of a bitch who wouldn't stop pawing you, I'd break his arms for you, Candace."

She couldn't resist the glow that spread through her chest, so she reveled in it. "Don't worry too much about it. For a while I didn't want anything to do with any guys, but I got over that. Obviously."

"Whatever happens with us, you can trust that all you have

to do is say the word and I'll stop. Hell, you don't even have to say the word. Unlike the dumbass who cornered you, I can tell when you're enjoying it and when you're not."

"I know."

"But I have to say." He trailed his fingers down her cheek, his eyes glinting wickedly at her in the faint light. "I didn't get nearly enough of you. You told me to do one thing, and I did it, but we didn't stipulate as to whether I could do it more than once. So with your permission, of course, I'd love to get another taste of you. Draw it out. Make it last." He pulled away, searching her face. "You don't mind how I talk to you, do you?"

So lost in ecstasy over his request, she almost missed the question. "I love it. There are things you want to hear from some people, but not so much from others."

"Mm-hmm." He coaxed her over onto her back again. With a stroke so soft and slow she could scarcely feel it, the tip of his finger slid up the middle of her sex, tantalizing every inch of her. She sighed and opened her legs wider. "That's good. Because I want you to know how soft and wet and perfect you are. How crazy you're driving me," he said, grazing her throat with his lips.

"Yeah, you can keep that up all night," she murmured, squirming against the sensations he was building all over again. His fingertip trailed from her clitoris to her entrance, dipped inside, and spread the wetness he found all through and around her folds. She arched upward, needing more, seeking a deeper contact, and he kept his hand between her legs as he kissed and licked his way down her body.

She threaded her fingers through his hair and left them there as he took position between her thighs again, holding them open as he'd done before. Just when she thought she couldn't bear another moment without his mouth on her, he lowered his head and leisurely built the pressure to a towering inferno all over.

Jesus, did all guys know how to do this so well? She doubted it. She liked to think that for her first non-self-induced orgasms, she'd found the absolute best.

He caught her at the edge of the precipice and slid his fingers deep inside. The sudden tight burn was all it took to push her over. This time, when her release swept her away, it was long, and rolling, and he knew just how to stoke it, just how to draw it out with the gentle thrust and drag of his fingers. She finally collapsed, utterly drained as the last contraction bled her of all remaining strength, her hands relinquishing their death grasp on the sheets because she couldn't hold on anymore.

Brian rose up over her. She managed to crack open one eye to peek at him. "Wow."

"Wow," he agreed. She could smell her own musky scent as he nuzzled under her jaw to kiss her neck. She tipped her chin to the side and bared it for him, noticing his erection still strained his jeans. He'd said she could see him, was he going to keep it zipped up all night?

Steeling her resolve, she made a bold move. She reached down between them and stroked it. Damn if he didn't do that sexy hiss sound again, right in her ear.

"Candace."

"Your jeans are still on," she pouted.

"They need to stay that way, honey. All that control I was bragging about just now? Yeah, it's pretty much hanging by a thread. If you get your hands on my cock, I'm afraid I'll lose it and fuck you senseless right here."

Her soft gasp was involuntary. His words at once thrilled and terrified her. Whichever emotion was more dominant, it caused her blood to hit flashpoint. She was about three seconds—and a whole lot of courage—away from begging him to do it.

"Is that really what you want? I'll hurt you." Even now his voice was shaky, and more savage than she'd ever heard it. Like this, he scared her, and she loved it. If only her stupid virginity weren't in the way, the two of them could have one hell of a time together.

"I know it'll hurt."

"I'm talking more about in the long run."

She ignored that. Now, at this moment, she couldn't ponder any future heartbreak he might bring her. "You're insinuating that I don't have good judgment in determining who I want to sleep with."

"I have the advantage. I think I know me better than you do."

"I don't see what the big deal is. You just gave me two orgasms. What difference does it make that it was with your mouth and not with your..." She snapped her mouth shut.

"Oh, please say it." He laughed.

"Fine. Your *dick*."

"Filthy-mouthed little minx."

"Ha! You're one to talk."

"I know how I talk. But you're so sweet, baby."

"You're changing the subject."

"I'm actually trying to talk myself down."

"Is it working?"

"Not really."

If the hardness pressing into her thigh was any indication, it definitely wasn't. And when she truly examined her feelings, she realized that all of her lust-charged courage had fled her now. "Brian, I could...do something else for you. Whatever you wanted. It isn't fair to leave you like this."

His breathing changed, becoming more ragged. "I should probably work this one out on my own."

She caught his face between his hands. "Let me do it. I want to, more than anything. Please?" Surely it went without saying she didn't know what she was doing, but how hard could it be? Sam had always assured her a stiff breeze would probably make a guy ejaculate if he was worked up enough. Candace had a feeling he was there now.

Chapter Seven

He should have left her at the first touch of her lips, but Brian couldn't regret having the taste of her innocence on his tongue. There was no way in hell he could ever wish he hadn't been the one to make her come like that.

This damn girl was going to kill him. How in the hell did he think he could spend all that time going down on her and not be dying to fuck her?

When she reached down and rubbed his cock through his jeans again, he knew he was lost.

Dumbass, he chided himself even as he surrendered, turning over on his back as she went to work on his fly. Feeling her mouth slicking over him was going to make him want to do nothing but lift her up over his hips and impale her. She was the most beautiful thing he'd ever seen, and if he said or thought the word "sweet" again he was going to lose it. But that's what she was. Too sweet. She'd been a sugar cube on his tongue. He wasn't accustomed to being with girls like her.

A virgin. He still couldn't wrap his mind around it. He hadn't had to worry about shit like that since he was eighteen. She'd been so tight around his fingers he couldn't even fathom attempting to push his way inside her. Couldn't fathom it, couldn't think of anything else.

But he knew one thing for damn frigging sure. The thought of some other guy trying it on her was enough to throw him into a blind, murderous rage.

She'd saved it for all these years, and now she wanted to

give it away? To *him*?

Funny thing was, he probably wouldn't have valued that quality as much in anyone else, if at all. But because it was *her*, he felt like a kid staring at a bright, shiny-wrapped present on Christmas morning. Dying to unwrap it, reluctant to destroy the beauty and purity of it.

And wasn't he just the fucking sap.

She seemed to be having trouble with the button on his jeans, so he reached down and popped it open for her, eager to feel her hands on him. And thank God he was about to. Another thing he hadn't feared since he was a teenager was blowing in his jeans. Watching, hearing and tasting her come in his mouth earlier had nearly done it to him. He was primed and ready for lift-off.

A little groan of pure feminine appreciation escaped her when she finally freed him from the hellish confines of his boxer briefs, and he loved her for it. He couldn't look anywhere else but at her mouth as she licked her lips, curling her hand around his shaft and stroking him. Her touch was so light and unsure—as if she was afraid of hurting him—that he leaned his head back on the pillow and groaned with more agony than pleasure.

Christ, the only thing hurting him was that this particular shiny-wrapped present didn't have his name on it. At least, it shouldn't. It should have some guy's name who was way better than him. Better for her, for her future, for her overall mental health. But whoever that other guy was, Brian wanted to maim the bastard.

Especially when her wet tongue suddenly stroked up the length of his cock. "Jesus *Christ*," he bellowed toward the ceiling. She laughed. And did it again. And again. Then pulled away and gave an embarrassed giggle.

"Um, I'm not quite sure how to maneuver around this thing."

"Huh? It's pretty damned self-explan—oh." Looking down at her, he realized she meant his apa, which she was staring at apprehensively. Something he always made sure to explain to clients was that particular piercing wasn't too conducive to oral if the girl had a small mouth, which Candace did. "Sorry. Do you want me to take it out?"

"You can?"

Ordinarily he didn't like to, but when his only options narrowed down to having a pierced dick or having Candace's mouth wrapped around it, there was no contest. "Some guys have problems with it, but I never have."

She sat back on her knees and watched as he unscrewed the barbell, and he found himself looking at her more than at what he was doing. Long blond hair streaming toward her breasts. Graceful fingers resting on her thighs. Flat belly. The sexy little tat he'd given her. He was so glad she'd come to him for that. The thought of some other guy marking her flesh made him just about as crazy as imagining some other guy fucking her.

That was a new one. He was really losing it.

"So the mystery is at last solved," she said out of the blue.

He gritted his teeth as he finished his task, the tugging almost too much for his overly sensitive erection. He shoved the barbell in the pocket of his jeans. "What mystery?"

"That totally wasn't you in any of those pictures."

He burst out laughing. She was too much. "Sweetie, have you been giving it that much thought?"

"Well...yes!"

"I'm not one to put my cock on display. You see it only if I want you to." He loved how she gave an affronted huff every time he said something crass. It was the cutest damn thing.

"I'm honored," she countered, and he was about to flip something back, but she leaned over and pressed the flat of her tongue to the underside of his glans, and the words died in his throat only to be replaced by two little ones.

"Oh, God."

Even in the darkness, he saw her gaze flicker up to his, and there was no debating: it was the sexiest fucking sight he had ever seen in his entire life. And he'd seen some crazy shit.

"You'll have to tell me if I'm doing this right," she whispered between delectable licks.

"Whatever you do, honey, I imagine it'll be right."

With that reassurance, her lips slipped over the crown and down his shaft. Damp heat engulfed him. Life ceased to exist, his surroundings receded...there was nothing left but the sensation of her mouth closing over him, swallowing him down until his tip nudged the back of her throat. His fingers wrapped in her hair, but he was careful not to force her to take more than she wanted. It was as frustrating as it was pleasurable; he couldn't get deep enough inside her this way. Goddamn, how he wanted to fuck her. Long and deep and slow. He wanted to be the one to show her so much more.

He took her hand and wrapped it around his base, holding it to show her how to stroke where her mouth couldn't reach. How tight he wanted her grip. The rhythm he liked. And oh, Jesus, once she caught on, he could do nothing but collapse in ever increasing ecstasy, unable to imagine how anything could ever feel better than this. She was a quick study. Her tight mouth would fuel his fantasies for the rest of his life. Probably beyond.

The pressure tightening his balls was reaching a critical peak. He willed it back, to prolong this a little longer. As much as he needed relief, he didn't want it to end. But she caught him in a suction that made lightning race along his spine, ripping his senses loose, until all pathetic attempts to stave off the inevitable were utterly annihilated.

"Back up, sugar. I'm gonna come. Oh, *fuck*." Something about letting go in her mouth didn't sit right with him, not this first time. She did as he said, keeping up the same motion with her hand until he erupted. And when he did, holy shit, the angels sang. The force behind the surge was enough to wrench him upward, and he grabbed her fingers to still their motion when it all became too much. She made a throaty sound as if watching him come all over their hands got her hot again—and God help him if it did—while he bit out curses until the violent throbs subsided and the last of his semen seeped out.

Decimated, he fell onto her waterbed, feeling like he was floating as the surface sloshed him around a bit. Candace tentatively released him and crawled from the bed without speaking. Even from behind his closed eyes, he discerned a sudden burst of light from her bathroom. Heard water running. A moment later, a soft towel dropped on his stomach, brushing gently as she cleaned him up. He left la-la land and came back to himself, opening his eyes to find her staring at him, blond hair haloed by the bathroom light behind her.

Goddamn. He was close to professing undying love and she was probably about to kick his ass out of her house. Her silence unnerved him and he had to wonder if she was embarrassed, or thinking this whole thing had all been a huge mistake. If that was the case, she probably realized how much greater of a mistake it could have been. That was good. For her, anyway.

She went to click the light off and returned to the side of the bed, fingers fiddling with one another. “Are you leaving?” she asked softly after a moment.

“Do you want me to?”

Her answer was immediate. “No. I just figured you probably would.”

He patted the bed beside him, leaving his arm down so she could lay her head against his shoulder. She climbed on, pulling the covers over the both of them, and snuggled against him. It was probably the absolute worst, stupidest, most idiotic thing he could do, but he kicked his jeans the rest of the way off and curled her naked body around his so that there was scarcely a square inch of them that wasn’t touching. He would most likely dream about her all night and wake up with a massive hard-on, and there she would be, tantalizingly close and warm and maybe still willing.

Dude, you are either one stupid son of a bitch, or you might just be the smartest motherfucker who ever lived.

“Are you okay?” he whispered.

“Mm-hmm. Are you?”

He stroked her hair. “I’m great, sweetheart.”

"Can I ask you something?"

He had to chuckle. Whenever anyone else said that to him, he groaned. With her, he could only look forward to what she was going to inquire with eager curiosity. "Anything."

"Did you quit smoking?"

For a moment, he was struck speechless. They hadn't talked about this at all. He hadn't talked about it with anyone. "I did, actually—well, I haven't had one in two weeks, anyway."

"I noticed. You never could go an hour without walking outside to light up."

Maybe it wasn't as big a deal as his mind—or his heart—wanted to make it out to be. Any observant person could've put it together. But his family hadn't. His friends hadn't. She had. She'd watched him that much.

He tightened his embrace on her and turned his face to brush his lips against her forehead. "Thank you."

She tilted her face up to his. "For what?"

"For being there. For being you. For everything."

"I'm glad you quit," she whispered.

"Me too."

She awoke to sunlight pouring in her window and a heavy leg lying on top of one of hers. The previous night came flooding back all at once, too vivid to have been a dream, and besides, the warm male flesh crowding hers in the bed was proof it had really happened.

She hadn't slept much, awakening several times during the night just to stare at him and marvel that he was here, next to her. Her virginity may still be intact, but he'd taken it down from "complete and utter" to "technical only". It was something, at least.

She lay on her side with Brian's arm over her waist. His breath tickled her nape, slow and languid.

How would it feel to wake up like *this* every morning?

She wanted to stretch and arch her back and purr like a

cat. The urge was almost undeniable, but it would probably disturb him, and she needed to savor these moments. There might not be any more of them.

The numbers on her digital clock said it was almost ten. She was dying for coffee. No class on Fridays, but for all she knew, he had someplace he needed to be. Sighing in resignation, she turned over in his arms and snuggled close, putting her lips on his throat and giving him a gentle bite. He chuckled drowsily and raised his shoulder, forcing her to pull back.

"You can't be ticklish," she said in disbelief.

"Mm-hmm. I am." She loved how he sounded, his voice all slow and sleep-roughened.

"I'll have to remember that." Even as the words left her lips, her heart sank. What if this had all really meant nothing to him? What if he wouldn't take her virginity because he suffered from that stupid male affliction of thinking she was going to want to marry him or something if she gave it up to him? Maybe she would, but that wasn't the point. The point was, if that was the case, then he didn't want her wanting him, because he didn't want her.

Is that really what you want? I'll hurt you.

It crushed her.

His hand came up to caress her cheek, pushing her tangled hair away from her face. When he looked at her as he was right now, she wondered what the problem was. He had to feel something. There was something there in his eyes she had never seen when he looked at her cousin. A...tenderness, lame as it might sound. As if the sight of her caused something in him to melt. She couldn't be imagining it.

He was so beautiful. Handsome was such a plain word, too plain to describe him. Here in the light of day she could see what she was touching. She trailed her hand over his biceps, tracing the lines of his tattoos. It could turn into a favorite pastime of hers. She sat up a bit and leaned over to press her lips against a beautiful blue rose on his skin. The movement pressed her breasts against him.

"Shit," he whispered. His arm came up behind her so he could clutch at her hair. His other hand gravitated toward her left breast, palming it and gently massaging. She sucked in a breath and her nipple peaked against him. Her tongue sneaked out to flicker against his skin, and he pushed his hips into her.

His cock was already as erect as it had been last night, a hard ridge in his boxer briefs. It ground into her abdomen and, before he could stop her, she plunged her hand down into the waistband of his underwear and deftly freed it.

"Candace," he said, his voice tinged with warning.

"I just want to play," she murmured. "Let me? One more time?"

His groan was a combination of frustrated pleasure and despair. She loved making him sound like that, as if he was torn in two over her, even though she knew she would be better off if she could take the "despair" out of the equation. "When you ask me like that, how the fuck can I resist?"

Giggling, she cupped both hands around his length and stroked, noticing he'd put his piercing back in at some point in the night. He was big and long and heavy, jutting straight out from a patch of jet-black hair. The thickness of his shaft and the silver glint of his barbell gave her a twinge of anxiety. If she ever got her chance, it would be enough trying to take him in without anything else going along. But at the same time, she wanted to experience everything he had to give her.

She continued rubbing him from base to tip, first with one hand and then the other. She circled the ball on the top of his glans with her thumb. His breath rasped, his grip on her tightened. He reached over and pushed her thigh up, burying his hand between her legs and groaning again when he felt how damp she'd grown.

A gasp ripped from her throat as his fingertip parted her folds and he dipped into her wetness and spread it, circling her clit and then gently probing her entrance. She clamped her thighs on his wrist, all the sensations too much for her to take. He stopped what he was doing only long enough to wrench her legs apart again, his mouth finding hers as his fingers dove back down to take their place between her labia.

"Oh, God," she said in a rush against his lips. He sucked her tongue into his mouth and stroked it with his own, sending her arousal spiraling into the heavens. One of his fingers breached her passage, pushing past her resistance until he was buried to the knuckle in her heat, his palm tight against her. Instinctively, she undulated against it, collapsing on the bed in sheer bliss as he moved in and out, hooking his finger to graze her upper wall.

When she relaxed for him, she felt him nudge a second fingertip next to the first and nearly lost her mind. So incredibly wet... Her body couldn't resist the intrusion, and she didn't want it to. The stretch as he pushed inside was exquisite, devastating, and she could do nothing but spread wider and let him go as deep as he could, her brow furrowed in agony as he did.

"Am I hurting you?" he whispered. She could feel his gaze intent on her face.

"I...just...please..."

"Please what?"

Stop. Don't stop. I don't freaking know.

"Surely you've done this to yourself before?" he asked, his voice dark and sinful. "Tell me."

"Brian, I..." She trailed off into a moan when he twisted his fingers inside her.

"What did you say to me last night? You wanted me to let you get a little bit dirty. Tell me, Candace. Tell me what you do and what you think about."

She'd fallen into the Twilight Zone. The world outside was bright and cheerful; birds sang, cars zipped down the street. This was her room, her bed, her belongings. Yet it was an entirely different dimension she'd fallen into. He was its gatekeeper.

"Y-yes, I've done this."

"What do you think about? Do you imagine someone else is here, doing it to you?"

She nodded, her entire state of being reduced to the sensual slide of his fingers in and out of her pussy. So many times, she'd wished it were him doing that to her. And now it was.

"Tell me."

The words burst out of her throat with an almost humiliating eagerness. "I think about— I think about you. I promise I'm not just saying that because you're here now. I think about you doing this to me. And kissing me there. I think about...you making love to me." She wanted to cringe even as she said it.

He lowered his lips to her ear, nuzzling the soft, sensitive shell. "And when I make love to you," he murmured, sending chills skittering madly down her arms, "am I gentle? Or am I rough?" He pushed his fingers hard when he said the last, driving a gasp from her. His palm connected with her clit and he pressed it firmly, still keeping up his torturous rhythm inside her body.

"If I'm having a—oh, God—having a bad day, or if I'm sad, I imagine you're gentle. But other times...I just want you to..." She sank her teeth into her bottom lip, lifting a hand to cover her face.

"Don't be embarrassed," he whispered. "Although I love the way you blush. Tell me what I do, how you need me. The darkest fantasies you have, in the last wild moments before you make yourself come, what do you imagine I've done to you?"

She shook her head on the pillow, not wanting to lend voice to those thoughts. He gentled his movements, and she grasped his wrist hard enough to make her knuckles go white, terrified he would stop if she didn't reply. "You tie me up," she said.

"Fuck." He moved his mouth to her shoulder, exhaling warmth across her skin, and then trailed it over to her breast. Her nipple slipped into his mouth, and he sucked it until she whimpered. All of it was too much for her, but she needed so much more.

Once the words were out there, she couldn't stop them. "You tie me up and I'm helpless, all spread out for you. You can take whatever you want and I let you have it all." His teeth sank into her soft flesh, and she cried out. It was the best pain she'd ever felt in her life. "S-so maybe I'm not as innocent as you think I am."

"Oh, you are," he murmured, releasing his hold on her nipple, leaving it shining with moisture. It was so stiff and aching and throbbing from his ministrations she wanted to touch it herself, to soothe the sting away. "But I do love that you fantasize about me. Maybe you'll call me next time you're in the middle of one and you need to hear my voice to get you through. I'll tell you what I wish I was here doing to you. However you need me, rough or gentle."

Her cheeks flamed at the thought of that deep, wicked voice purring her to orgasm as she stroked herself. Letting him hear her moan his name as she came for him, only for him, even if he was across town.

"I will," she said. "I think I'd love that."

Suddenly, he pulled his hand from between her legs and rose up over her, pushing her thighs down to the mattress so that she cried out and nearly had a panic attack.

Oh God I've set him off he's going to do it he's going to...

He dragged the tip of his cock between her labia, coating it with her moisture, but he didn't push inside. "Fuck, I want to," he muttered, and she had the feeling it was more to himself than to her. "I want to more than I've ever wanted any fucking thing in my entire life."

She was dying. Couldn't lie still, wriggling closer, tilting her hips, trying to get him to slip inside. It wasn't possible. Given his girth, it would take more than a mere "slip" to get him in. But he appeared to have complete control of himself, and he evaded her every move.

She let fly a string of curses she hadn't known she was capable of, calling him a choice name or two. He had the audacity to grin. He rubbed his crown over her clit, letting the little ball on the underside skim over it. Strong hands gripped her hips and lifted them off the bed, while he kept up the delicious back-and-forth motion across the aching bundle of nerves, his shaft cradled by her labia. Oooh, that was good. And it would make her come soon, but it wouldn't assuage the empty ache. She needed to be filled up by him. If he would only move down an inch or so, he could push in...

"Do it," she sobbed. "I don't care, Brian, just—"

"Baby, I don't have any condoms on me. I'm guessing you don't, either."

She shook her head, her brow furrowed with frustration.

"I'm not going raw in you."

"You were going to until you found out I'm a virgin."

"No, I was praying you had something. Or were on something. I told you, I didn't come here for this, and I meant it."

She thought it was a convenient lie, and wanted to argue further, but her muscles were tightening deliciously, shutting down the connection between her brain and her mouth. Brian's eyes closed and he groaned, grabbing his shaft and pumping it as he rocked against her. She had only a moment to appreciate how gorgeous he looked this way, muscles standing out in his arms and his abs, before the sensations in her sex overtook her entire body, exploding outward. She could only wish he was inside her to feel how she would grip him.

"That's it, sweetie, come for me," he murmured, the words dissolving into a groan that brought as much pleasure to her as everything else he was doing. She reached out and fisted the sheets as he ground out a curse and warmth erupted across her belly, though he had the foresight to move a bit so that her tattoo wasn't endangered. Unabashed, she arched against him, her head thrown back, feeling his gaze on her swaying breasts even though her eyes were closed. It wasn't often that she felt truly beautiful, but in that moment, with the lush pleasure he'd given her zinging along her nerve endings, she could have believed she was.

It was the only thought at the forefront of her mind as he eased her back down to the bed and back down to earth. All the heat had rushed out of her body and suddenly, she was cold. She just needed him to hold her. Again, she couldn't stop shaking.

His weight came slowly down on her and she wrapped her arms tight around him, feeling at once deliriously happy and more than a little furious that he'd made her beg like that. Helpless tears leaked from her eyes as she leaned her face into his shoulder. Maybe he would hold her until she could get control, and he wouldn't have to see her cry again. Was it too much to ask to maintain at least a shred of dignity around him? He'd about taken it all away.

Bullshit, he didn't have any condoms. She wanted to scoff. He probably had one in his wallet right now. But she didn't really want to know if he'd lied to her.

With some effort, she cleared her throat and prayed he wouldn't hear tears in her voice when she spoke. "I can get up and make some coffee."

"That would be awesome." He rolled away from her and pushed the hair away from his eyes, staring up at the ceiling. She took the opportunity to surreptitiously swipe at her cheeks with the sheet. Time to put on her big girl panties and deal with it. The consequences had been laid out for her from the beginning.

"Do you mind if I jump in the shower first?" she asked, considering the mess they'd made.

"Only if I can go right behind you."

"Sure." He could be in there *with* her, if he wanted to. Jerk.

The hot spray did little to clear her head as she rinsed away the last remnants of their interlude. But at least the water running over her face camouflaged the tears she finally let flow in earnest. Had to get them out of her system *now*. Get them out, get it over with. She didn't have any idea where this was going, but it hadn't hit a brick wall or anything. They had time. They were okay.

So why was she near sobbing?

She jumped and whirled when he entered the shower behind her, his chest brushing her shoulder. "Thought you were coming in later," she said, hearing panic in her voice. He was looking straight into her eyes, which she knew were red and weepy. There was no hiding that, or the trembling of her bottom lip.

Dammit. Caught.

Brian slicked the hair back off her forehead, as he seemed to be fond of doing, then put his hand to her elbow and gently moved it up to her shoulder. When he pulled her to him, she hated herself for going so willingly, and for breaking down when his arms wrapped securely around her, holding her tight to him as she sobbed.

Chapter Eight

Somehow, they fell back into an amiable manner with each other, drinking coffee out on her patio under a flawlessly clear sky. Candace had not only put coffee on, but whipped up a batch of pancakes and made him the best damn omelet he'd ever had in his life, and he was stuffed. The morning was mild, and she wore a silky white robe he'd love to strip off her, but that time had passed. Still, she was beautiful, her hair damp and her face clean of what little makeup she ordinarily wore.

He needed to stop these lightning-flash thoughts about how nice it would be to spend every morning with her. That way could only lay disaster. He didn't want to take the one thing she had left before he had time to examine this feeling, to see if it could turn into something real. It was tough getting her to understand that. She was such an all-or-nothing go-getter. He loved that about her, but damn. She was a handful.

And such a go-getter that she'd damn near gotten it this morning. One flip of his switch while he'd been poised at her entrance and he'd have been lost. The thought of having her tied up and at his mercy had almost been enough to do it. Imagining her gasping and sighing over his phone had compounded it. If she'd only reached down and run her fingertip along her clit where he could see, he'd have been a crazed beast. Seeing a woman touch herself was his trigger.

Hell, they'd pretty much done everything-but over the past ten hours. Her virginity really shouldn't have been that big a deal at this point. But it was. It was huge. If he'd lost control and taken her the way he wanted, he'd have left here feeling like a dog, because he would have hurt her. No question.

She deserved something special. She deserved candlelight and roses, shit like that. A promise, at the very least. Something he didn't feel he was in any position to give her.

Candace was silent as she sipped her coffee and stared out over the park across the street from her apartment building. Kids were running around and playing on the monkeybars and the rickety merry-go-round, challenging one another to swing the highest on the swingset. Brian could remember playing there with Evan and Gabby when he was little. The two of them had tortured him and kept him in tears. Now it was mostly the other way around.

He turned his gaze from the place of much of his childhood torment and watched the wind lift damp tendrils of Candace's hair and cast them across her face. She reached up to smooth them back and tuck them behind her ear, her hands slender and graceful, each tapered finger ending in a French tip. His fantasies of watching those fingertips slide over her nether regions went full-blown.

Okay, if just seeing her make the most mundane gestures was getting to him, he was definitely in trouble. But he'd never minded trouble, and it always seemed to find him. It was practically an old friend, but it had never been as sweet as this.

There was that damn word again.

"What are you doing today?" she asked.

It might have been a subtle hint to get lost. He didn't think he'd ever hung around for this long with a girl the morning after, and he felt awkward, conspicuous. He was so reluctant to leave her. "I imagine I'll go to work in a few hours," he said.

"You imagine?" She laughed. "Must be nice to be the boss."

"I highly recommend it. And I like keeping them on their toes, not knowing when I'll drop in." He grinned at her. "What's up with you today?"

He could have sworn her face darkened. "I have to get fitted for a bridesmaid's dress. Crap. I never did call to..." She checked her watch and frowned.

"Who's getting married?"

"Deanne and Tyler."

"Finally, huh. Well, good for them. They deserve each other. Let's just pray they don't reproduce."

Her eyes widened and her mouth dropped, and he got the biggest kick out of her split-second of dismay. Then she laughed. "That's my cousin."

He shook his head. "I feel sorry for you. I always did for Michelle, too, for ever having to live with her." He would also pity Tyler, the poor schmuck, if the guy wasn't such an asshole himself. "I should go to the wedding. Jump up when the preacher asks for reasons the two should not be joined and yell, 'Can't you *see*? Their child will be the anti-Christ!'"

She was still laughing and looking rather distressed about it, covering her mouth and ducking her head so that her hair fell forward.

He reached across the small table and tugged the sleeve of her robe. "Come on, you have to agree with me. Admit it. I won't tell."

"You're bad. That's my family."

"You won't find me keeping quiet about mine. I have no qualms about telling them to their faces how I feel, either."

She sobered, the corners of her mouth turning down. "Mine is..." Her cell phone suddenly chirped from its position on the table, and he wondered if she would have continued even without the interruption.

He'd forgotten about it until this moment, but Michelle had once told him she was concerned about Candace because of how stern and close-minded and positively medieval her parents were with her. According to his ex, they practically believed in arranged marriages. Candace's older brother was no better, but Brian didn't need to be told that. He'd gone to school with Jameson. If ever anyone deserved an ass-kicking more than Tyler, it was Jameson Andrews. If he bullied his baby sister like he did everyone else, it was no wonder she seemed so beat-down sometimes.

"Speak of the devil," Candace mumbled. "It's my mom."

He fell silent and sipped his coffee as she answered the phone, watching her expression travel the spectrum from calm to alarmed to outright panicked as the conversation progressed. Even before she hung up, he had a feeling he knew exactly what she would say, and his heart sank.

Sure enough, as soon as she snapped the phone closed, she turned rounded blue eyes on him, sitting straight up in her seat. "She's on her way to pick me up to go to lunch. She'll be here in like *two minutes.*"

"Guess that's my cue to disappear." Grudgingly, he stood. She shot up beside him and ran through the open patio door as if a rabid dog was nipping at her heels. He followed her into the living room.

"Oh, God, I'm so sorry, but no, you can't be here!" It was said as she rushed about, frantically grabbing empty beer bottles and the popcorn bowl from the night before off the coffee table. "Shitshit*shit.*"

It would have been cute to hear her curse like that under other circumstances. As it was, it seemed ridiculous. "Candace, you're a grown woman. So what if you had a guy stay over? I can understand not wanting to rub your mom's face in it, but Jesus, it's not that big a deal. This is *your* place, not your upstairs bedroom back home."

"You don't understand," she wailed, high-tailing it to the kitchen to bury the incriminating evidence as deep in her trash can as she could push it. How Joan-Crawford-*Mommie-Dearest* could her mother be?

"*Nooo wiiiire hangerrrrrs*!" he bellowed as he picked up his wallet and mobile phone from an end table, stuffing them both in his back pocket.

"Dammit, don't joke about it, Brian!"

All right, he got it. He'd never met her mother personally, and she would take one look at him and faint. Some inked-up, pierced metal-head-looking dude corrupting her baby girl. He knew the drill. Hell, his own mom looked at him in utter exasperation most of the time. He'd seen the paternal head-shake more than once. Even his brother didn't know what to make of him most of the time. And his sister? Forget it. But he'd never tried to hide who he was. He'd never been ashamed.

"I'm out," he called harshly, striding toward her door.

"Brian?"

The doorknob was in his hand. He should turn it and walk out of her life. It wasn't as if a fucking *husband* had pulled up to the curb outside, just her fucking *mother*. "What."

Candace stopped her frantic clean-up efforts long enough to rush over to him. "Are you okay? I'm sorry. I had no idea she was coming—"

"You know," he interrupted, and she stopped and retreated a step from the cold blast of his voice. "I don't see how you possibly think we could work out, when you're too embarrassed for your mother to see me here."

"I'm not embarrassed, I—"

"You are. Would you be quite so freaked out if I was some Ivy League preppy fuck? I doubt it."

"Please don't think that's what this is about. It isn't, I promise."

After all that begging for him to pop her cherry. What would it have really been for? A revenge fuck? A way to get back at Mommy and Daddy for sheltering her all her life? Because she damn sure wasn't ready to parade him in front of them and introduce him as her man, and judging by her actions in the past few minutes, she never would be.

He shook his head. Opened the door. "You're seriously deluding yourself if you think that." And he was gone. He didn't know if she made any move whatsoever to follow him, because he never looked back.

Sylvia Andrews swept into the apartment as if she owned it, not even bothering to knock. She eyed Candace sitting on the couch, staring off into space, and crossed her arms. "Candy, you're not ready," she said by way of greeting.

Candace turned blind eyes on her mom. "Hey. Sorry. Give me a minute, okay?"

She stood and padded across to her bedroom, wondering how she was going to keep it together for the next few hours under her family's scrutiny. Brian hated her. She couldn't forget that last look he'd given her before he walked out the door, as if she was scum of the earth.

She so was not ashamed of him. She'd be the proudest girl in the world if he were hers. But her parents had scared off more than one potential suitor, and she was so afraid of that happening now. Apparently, she'd already done it herself.

"Well, hurry up, dear," her mom called. "I never thought for a minute you wouldn't be dressed yet. They're only holding our table for twenty minutes. Are you ill?"

He couldn't understand. He hadn't grown up in the environment she had. He was stronger than she was. Candace pulled her closet door open and stared listlessly at her wardrobe, wondering what she could wear that her mother wouldn't eye too critically. Or outright criticize.

"Candy!"

"Ma'am?"

"I asked if you felt okay."

"Fine, Mom. Sorry. I'll hurry."

She rushed through dressing and reentered the living room. Her mother's gaze traveled up to her hair and she sighed. "Your hair is damp."

"I'd just gotten out of the shower when you called. I didn't have time to dry it."

"Well, the top is down on the convertible. Maybe that will finish it off."

Right. She would look like the bride of Frankenstein by the time they got there, while her mom would somehow look immaculate with nothing more than a quick pass of the brush. Right now she was flawless in her perfectly tailored peach pantsuit, carrying a Louis Vuitton the size of a briefcase.

Candace ran to the kitchen to grab her own purse and headed toward the door. "I'm ready." She held open the door for her mother, trying to turn her face away as Sylvia walked past. It was too late.

"Really, are you all right? You look on the verge of tears."

She was. Right on the cusp, about to fall. And maybe there really wasn't any reason to hide. Maybe her parents wouldn't have any objection to Brian. He came from a wealthy family, surely had a sizable inheritance. A shame that it was really the only thing that mattered to her family, but that's the way it was. If she could get their blessing, she could then go and see if she could get his forgiveness.

"I had a, um...I had a date last night that didn't go so well."

They were almost to the parking lot where her mom's car sat, and the clack-clack-clack of Sylvia's Blahniks ground to a halt. Candace stopped to face the music. "You told me you were with Macy."

"I was, for a while. Then I ran into, um, this guy I know, and—"

"Who?" That one word was practically an inquisition.

Candace took a deep breath, praying, praying... Oh, crap, it was useless. Looking into her mother's expectant, icy blue eyes, she couldn't even say his name. "He's one of Michelle's exes."

For a split second, Sylvia looked relieved. "Scott Chandler, maybe?"

"No."

"For heaven's sake, *who*, Candace?"

"Mom, promise you won't get mad at me, okay?"

Just like that, the relief was gone and her mother blanched three shades whiter. Candace's heart deflated. "Not Alexander's boy. What are you thinking? What was *Michelle* thinking?"

"What's so wrong about him? I mean, he's different, but—"

"Different? No. Different I could accept. Maybe. But that boy's been nothing but a stain on his family name for years. We finally got her away from him, and now he's moved on to *you*? Well, at least you said the date didn't go well. We don't have to worry about you seeing him anymore. Thank heavens."

We finally got her away from him?

Sylvia took her arm and steered her toward the car again. "At least you have Deanne's wedding to look forward to. There will be several eligible bachelors there, if you're looking. Do you remember Stephen Davis, who we introduced you to at Deanne's graduation? I was so impressed with him. And he seemed to like you. He'll be one of Tyler's groomsmen. He's coming in from *Yale.* Isn't that wonderful? Candy, I want you to find someone like that, someone with a real future. Maybe Deanne will pair you with him in the recession, and you two can get to know one another better."

Candace kept her jaw resolutely closed, but ice slid down her spine. Indeed, she remembered Stephen Davis who had been at Deanne's graduation with Tyler. He'd also been the one she'd told Brian about, the only other guy who'd ever had his hands on her body, and not with her permission.

She had another flash of remembrance. That guy had been obnoxiously arrogant, but somehow he managed to charm the pants off any and all parents. Hers had loved him from the moment Tyler introduced them. Her mom had been giving her that nudge-nudge-wink-wink look even then.

Candace smirked. He hadn't been able to charm *her* pants off. And he'd reacted violently.

But she already knew better than to try to explain to her mother what had happened with that guy. Sylvia would turn it around and make it her fault, somehow.

She could hear it now. *What did you do to tempt him? You were probably dressed like a whore, like all you girls are fond of doing these days.* Her mother had actually uttered words to that effect once, about a girl who'd accused a family friend's son of date raping her. Candace didn't see why she would be any different.

"I like Brian a lot," she said, without much hope. "One date didn't go exactly well toward the end, but we had fun. If he wanted to see me again—"

"Absolutely not, and if I have to call Alexander to tell him to keep that boy away from you, I'll do it. Poor man. Evan turned out so well...oh, why couldn't he be the one you liked?"

How Brian would love being called "that boy", as if they were all still in high school. "Mother, Evan is married. And he's almost ten years older than me."

"Age doesn't matter. Yes, I know he got married. Pity. And to Todd Jacobs's ex-wife, who's not even from here. I just think he could have done better. Courtney Miller was such a nice girl, and from a good family, too. Her poor mother was devastated when she and Evan broke up."

With a heavy sigh, Candace plopped down in the car seat and slammed the door shut. "You seem to forget Evan threw her out because she cheated on him."

"Well, now, we all make mistakes, dear. We mustn't judge."

Mistakes! Mustn't judge? Ugh! Candace wanted to grab the nearest sharp objects and jam them into her eardrums so maybe she wouldn't have to listen to any more of her mother's hypocritical BS. No use in explaining that Evan was, by all accounts, wildly in love with his wife and deliriously happy with their new baby, oh, no. How dare he dump a traitorous fiancée to marry a perfectly nice and lovely woman whose only crime was not sharing quite the same status in the community as he?

Candace would've described that question as sarcastic. It would've been legitimate and worth pondering to Sylvia.

She should have known better than to mention Brian. Despite his family name, he bucked convention and held up a middle finger to "status in the community". He didn't give a damn, and people like that confused and frightened her mother.

Today was shaping up to be the most trying day of her life. She was going to lose it, absolutely freaking lose it. Her control was stretching thinner all the time.

Deanne met them for lunch, and Candace groaned inwardly at seeing the lithe Barbie doll personified walking toward them in the restaurant, wearing a blinding smile. "Aunt Syl!"

Actually, Candace mused as she watched the two collide

with air-kisses, "Barbie doll" wasn't entirely apt. Unless it was "Southern Belle Barbie" or something. She'd always thought Deanne should walk around wearing huge, airy hats and petticoats. She had that look about her. Fresh, blond, busty…and of course there was that beguilingly sweet drawl Candace suspected she'd cultivated to perfection. It could go from syrupy to satanic in a heartbeat.

Sighing, she rubbed a hand over her face, certain her lack of a full night's sleep was registering there. She knew she was sporting evil dark circles and carried the aftereffects of her earlier tears in her red-rimmed eyes. She was surprised her mother still wanted to be seen with her.

"Candy! You look…great. I'm so glad you'll be in my wedding." Deanne's mouth was smiling warmly at Candace as she took her seat, but none of it reached her assessing, judgmental eyes.

Do I look like I was up trying to get laid all night and failing miserably? Good.

"Don't mind her weepiness. She had a bad date last night," Sylvia announced as she snapped her menu open, her mouth drawn into a tight, lipsticked slash across her face. She spat the word "date" as if it was dirty.

Jesus Christ. A series of curses that would've made Brian proud lit off in her head. If Deanne found out who it was, she would go straight to tell Michelle, and while she knew her cousin would find out eventually if she and Brian ended up together—yeah, right—she wasn't ready for that information to get back to her yet.

Deanne looked sympathetic, but Candace couldn't tell if it was fake or not. The inevitable question followed. "Who are you seeing?"

"Um…no one, apparently. I'd rather not say right now, if you don't mind." Candace shot her mom a glance and found Sylvia glaring at her over the top of her menu. She dropped her gaze to her own and thought about how *not* hungry she was.

And then Deanne dropped a bombshell. "Oh, Aunt Syl, I invited Michelle to eat with us and come to the fitting. She's just running a little late. I hope you don't mind."

"Of course I don't. I haven't seen her in weeks, it seems. But she's *so* very busy with school, the poor dear."

I'm so very busy with school too, Candace grumbled inwardly. *I've never been your poor dear.*

Okay, she was feeling entirely too sorry for herself. Her freaking cousin was coming, and Candace could still taste Brian's lips, still feel his fingers lodged inside her, still hear his erotic enticements in her ear to tell him all her fantasies...

"Hi, everyone!"

Blowing out a breath, Candace stood to face her ravishing cousin and waited her turn to give her a hug. When Michelle finally enveloped her in a cloud of perfume and chestnut brown hair and soft bosom, Candace held on tight for a second longer than she needed to.

"Hey, there, little cuz. Where've you been lately?"

"Here and there," Candace said, trying to sound bright and not as if she was about to burst into tears any second. She'd been a freaking moron to tell her mother about Brian. *Stupid stupid stupid...*

Michelle stepped back and her brown eyes—the same gold-flecked color as her hair—roved over Candace's face as concern filled her expression. "Oh, honey, are you okay? You haven't been sick, have you? You don't look like yourself."

No, and she didn't feel like herself either. Her mother was watching her like a hawk. Just waiting to hint at the bit of news she was privy to? If she said anything about Brian, anything at all, Candace was going to throw a glass of water in her face and tell Deanne to hell with the wedding. She was in no mood for their crap.

"I'm fine. Just tired."

"Better shape up in the next couple of weeks," Deanne chimed as Michelle and Candace took their seats across from each other. "You'll go with me and the girls for a spa day next week. We'll get manicures, pedicures, facials...the whole thing."

"I'm *so* glad you're in," Michelle said to Candace. It was

probably the first genuine thing that had been said at this table. "We'll have a good time. And we've got a lot of catching up to do."

"I'm looking forward to it," Candace replied, trying to pour some truth into the words. She'd love to catch up with Michelle, but preferably some other way that didn't involve a crappy pastel bridesmaid's dress and dyed pumps and hanging out with a bunch of people she couldn't stand. She'd have to train herself to walk in the shoes so she didn't wind up face down on the floor of the church.

Michelle turned to her sister. "So you never told me why Becky's out. What happened?"

Candace picked up her water glass to take a sip, thinking this was probably going to be a riot.

Deanne rolled her eyes heavenward, lifting her hands for emphasis as she bellowed: "She got a *tattoo*!"

The mouthful of water Candace was in the process of swallowing jammed in her throat and came back up. Frantically, she grabbed one of the heavy linen napkins and pressed it to her lips, certain she was turning beet red as she tried to catch her breath. Michelle was grinning knowingly at her, but Deanne and Sylvia were both too caught up in their horror over the situation to notice.

"It's on her *upper back*. Right *here*." Deanne indicated the spot on her left shoulder blade. "I said, 'Rebecca! Oh my God! The dresses are *off the shoulder*. I can't have you walking down the aisle like that! It's *trashy*.' I mean, you're all wearing up-dos. That thing will be right out there for everyone to ogle."

Sylvia was shaking her head as if being faced with all the suffering in the wide world. "How dreadful. Those things are hideously unattractive."

"Oh, Aunt Syl..." Michelle began indulgently. She'd always been so much better at dealing with Candace's mom than Candace herself. She was so easygoing about everything, taking it all in stride. Of course, that was the best way to survive in this family. "They're the norm now. You might as well face it."

"I will not. People are ruining their bodies with those

wretched things. Candace Marie, if I ever hear of you—"

"Aunt Syl, before you say anything, don't forget I have three." Michelle was laughing, having a great time. "Of course, you don't date a tattoo artist for over a year and not walk away with a few souvenirs."

"What did he do, hold you down and tattoo you against your will?" Deanne asked. A dreamy smile—remembrance?—spread across Michelle's lips and there was no denying the flush that crept up her cheeks. Her entire demeanor had softened.

Oh, crap. There were still feelings there. Candace had just witnessed Michelle silently go to pieces at the mere mention of him.

Thankfully, Sylvia's lips were currently sipping water, but her narrowed, accusatory gaze flickered over to Candace.

"At least yours aren't anywhere I can see," Deanne finished.

Michelle managed to pull herself out of her own Brian-induced funk. If only Candace could do the same. "So what are you saying? If they were, I couldn't be in your wedding? Your own sister?"

Deanne sniffed and pursed her pillow lips. "It would depend on what they were. I guess."

"What did Becky get?"

"I don't even know."

Michelle shook her head, giving Candace a wink as the waiter came to take their orders. Still feeling stuffed from her late breakfast, she ordered a garden salad and earned an approving nod from her mother that made her not want, but *need* to tear the woman's hair out and then order the most fat-laden item on the menu.

"Good for you, Candy. Better to have to take the dress in than let it out, I always say. And you do look as if you've put on a few pounds these last couple of months."

She did not just go there in front of everyone. Are you kidding *me?*

"I don't think she'll need too many alterations," Deanne

said, eyeing Candace critically from the neck down. "You're basically the same size as Becky, I think. Maybe take the bust in a bit."

Of course. Because I have no boobs. But remember, I've got ass.

If she didn't get through this day without hitting someone or screaming, she had far more self-control than she thought.

Chapter Nine

Brian must've been wearing one hell of a thunderous expression. When he stalked into the shop that evening, his employees glanced up at him, opened their mouths to speak, apparently thought better of it, and went back to whatever they were working on.

Shit. They were swamped. Everyone had a client and there wasn't an empty seat in the waiting area.

So much for going back to his office or his studio and unwinding by drawing and blasting the music until his eardrums bled, which had been his plan when he'd forced himself to leave his apartment. All he'd been doing there was pacing like a caged animal, thinking about calling Candace and apologizing for being such an ass this morning. He hadn't necessarily wanted to interact with anyone, but now that he was here, he couldn't go into the back and hide while his guys were working their asses off. That's something the old Brian would have done, the one he kept insisting didn't exist anymore. Hell, the old Brian wouldn't have gotten off the couch tonight in the first place. He'd have wallowed in his misery, or drowned it in booze.

Now he would drown it in work. He needed to put the mindfuck Candace had run on him out of his head. Of all frigging ways for it to end. If only he'd cut out as soon as he'd been dressed and ready, like he usually did in those situations, he might still be willing to stick it out and see what the future held. It was probably for the best it had happened the way it had, before he let himself get too involved.

"I'll be with you guys in a minute," he told the waiting group as he strode through toward the back. He thought he sensed a collective sigh of relief from his artists. It only took him a few seconds to grab his cap and his gum—damn, but he needed a smoke—and head back out to the chaos.

His first client of the evening wanted her navel pierced. She thought. She was petite and really pretty, and looked young enough that he made her flash her ID. Nothing irked him more than sixteen-year-olds coming in here trying to pass themselves off as eighteen—well, nothing except thirteen- or fourteen-year-olds who actually had permission from their parents—but his girl checked out.

She'd only ever had her ears pierced, and had about five bazillion questions. As he began to settle into the routine, explaining aftercare, helping her pick out the jewelry she wanted, he started to feel a bit better.

But his girl was so hung up on whether or not it was going to be unbearably painful that he was finally forced to give his usual spiel about the pain factor, only it came out all wrong. And ended with, "So, hey, it's all gonna hurt, there's no way around it. If you're deciding on where to get pierced based on where it's going to hurt the least, then it's not for you."

She looked at him in surprise. Great. He was supposed to put them at ease, not chase them away. But just then he realized where his statement had come from...it rang true with relationships too. They weren't for him. Too much pain involved.

Physical pain he could take. It came, did its damage, and was gone. He didn't know what to do about the ache that gnawed at his gut after everything crashed down around him. There'd only been a handful of times he'd experienced it, and today was definitely one of them.

After one night with the girl? No way.

It couldn't be just about her. The way she'd treated him was shitty, that was all, and he'd be pissed at any girl who screwed him over. God knew he didn't mind using someone, and he didn't mind being used. But that shit was supposed to be understood from the start. There were ethics involved. Two people getting each other off was one thing. But she couldn't ask him to be her first, she couldn't look at him as if she wanted to crawl inside him, she couldn't cry on his shoulder for ten minutes in the shower only to turn around and treat him like dog crap afterward.

But she wouldn't know a damn thing about how any of this works, dumbass. Remember?

That was the exact reason he was better off without the hassle.

His girl finally stopped fretting and went ahead with the piercing. The clamps seemed to freak her out more than the needle. She did better than he expected, but then, he knew he was good. Most of his clients said they felt a pinch and that was it, but he had the occasional one get light-headed. It always made him feel like an ass, and he ended up buying them a drink from the machine and talking them through it until he was sure they were okay to leave.

That was actually how he'd met Michelle at his old workplace, the one and only client he'd ever let himself get involved with. As soon as she jumped off the table after getting her navel pierced, she'd gone dead white and swayed. He'd taken her arm and steered her to a chair before she could hit the floor. It had been such a slow weeknight, he'd ended up sitting with her and talking until closing time. Her friend had finally grown exasperated and taken off.

They'd continued the conversation over beers and tequila shots at a bar up the street, and then at her place, where they'd had marathon sex until well after the sun came up. It wasn't his normal MO at all, but that night, he'd figured what the hell. She was hot and funny and she'd been all over him as soon as they'd reached his truck at the bar. Fond memories.

Too bad those from last night and this morning were tainted from Candace's subsequent freak out. He could've still been drifting on the euphoria of it all. Even now, he could still smell the scent of her skin, still taste her on the back of his tongue. Still feel her wrapped tight and wet around his fingers. He'd been walking around all day at half- mast from that memory alone, and it was beginning to wear him down.

When he went back up front, someone had turned up the tunes, but the sounds of Static-X were doing nothing to soothe his savage beast. He got the next person in line—who wanted a tat, thankfully, because it was his favorite thing to do to mellow him out—and got her prepped and under the needle in no time. She wanted a fairy on her shoulder blade, and it would probably take a good hour or so. Plenty of time to clear his head.

Until Starla stuck the phone under his face, totally destroying his already feeble concentration. "Here. It's your brother."

He frowned and leaned away from the offending instrument. "He can get me on my cell later."

Starla rolled her eyes and brought the phone back to her ear. "Evan, he's tied up, can you call him later?" She listened for a second and then held it back to him, laughing. "He says you need to learn how to multitask." Even the girl he was working on giggled.

"Dammit." He grabbed the phone, crammed it between his ear and shoulder, and picked up the line he'd left off on her skin. "We're swamped, brother. I don't call for you and tell them to drag your ass out of court, do I?"

Evan cut right to the chase. He and their mom were alike in that regard, at least when it came to Brian. "Why is Sylvia Andrews calling me out of court asking me to help her keep you away from her daughter?"

"The *hell.* Are you shitting me?"

"What have you done now?"

"Man, I ain't done nothing. I can't even begin to tell you how much nothing I did." Well, okay, he'd done a little, but that was no one's business but his and Candace's.

"Ordinarily I wouldn't believe that for a second, but because it's Candace we're talking about, you might be telling the truth."

Did everyone know this girl was a virgin except for him? Did other guys have some kind of built-in hymen alert mechanism he was lacking? He never would have taken Candace for someone who took frequent trips around the block, but hell, at least once or twice. She was in college and she was hot, for fuck's sake. How had she managed to keep that smokin' body under wraps all this time? Were the guys over there blind?

I'd still want to wait for you.

Shit.

"Why do you say that?"

"Her parents guard her like she's Fort Knox. If they had snipers stationed around her place to take out anyone who dared approach her door, I wouldn't be surprised."

Then they must have fucking surveillance cameras mounted somewhere across the street. Or spies. "I kinda get that now," he muttered. "I'd already heard, but Jesus, I thought Michelle was always exaggerating at least a little whenever she talked about it." Damn, it must have been hard for Candace growing up. Guys probably ran screaming from her at the very thought of facing down her parents.

Well, *he* wouldn't have. He'd have proven it to her this morning, if she'd given him a shot.

"She wasn't, trust me. I didn't even know you were hanging out with Candace."

"I'm really not. And I doubt I ever will be. So ease your mind."

Evan paused for a second, and lost the sharp prosecutorial edge to his voice when he spoke next. "You don't sound too happy about that."

"Look, does it matter?"

"I was already itching to tell the woman to take a flying leap. I would've done it, but I didn't have the details. She didn't like what I did tell her."

"And that was?"

"I said I wasn't aware of the situation with you and her

daughter, but if she had a problem with it, she needed to take it up with you and Candace. Not me."

Brian blew out the breath he'd been holding. Just when he thought he had his brother pegged, Evan surprised him. Evan could've shown the same outrage as Mrs. Andrews and trashed him on the phone to her for half an hour and promised her he wouldn't let his evil thug of a brother near the poor defenseless maiden again. He could have, but he hadn't. "Bless you."

"They have to start letting her live her life sometime. But I have to say, if you're trying to add a notch to your belt, then she really is better off without you."

There was the Evan he knew. No matter what, he was always hiding in there somewhere. "Hey, just drop it now. All right? I appreciate what you said to her, but I can handle it from here without your input on who I should or shouldn't hang out with. What the fuck am I, fourteen again?"

Evan sighed. "Sometimes you act like it."

He bit down on a crude, juvenile comment that would only have proven his brother's point, something like *I got your fourteen right here*, but suddenly, he was exhausted. Spent. He didn't want to deal with it anymore, just wanted to get through tonight and post up at home. For days.

"I gotta go. I do work, believe it or not."

"I know you do, Brian. And believe it or not, I'm proud of you."

He nearly choked. It was the first time he could ever remember hearing those words out of anyone's mouth in his family. *Focus, dude*, he told himself, struggling to stay in the purple line on his client's skin. Any second now it was going to start to blur, and how uncool would that be? Christ Almighty, he was a sap lately.

"Damn, for once I've stunned you into silence." Evan laughed. "Hey, don't be a stranger, okay? I dread to see you walk in the door, but Kelsey likes for you to come around, for some reason."

"How's the baby?"

His brother seemed taken aback that he would ask. "He's great. He's amazing. Come see him anytime you want, all right?"

"I will soon. See you."

He clicked off the phone and tossed it back to Starla behind the front desk before things could become any gooier. He had a girl fully lodged under his skin and his brother trying to make him cry. What the ever-loving hell.

Who did Candace's mother think she was? The Andrews family might be affluent, but the Rosses could buy and sell every one of their asses. Did they think he'd paid for this establishment by standing out on the street slinging rocks? That old shrew had no clue who she was dealing with. And as far as moms getting dragged into this thing...

His outraged line of thinking derailed, and he stopped before he could screw up the tattoo. He put up the pretense of straightening his cap and popping another stick of gum in his mouth while the wheels spun in his head.

Seriously, how had Sylvia Andrews known? Had Candace told her? Surely not. Not after the way she'd reacted. Some PI wearing dark glasses and sitting crouched in a car across the street taking notes seemed more feasible than her fessing up to hanging out with him. Candace probably mentioned it to a friend, who took it upon themselves to report her bad behavior to her parents. Something like that.

He had to believe it. Because the thought of her biting the bullet and facing down a mother who obviously terrified her started a melting in his chest that he didn't want to examine right now.

"Hey, B," Ghost called out to him as he was leaning down to get back to work. "You did know that Korn is coming to Dallas in a couple of weeks, right? Big rock festival up there."

"Yeah, I'd heard."

"Kara called earlier today while you were out and said they have tickets and want us to come up. Said we could crash at their place."

"Man, I've already seen Korn eight times." But he mulled it over. The "Freak on a Leash" video was playing on the HD flats, one of his favorite songs of all time, and the lyrics sank in at that moment more than they ever had before.

When he'd first heard about the concert, he'd been tempted, but figured there was too much stuff to do around here to take off for a day. The show was on a Saturday, their busiest day.

"Come on. You can never see Korn too often."

True. Maybe it was exactly what he needed. To get lost in the pit, work out some of this anger, do permanent damage to his hearing, and quite possibly get shitfaced drunk. Old habits were threatening to rear their ugly heads and wreak havoc.

"Is it on, dude?" Ghost asked.

How would Sylvia fucking Andrews feel about *that*?

"It's on."

If he could see her right now, he would think she was a crazed stalker. She'd reached new lows of wretchedness, sitting outside his parlor like this, but in her own defense, she'd come here hoping to grab him as he left and try to explain. Not to spy on him. The longer she sat, though, the more her courage ebbed. It really was shaping up to be a spying session, after all.

"So what's going on now?" Macy asked over the cell phone Candace had pressed to her ear. She was gripping it so tight, her knuckles ached.

"Nothing yet."

"Candace, please. Just go home. Forget about him."

"That isn't possible."

"You told me how your mom reacted. She freaked. They'll never accept him. Think of how hard your life is going to be if you end up with a guy your parents hate. With any other parents, it might not be that big a deal, but with yours...whew."

"Whose side are you on, mine or theirs?"

"I'm on yours. That's why I'm telling you this. Find someone all of you can agree on."

"I don't want to *agree* with them on someone. I want to be madly in love, and if they like him, great, and if they don't, tough. I wasn't ready for it all this morning. I panicked. I won't make the same mistake again."

"I hope it's because you won't see him again. It's not just your parents, you know. There's Michelle to think about. Maybe she won't like the idea of you with her ex. Taking him around her at holidays and stuff might be uncomfortable for everyone."

Then we won't go, her mind returned immediately. But the truth was, Michelle was her primary concern. If her cousin hadn't been with her today, she'd have lost her damn mind hanging out with her mother and Deanne. Michelle had saved her sanity so many times, and if she truly had a problem with Candace seeing Brian, it was going to be devastating. Because of that, she hadn't been able to confess. She wondered if she'd ever be ready.

The silence stretched out until Macy finally spoke. "Please don't lose your head over him."

"I'm not. I just..." *I just want to live my damn life. Is that so much to ask?* She didn't want her parents making any more decisions for her. Brian wasn't the only issue here. The situation with him was only dredging up emotions that had been festering within her for years. Giving them an outlet.

"Candace, everyone else aside, I don't think he's good for you, either."

Her vision was momentarily washed in red. "Why not? Yes, he's different. But other than that, what's really wrong with him?"

"Because he *is* different. I've known you for a long time. I've known what your dreams were since we were twelve years old. You wanted the white knight on horseback coming to rescue you. You wanted a romance novel hero. You wanted a guy like John Cusack in *Say Anything,* standing under your window, holding up a boom box." Macy laughed. "Remember?"

It was hard not to chuckle at the memory of them sneaking out of bed to watch movies in the middle of the night, comparing notes over which movie star they were going to grow up and marry. "I can see Brian doing that. Except instead of Peter Gabriel, he'd be playing, I don't know, Slipknot or something."

"I don't think you'll ever have your fairytale ending with him."

"Who needs a fairytale? In the end, I only want to be happy with a guy I love, and who loves me just as much. That's all I need. As far as sweeping me off my feet...he did that last night."

"With all due respect, you haven't been swept enough to know. Don't confuse lust with something deeper. As far as your parents, they're like me, just trying to protect you."

"It's not their job anymore. Or yours."

Macy was depressing her so much, she finally had to hang up to keep from bursting into tears. Was she really crazy, and everyone else totally sane? Should she simply lock last night up in her heart, keep it a delicious secret she could revisit whenever she was enduring sex with a man she and her parents could *agree* upon?

Hell, no. She shuddered, thinking of allowing someone else to do all the things Brian had done to her last night. She couldn't live like that. She wouldn't. She'd rather die a virgin. Her parents could send her to a convent and she would gladly go.

But oh, God, she didn't want that. She wanted *him*. His gaze gently roving her bare flesh. His mouth on her breasts, his fingers invading her body. He had to be the one. It had to happen. The very thought made excitement zing through her as she wondered if he would be sinister and aggressive and push into her hard and fast, getting it over with in one blinding instant of pain and ecstasy. Or if he would be gentle and considerate and take all night coaxing her through. Some moments last night and this morning had been so intensely sweet, and some so dark and frightening, she had no idea what to expect of him. And she didn't know which she'd prefer. The mere speculation stirred an ache deep inside her and made desire pool anew in her breasts and lips. When she saw him tonight, she might not be able to control herself.

What if he didn't forgive her for her hasty overreaction this morning?

Minutes ticked by. Another hour passed. She couldn't remember what time the place closed, and she didn't dare get close enough to see if their hours were posted out front. There were still cars in the parking lot, so she imagined they operated until the last customer walked out the door.

Her eyes were beginning to drift shut and she was contemplating going to get a coffee when movement caught her attention, and she sat straight up. Brian was leaving. She knew it was him from his tall, lean figure and the way he walked, with a loose, easy confidence that sparked off a tremor from the roots of her hair all the way to her toes. Her heart rate doubled, and she reached for the door handle, only to stop cold when the door opened behind him and a girl rushed out. A girl he stopped and waited for.

Damn. Was she an employee? Candace couldn't remember seeing her in there the day she'd gotten her tattoo.

She squinted, leaning as close to the driver's-side window as she could, but it made no difference. It was too dark, but the lights from inside haloed the girl's blond hair. She fell into step beside Brian as the two of them headed toward the vehicles in the side lot, where the employees parked. Brian's dark blue truck sat in a pool of dim light cast down from one of the overhead lamps.

She was an employee, then. They were leaving for the night. Candace nearly collapsed in relief. But unfortunately, it dashed her plans on the rocks. She wasn't about to rush up on him when there were other ears in the vicinity. She would just have to find the guts to call him.

Once Brian and his companion reached his truck, they lingered, talking about something the girl seemed especially passionate about, given her wild gestures as she spoke. Candace fought down the urge to crack open her window. She wasn't going to eavesdrop. She *was not* that far gone yet.

Brian listened to the blond girl, occasionally laughing and interjecting. Candace began to get a sinking feeling. Especially when he hooked a thumb toward his truck and she nodded. He popped open the door for her and she climbed in, making sure to put her ass in his face as she did. It was already half hanging out of the skirt she wore.

No!

It took everything she had not to fly out of her car and run screaming toward them. But all she could do was sit and fight tears.

And follow them, of course.

What was that about not spying on him, you psycho?

She ducked frantically before his headlights could sweep over her car, letting a couple of seconds tick by before she dared to pop up and crank it.

Macy's voice still echoed in her head. *Go home. Just go home, Candace. You don't want to see this.*

But she did. Maybe it was nothing and she could ease her mind. If she didn't go see what was going on, how would she be able to sleep tonight? She would find out where they were going, that was it. That way, it would be decided whether she should try to pursue this or settle into the life of agony her parents had chosen for her. Agony would be any life that didn't include him.

She didn't pull away from the curb until Brian's truck made a left at the intersection up the street, and then she sped to catch up, making sure she kept several car lengths between them. Speculation over what was being said in that cab started a burn in her chest she feared would turn into tears if she couldn't get a grip on herself. If he was moving on to someone else the very damn night after staying with her, he was a colossal asshole, and she wouldn't mind telling him that in front of his skank.

She was working on gnawing a hole in her bottom lip when his right blinker flashed to turn into a sports bar.

"Damn him," Candace murmured, quickly hitting her left blinker to zip into the lot across the street from the bar. It didn't take an expert in quantum physics to realize what would happen here tonight: they would get drunk, go back to his or her place, and do all night the very thing he'd denied her over and over again.

Well, he would do it with the knowledge that he'd been caught. Candace screeched to a stop in an empty parking space and grabbed for her cell phone.

Chapter Ten

Brian slammed back his whiskey and tried to ignore whatever Starla was jabbering about.

This might have been a huge mistake. He'd known her for years, but he could imagine it wouldn't take too many shots before the flicker of her tongue ring would begin to get more and more enticing, and he might end up taking her home and putting it to use. Crazier shit had happened, and he was damn sure frustrated enough.

But Starla had love life problems of her own and she loved to dump them on him, for some reason. Or anyone else who would lend an ear. She'd wanted to come here because she was hoping to find a distraction, but if he had anything to do with it, it damn sure wouldn't be him.

She was pretty enough, with white-blond hair shot through with pink and purple and lips that could give Angelina Jolie a run for her money. Three years ago, there wouldn't have been a problem. Not now. Not when she worked for him. And not when there was Candace smoldering in his thoughts.

"I'm probably cramping your style," he informed Starla, amidst howls of excitement when the Astros hit a homer on the flat screens mounted around the bar. It was getting close to midnight, and the game was on so late because of extra innings and the two-hour time difference between here and San Francisco, where they were playing.

For probably the first time, he was thankful for the smoking ban, so he didn't have to sit and watch in misery as people lit up all around him. Otherwise tonight might have been the night he fell off the wagon.

Starla craned her neck to look around the establishment. "Oh well, it's a dog fest in here anyway."

He laughed and gestured toward her AMF. "A few more of those will help the situation, I'm sure."

"I figured that asshole would be here, but I don't see him. I see one of his scummy friends, though. I should go throw a drink in his face."

"Just don't get me arrested."

"Thanks for bringing me. You're an awesome boss. You can take off, if you want. I just hate walking into one of these things by myself."

"I hear you. But you'll need a ride back to your car."

She waved her hand dismissively, still twisting around on her barstool to assess the situation. She wasn't paying much attention to him, anyway. "Nah, I got it. I'll either hook up with someone or find the asshole if he shows up or get a cab. No biggie."

"Are you sure?"

"Yep."

"Cool. But while I'm here, I think I need a few more of these." He signaled the bartender and ordered a beer.

With a sigh, Starla turned around and faced him, toying with her drink glass with black-tipped fingers. "So what's got *you* down, Bri? I noticed you were in full-on funk mode all night."

"Was I?" he grumbled, hating that he was such an easy read. "More than usual?"

"Yeah, way more. Who is she?"

He grinned before taking a swig of the beer the bartender set in front of him. "Has to be about a girl, huh?"

"Unless you swing the other way."

And the drink he'd taken nearly ended up sprayed all over her. He cringed and wiped his mouth with the back of his hand.

"Uh, no. That wasn't what I meant."

"Just making sure what I was dealing with, here. So, who is she?"

"Someone I'm sure you don't know."

"Has she ever come in Dermamania?"

He shifted uncomfortably. "She's been there. You were off that night. But she's not a regular or anything."

"You don't want to talk about her. Dude, I wish I could be like that. I dump my drama all over anyone who'll listen whether I think they care or not." She laughed. "But I like to listen to others. And I do give great advice. I'm renowned for it."

"She's a sheltered virgin princess."

"You are *so* on your own right now."

"I figured." He leaned forward on his arms and heaved a great sigh.

She stared at him for several seconds, seeming to read something in his face, then leaned toward him conspiratorially. "Okay. Let's break this down. Which bothers you most, the sheltered virgin part or the princess part?"

"They both pretty much suck equally."

"Well, the virgin part can be easily taken care of. Then you won't have that hanging over your head anymore, because the deed'll be done. Unless she's not willing to give it up, in which case I'd have to say you really are on your own with that one."

He shrugged.

"But I sense she's more than willing?"

"She probably *was*."

"Then give the poor girl credit for knowing her own mind and take it, Brian. What is it about the fact that a girl hasn't been handing her cooter out all over town that skeeves you guys out so much? I realize you feel pressured to make it good for her and all, but most likely? It's gonna suck for her, it's gonna hurt, but she doesn't have anything to compare it to anyway, so you're in the clear." She rolled her eyes, taking a long drink before going on. "My first fucking time was in the backseat of his mom's Ford Taurus in the parking lot at a high school football game. A cop busted us. At the time, I was glad he did. I aimed high, didn't I?"

He nursed his beer again, thinking back to his own. "If you can remember the guy's name—or if you even knew it at all—then you're one up on me." He'd been fifteen and drunk. It hadn't been with anyone he loved, or even had lukewarm feelings for. Just a random girl at the party who'd been willing to give it up to a horny teenager. He'd aimed pretty damn high himself.

Starla was going on. "See, I wish I'd held on to it for a while like your girl. Some people have no regrets, but I do. So, props to her, Brian. I've never met her, but I think you're really lucky, if she has her shit together like that."

"Well, you don't know the whole story. She doesn't have it completely together yet. But she is pretty incredible."

"She has you turned out, obviously, if you're this worked up about it. Even if you guys don't work out, you'll at least leave her with fond memories. It's more than a lot of us get."

"Problem is, I doubt it'll ever happen. That's where the princess part comes in. When I say her parents make Hitler look like Mother Theresa, I'm only being somewhat hyperbolic."

"Oh. Ohhh. That's not good. She still *lives* with them?"

"No. She's got her own place, but she's still under their thumb. She's finishing up her junior year of college."

"So hang in there. Before long, she can graduate and get a good job and be able to pay her own way and tell her parents to fuck off."

"Yeah. If she would." He wondered at that moment if Candace had never had sex before because deep in her mind, she worried that her parents would somehow find out. Maybe they'd struck such fear in her they were an omnipresent force in her life, like the Eye of Sauron or something. And that pissed him the hell off. He would call it outright abuse. It had probably done some psychological damage. He'd have lost his fucking mind, if he were her.

He was probably catastrophizing. She had been more than

willing last night. It had probably taken so much courage for her to allow it to happen, in opposition of everything she knew...and he'd shot her down.

Images of her in her baseball caps and T-shirts, looking like anybody's sweet kid sister, swam through his thoughts. She'd never had a man to tell her how beautiful and sexy and desirable she was, and when she'd finally found one, he'd said all the words but hadn't followed through.

Not only that, but he deserved the Asshole of the Year award for the way he'd treated her when he left. He hadn't known how dire the situation was.

That melting sensation was back in his chest. Either it was worse or the alcohol exacerbated it, because he felt as if his whole damn heart was about to spill out on the floor.

He had to get out of here.

"Starla, I need to jet," he said, fishing his wallet out of his back pocket. He threw down enough cash to cover their drinks and a hefty tip.

"Going to see her?"

"Thinking about it."

She gave him a sly wink. "Well, I hope you two have a *wonderful* evening."

He returned her grin and stood from the barstool, only to sit his ass right back down when he saw who was in the booth nearest the door. "Holy shit. She's here."

Starla gasped, sitting straight up. At least she didn't whirl around to look. "Oh, no, I hope she doesn't get the wrong idea. Did she see you?"

"She wasn't looking at me. Looks like she's with someone."

"Well, go invite her over or something! So she knows this isn't anything shady."

"Nah, it's cool." He really wasn't worried about her getting the wrong idea about *him*. Who in the fuck was that guy sitting next to *her*?

"This isn't funny at all," Michael fretted at Candace's side.

"You're going to get my ass kicked, Candace."

"Oh, please. It won't come to that, I promise."

Sam giggled from her seat across from them. "Hey, we're three buddies out for a drink. Besides, he can't say anything since he's here with some other chick." She threw a surreptitious glance over her shoulder. "Although I have to say that looks pretty platonic from where I'm sitting. You could fit a bulldozer between them. Still, it won't hurt for him to get a teensy bit rattled."

"If he'll bother," Candace murmured.

Michael shook his head. "It might hurt if he rattles *me*. Oh, shit, here he comes."

Candace fought down the desperate urge to look up. To gauge Brian's expression. To see if she really needed to keep her body between him and Michael in the name of her good friend's safety.

"Michael," Sam whispered. Although a whisper in here was practically a shout. "You should put your arm around her or something."

"So he can break it off?"

"Man up, dammit," Sam snapped, her eyes twinkling with amusement. She leaned across the table toward Candace. "No matter what happens here tonight, don't you dare leave with him. You gave him a taste last night, now you want to make him sweat. The man hasn't even taken you on a proper date yet."

She could excuse that. Brian just didn't seem the dating sort. "I'm not into the whole hard-to-get thing," she fretted.

"Honey, that's so freakin' obvious, but this isn't a game. Wanting what you can't have is a fundamental of human nature."

Was that all her feelings for Brian were? Nothing more than a base reaction to the untouchable, the unattainable?

Michael was still hung up on Sam's previous comment. "Hey, I am a man. But getting the shit beat out of me so *she* can make some dude jealous does not a man make."

"Okay, shhh," Candace hissed. She allowed herself to glance up then. Her gaze tangled with Brian's as he approached, and she forced herself to school her facial expression to show only genuine surprise to be bumping into him. An oh-what-a-wonderful-coincidence look. Not an oops-I'm-caught-spying look.

He didn't seem to be trying to conceal any feelings at all. There wasn't joy to see her. There wasn't anger, either. Did he feel *anything*? He was so frustrating.

"Hi," she greeted as he reached them. He gave them a smile, but it was scarier than it was friendly. "Do you know my friends, Michael and Samantha? Guys, this is Brian."

The three of them exchanged greetings, and she thought Brian's appraisal lingered on Michael longer than on Sam. Sizing him up. Michael seemed to notice it too, because his foot prodded hers hard under the table. She kicked him back.

"It's great to meet you," Sam piped up, scooting over to make room for him in her booth. "Candace has told us a lot about"—Candace shot her a withering look—"about getting her tattoo. She said you did a great job. I've been thinking of getting something myself."

Brian's gaze lingered on Candace even as he and Sam struck up a conversation. She felt it like a physical caress, though she didn't dare to meet it directly. Anger still simmered in her blood. His blond companion had found her way over to the pool tables, chatting up a few of the guys shooting a game and occasionally swigging her beer. Candace could see her only from the back, except for when she turned to glance in the direction of the door and flashed a pretty, delicate profile. Lips to die for. She had different colors threaded through her hair. Her denim skirt was slung low enough on her hips to reveal what Macy would call a tramp stamp...and a peek of a thong of some indiscernible color. One of her legs had what looked like a gorgeous sunburst on the calf, but half of it was obscured by her black cowboy boot.

Maybe he'd given her the tattoos. Maybe that's the kind of girl he really wanted. They would make a beautiful couple, she thought miserably. She was something Candace could never be.

"Here with your girlfriend?" she asked innocently, when the simmer threatened to turn into an outright boil.

Sam's eyes grew to the size of quarters. Brian had been saying something to Michael—who had relaxed considerably—but he calmly turned his attention back to her. She smoldered under the scrutiny of those blue eyes, and felt stirrings beneath her own micro mini-skirt that did not bode well for Sam's directive not to leave with him. His hair looked so sinfully silky her fingers could still feel it sliding between them. Her lips could still feel the tickle of his goatee.

Damn you, why do I have to want you so bad?

He grinned as if he knew exactly what she was thinking. "That's Starla, one of my artists. She's here to confront her on-and-off boyfriend about something, who the hell knows what."

"She can't call him? Go to his house?"

"Not when he won't answer the phone or the door."

"Sounds like she's stalking him, then."

"Hmm, doesn't it? Stalking is such a deplorable thing." His gaze leveled her, vaguely mocking, infinitely infuriating.

Oh, the nerve! Was he actually insinuating...accusing her of...?

Well, he was right, after all. She hadn't called him. Hadn't gone to his apartment. She'd followed him here. But to call her out on it! How dare he!

It was official. She hated him.

Brian nodded in the direction of the door. "Let's go out and talk for a minute."

She hated him so much, her heart kicked into triple time after his suggestion. She shot Samantha a glance and read in the other girl's face everything she wanted to say. *Don't leave with him. Do. Not. Leave. With. Him.*

"Fine." She stood, resisting the urge to wipe damp palms on her skirt. Brian followed, leaving Sam and Michael staring up at them with knowing little smirks. Candace had one moment of satisfaction when Brian looked as if his eyes might roll out of his head at the sight of her outfit. It didn't involve much more fabric than Starla's. Stupidly, she'd worn it to entice him when they talked, hoping they'd end up back at her place again. Or his.

"Have fun," Michael said. The three of them exchanged nice-to-have-met-yous as Candace roamed toward the door, arms wrapped around herself, trying to get a grip. She was shaking, and she had no idea why...whether it was from anger or arousal or the memory of what had happened between them only last night. The desire for it to happen again, knowing that it couldn't.

She did know it, didn't she? Deep down, didn't she realize that Macy was right? That her parents would make her life a living hell from now till eternity if she ended up with someone like him? She didn't want to end up disowned. She didn't want to end up used and discarded by him. It seemed there was no happy medium: sleep with him even though there was no future, or sleep with him knowing there was a future and it alarmingly resembled the seventh level of hell. In that case, was she willing to run away from everything she'd ever known to be with him? It scared the bejesus out of her to consider it.

Of course, either option assumed that he *wanted* her. She should say her goodbyes to him now, go home, let the tears out and soothe herself with a tub of Häagen-Dazs and half a pound of Godiva. Then fill the lingering emptiness not assuaged by comfort food and *Desperate Housewives* reruns with a shoe-and-handbag shopping spree tomorrow with her best friends. Retail therapy. It had always helped.

Brian caught up and pulled open the door for her, waving goodbye to his female friend. Candace had nearly forgotten all about her. She supposed that meant she believed his story, foolish as it might make her.

They strolled out into the cool spring night, leaving the chaos of the sports bar behind. Candace breathed deep as they walked, trying to clear the muddled confusion of her thoughts. At least, that's what she told herself. She was really trying to calm the jitters that raced along her nerves. Being with him made her feel as if mad little beasts were trying to eat her alive from the inside.

"Where are we going?" she asked softly.

"I'm parked in the back."

She stopped walking. "I'm not leaving with you."

"That's fine. I just want to talk." His gaze raked down the length of her body, taking in her short skirt and tight baby tee. "Is this my influence, honey? Because I think I like it."

He might as well have touched her. Her nipples hardened and pushed against the silk of her bra. She fidgeted and tugged the hem of her shirt outward, hoping he couldn't see the peaks through her clothes, fighting the urge to cross her arms over herself.

When he saw she wasn't going to reply, he reached for her hand and pulled her into motion again. Maybe he had his own version of "goodbye" well rehearsed and ready to deliver, rendering all her agonized indecision moot.

The inside of his truck still had that new-vehicle smell. He'd bought it after he and Michelle broke up, so she'd never been in it before. It was nice and roomy, a quad-cab. She made sure to stay scooted as close to the passenger door as she could even when he raised the console and left the bench seat open.

A snicker sounded in the darkness when she made no move to get closer to him. "Afraid I'll bite?"

She stared straight ahead. "Something like that."

"You're a riddle to me, sunshine."

"Why do you even call mc that?" she blurted.

His surprise was almost palpable in the air between them. He cleared his throat. "It's stupid. Don't worry about it."

"Tell me. Please?"

"On one condition."

"What?" she asked warily.

"That you scoot over here next to me."

Her fingers were twisting into knots with one another. "After you tell me."

He sighed as if dealing with an insistent child, and began toying with the steering wheel. “One day when I was at Michelle’s apartment, the weather was crappy and cold and she seemed to have a galloping case of PMS or something. I was ready to take off, but then you came over. You walked in the front door, wearing a bright yellow T-shirt and a pink cap with your hair pulled through in a ponytail, and you gave me the biggest smile. It was...almost blinding. You lit up when you saw me. And I thought you were like a ray of sunshine that had wandered in from the rain.” He scoffed. “Told you it was fucking stupid.”

She picked at her nails, feeling her bottom lip quiver and hoping it didn’t portend a torrent of tears. “It’s not stupid. I remember that day. You stayed around and we ended up all going out for a movie and pizza. But why do you say I’m a riddle?”

“Damn, what’s with the questions?” He sounded far more amused than annoyed.

“You can’t just throw that out there and not expect me to wonder why.”

“I see.” Out of the corner of her eye, she could see the side of his leg and his hand resting on his thigh. How she wanted him to touch her. But if he did, she was lost. “If you don’t come over here, I’m coming over there.”

“Brian—”

“Hey, that was our agreement. It’s okay.” He patted the seat next to him. “Promise.”

Sighing so that he was well aware of how unhappy it made her, she slid across the seat until they were scant inches away from touching sides. Now his nearness washed over her, his heat battering her entire left side, and any trembling she’d recently wrestled back control of promptly returned. And then some.

“That’s better, isn’t it?” he said.

“You didn’t answer my question. Why am I a riddle?”

“Because last night, you didn’t seem to be able to get

enough, and now you're looking at me like I'm a leper. And you're running games on me."

"Running games?" she asked, looking at him directly for the first time since they'd left the bar. There was only one overhead lamp in this parking lot and it gave scant illumination, casting his face in shadows. "What am I doing?"

Brian gestured toward the establishment. "That guy in there. You had to make damn sure he was sitting next to you, huh?"

"I have no idea what you're—"

He laughed. "You can give it up, sweetie. I knew from the second the dude laid eyes on me that he knew exactly who I was to you. Obviously the whole thing was a set up. Did you follow me here?"

She couldn't speak because there was nothing to say, and besides, her jaw had come unhinged.

He went on. "I'm sorry you saw me hanging out with another girl, but honestly, don't let it bother you. She's a friend only. I've known and worked with her for years, and that's all she's ever been."

"You're free to do whatever you want." Even if she was only realizing it as she spoke it, it was the truth. She'd had no right to go off the way she did. Drag her poor friends into it.

Shame settled heavy and hot on her shoulders. God, way to overreact. She really was going to die a virgin, if this was the way she behaved when a guy she liked showed the least amount of interest in her. "You didn't make any promises to me, Brian."

"But," he said, almost interrupting her before she could finish speaking. "Those first few seconds when I saw you there with him... I guess you got your point across. I didn't like it."

"He's Samantha's boyfriend."

"I figured out there wasn't anything to worry about. But I still didn't like it."

"I didn't make you any promises, either," she said, almost muttering the words because she didn't have the courage to put any force behind them.

"I know." He traced the line of her shoulder lazily with one finger. "And we ended on bad terms this morning. I feel real shitty about that, and I'm sorry I was such an asshole."

She closed her eyes as that finger traveled gently up her nape, raising gooseflesh on her arms. "Maybe you had a point, as far as how my parents are going to react to you. Maybe it'll always be that way."

"Does it have to be?"

"How else could it ever be? There's no changing my situation."

"Sweetie, there's no way to say this without sounding condescending, but you're young. Right now this is all you can see, but trust me, this won't always be your reality. Pretty soon you'll be able to make your own way in the world no matter what they think."

"You don't know them very well, do you," she said flatly.

He cupped the back of her neck in his hand, bringing his other over to tilt her chin toward him. Trapping her for the kiss she knew was coming if she didn't do something fast. But he just held her that way, stroking her cheek with his thumb, his gaze searching hers as if all the answers were inside her somewhere.

If only that could be the truth.

"I don't. But I think I have a pretty good handle on *you*. You're going to be okay."

He stared at her so intently. His eyes were a dark, turbulent ocean, and she wanted to drown in it. Suddenly she became aware of the aching fullness of her lips and the weight of her breasts pushing against her bra.

This skirt was so short, and she'd chosen it for that reason alone, but maybe it had been a huge mistake. Reaching under it *and* her black G-string would take absolutely no effort on his part. Not good, though she wanted that so, so badly, she couldn't resist rubbing her bare thighs together as his gaze continued to melt through all of her defenses.

Just when he knew she was about to go up in flames or melt right there in his truck, he leaned in. Warm lips slanted over hers as a breathless cry rushed from her mouth into his. She brought up her hands, clenching his shirt in her fists as his tongue stole past her teeth and plundered her mouth. His was the kiss she had dreamed of all her life, deep and somehow as fierce as it was gentle. It opened the gates to a flood of emotion and erotic sensation that had her almost writhing against the seat.

His hand finding her breast seemed the most natural thing in the world. Even through two frustrating layers of fabric, she could feel his heat as he palmed her and circled the tight bud of her nipple with his thumb, forcing it to pull even tauter. When he pinched it, she moaned into his mouth, clasping his wrist in her hand. But not to stop him. To make sure he didn't stop. The little jolts of pleasure/pain sent lightning zipping all through her body, striking at the juncture of her thighs. Her skimpy underwear was no barrier to the growing wetness there. She began to fear making a mess on his seats.

She pulled away from his mouth to breathe, and he attacked her throat with his lips, his heavy breathing the sexiest sound she had ever heard. He was shuddering as hard as she was. His teeth raked her throat and an involuntary "Oh" slipped out before she could stop it. It seemed to only enflame him further, and he plunged a hand under her top, pushing up the cup of her bra as he finally brought his fingers flesh-to-feverish-flesh with her aching nipple.

She had no anchor, nothing to buffer her from these insane sensations. The worry of getting caught was only a minor flicker in the back of her mind...they were in the back of the lot, it was dark, and his windows were tinted. She turned into him as much as she could, trying to bring her right leg over his, to straddle him. If he would only pull her into his lap so she could grind against him...

He got the hint. Almost before she could cry out in frustration, he pulled his hand out of her shirt and plunged it beneath her ass, yanking her hard over him as if she weighed nothing. The new position, legs splayed over him, pushed her skirt the rest of the way up over her hips. She was bare except for a scrap of fabric he could easily rip. Instead, he ran both hands down the small of her back, allowing his fingers to become entangled in the strings as he cupped both her bare cheeks in his palms.

"Jesus Christ, Candace," he groaned, leaning his forehead against her shoulder as his hands massaged, soothed, played and tantalized. It felt so good, so good...

"Oh, God." The words were a shuddery sigh. Spread open this way, with his fingers only inches away... "Please."

"Please what?"

She ground her pelvis into him hard, so that her clit barely rasped across the fabric of his jeans. She couldn't get close enough. His hands continued tormenting her, squeezing her ass, tugging her panties, but making no move to address the need burning hot and wet at her center. "Touch me."

"Where? Let me hear you say it."

He didn't have to ask twice, but her mouth—so squeaky clean until she'd started hanging out with him—tripped over the word she didn't think she'd ever uttered out loud in her entire life. "My...pussy."

Pressed cheek-to-cheek with him, she felt him smile. He ran one fingertip lightly down the crease of her bottom, reaching under her until he found the source of all her torment. His other hand wandered up to her breast again, still bare under her shirt.

She wrapped her arms tight around his neck and sobbed as two of his fingertips trailed through her wetness, finding her entrance and nestling there until she wiggled and pushed down against him. He evaded her, chuckled maddeningly. She was caught, and it was torture. Did she push back and give him easier access to her slick channel, or lean her hips into his and grind her clitoris against him?

"Hasty little thing. I've got to teach you to slow down and savor this."

She didn't want to savor it. Not now. He couldn't understand. She'd denied herself this for so long, too long. She'd bought this skimpy freaking underwear dreaming of the day some guy would rip it off her in crazed lust. Her pent-up frustration had her running in the red, and she was about to burn down.

He had mercy on her, snuggling his fingers into her tight passage as she let her head fall back, groaning as loudly as he did. He withdrew and reentered, slicking through her, soothing the sting that was briefer and much less intense than it had been last night. She rocked her hips gently against his hand, bringing her head forward again to kiss him and struggling to open wider to his invasion of both her mouth and her pussy. He thrust his tongue between her lips in the same rhythm that his fingers plundered her body, and she nearly flew apart. "Ohhh, Brian."

His answering sigh formed into the most beautiful words she'd ever heard. "Candace. Come home with me right now and I'll give you everything you need, sugar. Everything you want. If it takes all night." His fingers plunged deep, as if to show her exactly what he meant, and she cried out.

But Samantha's earlier words were somehow filtering through her frenzied thoughts, making her want to scream. *Make him sweat.* Then Macy's, telling her how insane she was. Her mother's haughty, disapproving face.

Michelle's expression softening with yearning and traveling a million miles away at the memories of him.

All at once, she was barraged with all the voices of reason in her life, every one in direct opposition to what her body was begging her to do right now.

"I can't," she whispered, pulling away from his lips to cram her face into his neck. Praying he would understand, but that he wouldn't stop. Selfishly trying to claim what she couldn't have.

"I feel how wet you are," he murmured sinfully in her ear. "How much you need this. To hell with everyone else. Let me give you what you need." His tongue flickered against the soft shell, and she moaned as his talented fingers continued to work their magic. But he was slowing his pace, touching her too shallowly, holding her teetering on the edge of a devastating orgasm. Trying to make her give in. And she couldn't. "No one has to know," he cajoled.

"Please don't do this to me," she cried, fearing the dam stopping up her emotions was about to burst. She couldn't let it, couldn't do this. And Brian froze, pulling his hands away from her as if she'd seared him.

Chapter Eleven

Though it killed her soul, she jerked herself away from him and back to her original position crammed against the passenger door, frantically trying to right her disarrayed clothing. Humiliation burned almost as hot as her unsated arousal.

"Hey," he said, his voice gentle but with a rough edge, as if it was a struggle for him to contain his anger. She was a riddle to him, huh? What an understatement. She was outright insane. "Don't do what? What is it you want, Candace? Because I'm trying here, but I really don't get it."

"I..."

"Are you scared?"

Yes. Of everything. She shrugged. "I thought you didn't want this," she said a little more nastily than she'd meant. "I *begged* you this morning, Brian."

"I know you did, and I'm sorry. I haven't been able to think about anything else all day."

She pressed her fingertips to the center of her forehead, where she could feel a headache beginning to blossom, and refused to let herself look at him. "I came out here thinking I need to tell you goodbye," she said, hearing the flat exhaustion in her own voice. "And then I was terrified you were about to do the same to me. That's how screwed up I am right now. That's why it's best if we not see each other again. It's not what I want, but I'm a mess. I have enough pressing in on me from all sides. I can't be like this."

He was silent except for his breathing, slow and steady where hers was still thin and shaky.

"Is that what you're really prepared to do?" he said after several uncomfortable minutes ticked past and she steadily swiped at her insistent tears. "After everything that's happened since you walked into my parlor, after last night, after you followed me here tonight, you want to tell me to forget it, it was a mistake? Because you're feeling something wild and crazy you can't explain?"

"It can't happen, okay. You said no one has to know. I understand that, and you're right, but I don't ever want to have to hide the fact that I'm with you. No one would ever accept us."

"What the fuck does that matter?" He did sound angry now, his words a crack of thunder. She realized she'd essentially insulted him. Again.

Oh, she needed to get out of here. Not because he scared her, but because she couldn't take seeing him in any kind of pain, especially if she was the one inflicting it. "It matters to me," she whispered.

"What did your mother say to you? She knows about us because she's already called my brother freaking out."

"*What*?" She'd called *Evan*? Already? Disbelief choked her. Oh, dear God, it didn't stop. Humiliation burned even deeper into her chest, as if she'd swallowed sulfuric acid. She dropped her face into her hands. *Calm down, don't lose it...*

"Did you tell her?" he asked.

"Yes."

"Tell me what she said, baby."

His gentle command didn't register through the chaos. "Don't you see?" she asked, hearing the high-pitched edge of panic in her voice. "It's hopeless. I can't do this. I'm sorry."

Before he had a chance to reply, she yanked the handle and flung herself out of the truck, slamming the door on his protest. Instead of heading back inside where her friends were waiting, she ran to her car, sending up a prayer that she wouldn't hear the sound of his footsteps pursuing her. She didn't.

He would be a fool to do that, anyway. Or to ever speak to her again at all.

Once in the quiet safety of her car, she dialed Sam from her cell phone, trying to catch her breath, trying to ignore the fact that Brian's truck was still sitting across the lot, dark and still. Was he going to sit there all night? Or go back inside and get Starla to finish what he and Candace had started?

The thought forced out more hot, helpless tears just as Sam answered.

"You're leaving with him, aren't you?"

"No," Candace sobbed, despite all resolutions to keep it together.

"Oh, sweetie. What happened?"

"I don't want to talk about it now. I just wanted to tell you guys you can take off. I'm not in any shape to come back in."

"Sounds like you're in perfect shape. Come in, let us buy you margaritas all night, we'll chauffeur you around and you can crash at my place."

"Sammy, I really appreciate it, but I need to be by myself. Okay?"

"Are you sure you're all right? You sound so awful, I'm worried about you driving."

"I'm fine, honest. I'll call you tomorrow."

"Well, call before then if you need me. I mean it. We love ya."

"Love you too."

Even her friends thought she was a basket case. She chucked her phone back into her purse, sniffling. Well, that might all change if she could quit acting like one.

Wretched. She felt absolutely wretched. And embarrassed. And confused. And...she shifted in her seat, remembering his touch tunneling deep inside her. Um, yeah. She was unbelievably horny on top of everything else. Every inch of her skin was so sensitized even the graze of her clothing was almost too much to bear. She knew the reason. She wanted to be naked and pressed against every hot inch of *him*. It's where she could be tonight, if she could only stop freaking out. She wanted *sex*, dammit. Raw, scorching, amazing, merciless sex.

The irony wasn't lost on her. She'd just made one guy go from zero to sixty in two-point-five seconds. A bar full of guys who would probably be more than willing stood a few dozen feet away from where she sat. She should take one home and get the whole thing over with already. Lose it to an anonymous stranger, no strings attached, and come away from it with her heart still fully intact and worth giving to somebody, someday. Brian would only take a piece of her with him, and right now she didn't own enough of herself to share.

He still hadn't left. Maybe he was hoping she would change her mind and run back to him. She wanted to. One night, if nothing else. Even if she left his apartment tomorrow morning and never saw his face again, would she really regret it more than taking home a complete stranger? It didn't make any sense. He was someone she liked and respected and...well, she loved him.

Other people might struggle with admitting that particular emotion, but to her, it was quite a simple truth, and at the root of all the confusion. She loved him. Probably from the moment Michelle had introduced them almost two years ago, her heart had been his for the taking. The first time their eyes met, the helpless organ had lost its steady, sure rhythm. It had tripped over itself, and she'd been following suit ever since.

Her fingers tightened around the door handle before she realized she was gripping it.

See? Even your body knows what to do. Go back, you stupid girl. Go.

Brian's taillights suddenly flared red and she jumped in her seat, thinking it was now or never, do or die...but he whipped out of the parking space and lurched forward so fast she could imagine he would run her down if she tried to stop him. Releasing the door handle, she collapsed in her seat and stared down at her hands while his truck zoomed past. She expected him to lay rubber when he hit the street, but he didn't. He eased out and was gone.

Well, you did it. Are you proud? Now go home and drown in misery.

Goddamn it all to fucking hell.

So many things he wished he had or hadn't done. He shouldn't have let her chase him away. But since he had, he should have gone back in the bar and drank until he puked.

But he couldn't. No, he was going to have to go back to his frigging apartment and jerk it so he didn't end up with a case of blue balls to go in the books. Finding another girl to slake his frustration wasn't an option. He would hate her for not being the one he wanted, the one he could've been bringing home tonight. And he wasn't up for the hate fuck tonight.

Home was his destination, but as he passed his parlor—all darkened and closed up tight—he whipped his truck into the parking lot without really thinking about it. Home would depress the hell out of him right now. If he watched a movie, he would only wish she were there watching it with him. When he went to bed, he would only remember that she could've been there with him if he wasn't such an asshole.

There was stuff at work he could do to mellow him out, keep him occupied. Several designs were dancing through his thoughts even now, all of them involving splattered, stabbed or otherwise mutilated hearts. He'd inked his own onto Candace the day she'd come in here. There was really no denying it.

Entering the front door and closing and locking it behind him, he sighed with relief. This was his sanctuary. It was the very thing he'd dreamed of since he was eighteen years old: helping other people achieve their self-expression. And while he was still pretty much in Candace's boat and in debt to his dad for helping him out, the old man was getting back every red cent. Thank God he didn't really keep Brian under his boot heel like Candace's folks did her.

He guessed he didn't have a whole lot to complain about, when he stopped to consider it. They were all looking out for him, in their own obnoxious, meddlesome way.

Leaving the front lights off, he headed to the back and got a Monster out of the fridge in the break room. His employees left crazy messages to one another on the bulletin board in there, a little running joke. There was a new one for him: "B: You totally need to get laid." It looked like Ghost had written it. He smirked. Apparently he really had been in a funk all night.

Grabbing a Post-It from the counter, he scribbled, "Talk to your sister, she's not fulfilling my carnal needs of late," and tacked it up amid all the other good-natured insults and name-calling.

Yeah, he often complained of being treated as if he was fourteen again, but he damn sure enjoyed acting like it. Something else there was really no sense in denying.

Except where Candace was concerned. She called forth a violent protectiveness in him he'd never known before, and it was kind of freaking him out. Oh, he'd always been capable of the alpha male bit, had never liked another guy sniffing around his turf, but this was...different. Those feeling had been about marking his territory. These were a deep, primal need to defend something precious to him.

He wanted to be with that girl. He wanted to take care of that girl. He wanted to give her whatever she wanted in life and beat the ever-loving shit out of anyone who ever hurt her. That included pretty much her entire family right now.

Shit. Ordinarily he would think there was no way she could have him so sprung after one night, but this had been ongoing for a while, hadn't it. He just hadn't realized, and he damn sure didn't want to think about how long it had been or he might feel more wretched.

Once he left All That Remains' "Two Weeks" playing so loud on the stereo system it drowned out most of his chaotic thoughts, he carried his energy drink to the drawing room, prepared to spend the night there until he exorcised some of this aggression. If he was here until the sun came up, so much the better. Maybe the harsh light of day would kill some of this dark passion he had roiling inside him. Drill some sense right between his eyes when he walked outside in the morning.

The process was just beginning to flow when his cell phone vibrated in his pocket. Damn. He'd forgotten to leave it in the truck, and he could have ignored it, but his damn traitor heart leapt. Leaning back and fishing it out of his jeans, he cursed when he saw the name on the display.

Michelle? It all just kept getting weirder.

For a split second, he wondered if it could be about Candace, but that didn't make any sense, did it? How much did everyone know by now?

He flipped it open and raised it to his ear as he headed over to turn the music down. "Hello?"

Michelle's voice was soft, lacking its usual confidence. "Hi."

"Hey. Wow, it's been a while."

"I hope you don't think I'm weird or anything. I was reminded of you today and thought I would check in on you. How are you?"

"I'm great. Parlor is running smoothly, and everything's...great." He ended on an awkward note, but he didn't know what else to say. "How are you?"

"Oh, fine. School is kicking my ass, as usual, but I'm hanging in there."

"That's good." They were both silent for a moment. "So...you were reminded of me, huh? How so?"

"I was having lunch with Deanne, Aunt Syl and Candace today. We were talking about tattoos. Made me remember when you gave me mine." She gave a girlish giggle. Oh, damn, he remembered that too. It had been here, after hours, the night of their grand opening. After they'd christened this very room, so to speak. More specifically, the wall in this very room. "Of course, I think about it every time I look at them," she said.

He frowned. Was she seeking information? Was this a set-up?

"Are you seeing anyone?" she asked.

It had to be.

He cleared his throat. It would've been so easy to take the easy way out and say there was no one, but for some reason it seemed very important that he not lie, not dismiss Candace just because things were rough right now. She deserved more from him than that. "Actually, there is someone I'm interested in."

"Well, that's good. I'm with someone too. I actually have no idea why I'm calling you so late at night, I just...I care about you. I want to know you're happy."

It was nice that someone did. "Are *you* happy?"

"Really, I am. He's not anything like you, but then, not many guys are, at least around here." She laughed, a little sadly. "So is this girl anyone I know?"

Shit. He didn't want to get Candace in any more trouble than she was apparently already in with her folks. Cryptic was the way to go. "I'm not sure if anyone here really knows her. She's beautiful and amazing and someone I care about very much, and I'd do anything for her. But she apparently has her doubts about me now."

"That's a shame. The way you talk about her...wow. I have to say I'm a bit jealous. But I really hope it works out for you."

Yeah, you say that now...

She must truly have no idea.

He couldn't help but smile at her sincerity, though. Loneliness must be in the air tonight. He settled back on his stool and raised his hand to the board to put the finishing touch on a drawing. "No need for you to be jealous, sweetheart. You rocked my world for as long as you wanted to be in it."

"As long as you let me be in it."

"Hey, neither of us is to blame. We discussed it for days. In the end, we agreed it was mutual."

"Yeah, that's what we said, anyway. But I think those were possibly the most heartbreaking days of my life."

That was a revelation. Michelle was always cool, always totally together. She wouldn't have let on to anyone that she was hurting, especially not him.

Candace would. He wondered if that was the drive behind this blinding need to hold her close and protect her from all harm: that she might actually let him do it. If she hadn't just basically told him goodbye in his truck.

She couldn't have meant it. Give her a day or two to cool off, and hopefully she would be okay.

"I didn't know that," he said to Michelle. "You should have told me if you were having second thoughts."

"Would it have made a difference?"

Good point. "I'm sorry."

"Oh, Brian, I really didn't call to get into all this. And I'm glad everything is going good for you. I hope you and your girlfriend get things worked out."

"Yeah, me too. Good luck with everything you've got going on."

They hung up soon after, and then he was left with an extra layer of melancholy weighing him down. That relationship had been like a skin he'd needed to shed, but he was grateful for it. It had served its purpose in his life. He thought maybe it had prepared him for the one he could have with Candace, shown him that he wasn't a reptile; he could have feelings for someone.

That night he'd given Michelle her tattoos had been one of the most memorable of his life. His parlor had finally opened, his dream realized. He'd had a beautiful girl at his side. She'd told him all along that he could give her ink when he could do it in his own place. Then she'd changed the rules in the middle of the game that night and told him as they were getting hot and heavy in here that he could give her a small one for every orgasm she had.

He'd let her off easy and called it after three. She'd started to look a bit panicked.

Damn it to hell, now he didn't really feel like being in here, either. Everywhere he looked, there was a phantom.

"What are you doing here?"

The sudden bellow from the doorway startled him so much, he nearly dropped his pencil. "Fuck! Starla? The *hell*!"

She laughed merrily as he wondered if it was too frigging much to ask for some privacy. But then, he guessed he should've gone home for that. "No, really, what are you *doing* here?" she repeated.

"Working, damn it. Is that all right?"

"Not when you're supposed to be with your little love muffin."

He scoffed. "What are *you* doing here?"

"I'm with the asshole. He brought me to get my car so we could go home. Together."

"Congratulations."

"Whatever, like it'll last a week. Although I did tell him if he fucks me around again, I'm gonna give him that apa he's been thinking about. In his sleep."

"Damn, girl. That's not even right."

"Anyway, I saw you were here. I wanted to check on you."

"I might've been in here getting busy with her, for all you knew."

"Yum. Did I ever tell you I have voyeuristic tendencies?"

"Oh, God."

Starla waved and disappeared from sight, her voice growing fainter as she headed for the door. "Good night, Brian. Don't mope. She's not worth it. Go get laid or something."

That was the big cure-all with these people, wasn't it? Girl got you down? Get laid. No money? Get laid. Armageddon ensuing? Get laid a lot.

He sighed and hollered, "I'm not moping!" just as the door closed behind her. He hoped she remembered to lock it. Getting laid damn sure wouldn't cure an armed robbery and a bullet in the brain. They might argue that point, however.

At least he had the concert to look forward to. The more pissed off at the world he got, the more he felt inclined to shut down the parlor completely and let everyone make a day of it. In fact, that's exactly what he needed. A long weekend with his best buddies and all the debauchery they could handle. His father would probably have a coronary that he dared to shut down. To hell with it. The day the old man didn't get paid on time was the day he could bitch.

Chapter Twelve

Candace was drowning. Slowly. Choking, gasping, dying. A little more each day.

Oh, stop being so damn melodramatic.

Picking up her silverware and stabbing blindly at her food, she tried, she *tried* to tune out the polite chatter around her. It was impossible. Her mother's voice had become like the scrape of fingernails down a blackboard in her mind. Deanne's fakeness compounded the sensation, and her sugary sweetness grated Candace's nerves until they were naked live wires. If the wrong one got touched, someone was going to burn.

She'd just had to walk down the aisle with her arm linked through Stephen's, and now he sat beside her at the rehearsal dinner table, keeping up his oh-so-charming appearance to the other guests. Only she saw the way he leered at her breasts. She wasn't even wearing a revealing top. No hint of cleavage, no straining fabric. He was probably remembering the night he'd had his hands all over them without her consent, if he could even recall that particular drunken stupor.

When she nearly choked on the forkful of bland something-or-other she'd shoveled into her mouth, she quickly sipped her wine before her eyes could start watering.

Yes, dying. Get me the hell out *of here. Someone. Anyone.* It didn't even matter anymore.

"How is school going?" Stephen asked her. "What's your major again?"

"Social work," she replied softly, hoping it wouldn't get her mother's attention. No such luck. Sylvia's gaze whipped directly to them across the table.

"Can you believe that, Stephen?" she fretted, lacing her fingers together. "We pushed so hard for Candy to be an elementary school teacher. She's so good with children. And Lord knows many of them need a positive role model."

Candace schooled her voice carefully, desperately trying to keep the deadly edge from gathering too much notice from the other guests. "Mother, I can still be a positive influence." Without looking at Stephen, she muttered, "My ultimate goal is to be a LPC. But I could work for CPS, or do any number of things. Helping people who need it."

She saw him nod in her peripheral vision, but couldn't tell how interested he looked. She didn't really give a damn.

"I don't know," Sylvia went on, more to Stephen than to her, "but I don't like the thought. Consider the element she'll be coming in contact with."

"Well, it's a noble aspiration, Mrs. Andrews. You should be proud of her."

"Yes, of course, of course. We are."

Right. Her mother would've cut off her tuition when she changed her major if Dad hadn't talked her out of it. Which surprised her, because he was usually right up her mom's ass controlling her every move, the master puppeteer. That they'd actually disagreed on something like that had floored Candace.

"Stephen, I have a wonderful idea," Sylvia twittered suddenly. "We'll be going to our lake house for the weekend after the wedding. You should come by for a visit, and of course you're always welcome to stay if you don't already have accommodations. Maybe you and Candace can get better acquainted then."

"Thank you, Mrs. Andrews," he said smoothly. "I'll probably take you up on that."

He hadn't looked away from Candace. She felt like a caged mouse under that stare, and it made her seethe. Taking a breath, she reached for her water glass and hated how her hand trembled. Hated how that breath had been like trying to inhale through sludge.

Drowning. She was going down.

"I figured someone as beautiful as you would be seeing someone by now," Stephen said.

The glass froze on its way to her mouth. *By now.* He remembered her, all right. But that wasn't what caused her to shudder. All night, she'd tried not to think about Brian. His image in her mind would've been her final desperate gasp, the one-two-three count until sweet oblivion...because she figured she would completely lose her mind. In front of all of them.

At that moment, it felt as if every set of eyes in the room was trained on her, though truthfully it was only Stephen's and her mother's. Everyone else chattered right along, sucking up to the happy, too-perfect couple beaming at each other over champagne and filet mignon at the head of the table. She watched it all as if from a separate plane of reality.

Slowly, Candace put her glass back down without ever taking a drink. "There is someone," she said quietly.

"Nonsense," her mother announced, earning herself a murderous look she easily ignored. "She isn't seeing anyone, Stephen. Not at all."

It was the truth, wasn't it? She wasn't. At all. But...

"I am in love with someone," she said firmly, staring daggers at Sylvia Andrews. "I may not be *with* him, but in my heart—"

"Stop this right now," her mother said, her voice practically a hiss, every word its own sentence. "If I hear one more word about that boy, so help me God—"

It took only one innocent question to bring the world to an end. Michelle was the one who asked it, leaning over the table from her seat on Stephen's opposite side. "Who?"

Horrified, Candace looked past him at her cousin's lovely, inquisitive face. "Michelle, I— Can I talk to you later about that?"

Michelle's brow furrowed. "Well, of course, if that's what

you want. I was just curious. I wasn't aware you were that interested in anyone."

"She still doesn't know?" Sylvia demanded. Now they were starting to get some uneasy glances. "Well, that's reaching a new low, isn't it, Candace? I thought she at least knew what you've been trying to do."

Candace's voice was scarcely a whisper. Given the sound of her own pulse thundering in her ears, she could hardly hear it herself. "Mother, please don't."

"Ashamed of yourself? You should be."

When Sylvia's face began to swim in her vision, Candace calmly picked her napkin up out of her lap and laid it on the table, scooting her chair back as she stood. Stephen half rose next to her. "Excuse me, I need some air."

"Candace Marie, I'm not done. Sit down."

"*I'm* done. If you have something to say to me, then you're going to have to drag your ass out of that chair and follow me." Amid some gasps but mostly shocked silence, she whirled and strode for the door, her hands clenched into fists at her sides. Several chairs scraped against the tiles behind her. Wonderful. How many were coming outside to witness this? She was shaking so hard, her heart beating so fast, she feared she might faint. The hot tears that had been building spilled over, agitated by her pounding steps, leaving warm trails on her cheeks that were oddly comforting.

Finally, blessedly, she emerged into the muggy air outside her aunt and uncle's palatial home. It was stifling, but far less so than the atmosphere in that dining room. Out here the sky was huge and stained with twilight. The crickets were joyous, and she felt she could finally breathe again. Until her mother seized her arm and jerked her around to face her. Michelle was at her side, along with Candace's father, who looked stern and way too tall and mightily pissed off. A few seconds later, her older brother Jameson stormed out.

"I can't believe what I just heard in there," her dad thundered. "If I ever hear you disrespect your mother again—"

"What about my respect, Dad? As an adult, and a member

of this family, not to mention your *daughter*? When in the hell is it my turn to get some respect?"

"When you earn it," Sylvia snapped. "When you learn to *act* like an adult and make adult decisions. When you can refrain from episodes like the one we all just witnessed, maybe then it'll be 'your turn'."

"Aunt Syl—" Michelle began, trying to get a word in. Candace's parents promptly drowned her out.

"You still technically reside under our roof," Phillip warned, putting a finger in her face. Michelle tried to lay a calming hand on his arm, but he ignored her, every iota of his focus trained on Candace. There had been moments in her childhood that look had terrified her. Now, it only infuriated her more. *Here comes his all too familiar "respect my authoritah!" bit.* "As long as that's the case, we're the authority figures, Candace. I'll not have you running wild and embarrassing this family while we still foot the bill for it!"

"What have I done?" she shrieked. "I go to school and I go home! I'm not out partying and blowing your money on booze and male strippers, Dad. And really, so what if I was? I still have a fucking four-point-oh average—"

"*Candace*!" both her parents bellowed in unison. Even Michelle's eyes grew to the size of salad plates. Jameson, holding his tongue so far, crossed his arms and stared at the ground, frowning. She knew better than to expect any help from that quarter.

"Listen to me!" She ticked off on her fingers. "I have a four-point-oh, I'm not out getting myself knocked up, I don't drink, I'm not doing drugs! I am *freakishly* boring. All because of you, and not wanting to embarrass you, and being terrified of what you might think or say or do to me. I do *everything* for you. But I don't want to be a freaking school teacher. Please get off my ass about that. Do you want me to be miserable my entire life?"

"I'm sorry to say you're on the fast track for that, considering the lowlifes you're keeping with—"

"Lowlifes? I always wondered what you'd say if you knew your precious *Stephen* tried to sexually assault me at Deanne's graduation party. You want to talk about lowlifes?"

"Oh, Candace, please."

"He did, Aunt Syl." Michelle's voice was quiet, but firm. "We had to pull him off her. I told him to leave, but he wouldn't, and none of the guys would stand up for her and make him go. I brought her straight home, but she didn't want to tell you what happened."

Her mother's demeanor cracked, just a little. Not enough to give her any hope of a change. Then Jameson spoke up. "Aw, hell, he'd had too much to drink. We all had. Stop blowing it out of proportion, Candace. You were only in a roomful of people."

Michelle looked as if she were grinding her teeth into dust.

"That's something else," her mother said, fired up all over again. "I know you still run around with that Sanders girl, with the alcoholic mother—"

"Don't bring Sam into this! She has nothing whatsoever to do with it."

Sylvia swept on, unheeded. "And this new development..." She glanced at Michelle. "I'm just stunned."

Michelle planted both hands on her hips, her voice suddenly blasting through the continuing argument and commanding attention without her having to make a single move. "*Hey*! Stop it right now, and someone tell me what's going on. Aunt Syl, you made that comment at the table, and ever since this conversation started, everyone has been throwing me these weird, secretive looks and I can't take it anymore. *What is going on*?"

Candace turned to face her dear cousin, the words piling up in her throat until she almost choked on them. She had to spit them out before they strangled her. "Michelle, it's Brian." She drew a sobbing breath as Michelle only looked confused. "Brian is the person I was seeing, for all of *two nights*. He's one of the 'lowlifes' my mother is talking about. I'm sorry, and I love you, but I love him too. I have ever since you introduced us. All I can tell you is that *nothing* ever happened between us while you two were together, and I'll swear that on anything you want to put in front of me. This has all only happened in the last couple of weeks." She threw a glance at her parents. "When I went to him to get a tattoo."

Sylvia stepped back, and Phillip grabbed her as if he expected her to pass out. She even fluttered a hand up to her throat. "You did what?"

Candace felt her lips curl with a little more wicked glee than she should probably be displaying at the moment. "I would show it to you right now, Mother, but it might violate a few public decency laws."

Michelle ran one hand through her hair, holding it back off her forehead for a moment. It was her signature gesture of distress. Candace immediately regretted her careless words for her cousin's sake, but she enjoyed the stricken horror both her parents were wearing. Someone could have just told them she'd died. No...actually, they probably wouldn't have been as upset over her demise.

"I'm sorry," she said softly to Michelle. "I..." Fumbling, she gave up. "Please don't hate me."

Jameson scoffed, shaking his head. "You girls must really enjoy scraping the bottom of the barrel, messing around with that one."

"James," Michelle snapped as Candace's mouth fell open.

"You have the audacity to say that about him while you defend the scum sitting in there?"

"Don't forget I went to school with that no-good punk. When he wasn't living half his life in detention, that is, or his parents weren't shipping him off somewhere. Bad enough he was with *you*, Michelle, but I'll be damned if he's going to get his hands on my baby sister. I'll beat his ass into next week."

Candace tried to keep her cool, though she saw red, especially when she noticed the all-too-pleased smile on her mother's face. "Oh, please, Jameson, he'd wrap you into a pretzel."

Michelle smirked her agreement as the door swung open. Deanne flew out, her eyes nightmarish, seeking and finding Candace with unnerving precision. The sweet Southern belle act was long gone, and in its place was the true bridezilla Candace knew she could be. Deanne plowed between Candace's parents to face her front and center. "I've just now stemmed the freaking riot in there, Candace. What in the hell are you trying to prove, pulling that stunt at my rehearsal dinner? Are you trying to *ruin* this for me?"

"Hey." Michelle, ever the referee, grabbed her arm. "Lay off her. Candace, go home. I'm not mad at you, honey, but it's best if you leave."

More tears spilled, dripping on her blouse, as the five of them stood there looking at her. Michelle's gaze was the only one that wasn't openly hostile. But her mouth was set in a grim line, and there was a troubled wrinkle between her brows. God, of them all, she couldn't have Michelle hate her. She couldn't.

Deanne crossed her arms and eased her defensive stance a bit. "Whatever. I don't know what's wrong, and I don't care. But if one more thing goes foul in this wedding, I'm going to shoot first and pull my freaking hair out by the roots later. Candace, do you think you can manage to be at the church by two tomorrow? That's two p.m., honey. Just so we're clear."

"Deanne," Michelle said with a warning tone.

Candace didn't wait to hear more. The hurt was settling deep into a dark, scary part of her soul she didn't dare examine too often. A part of her that wanted to wreak all the havoc she possibly could to the ones who had hurt her. She turned and walked toward her car, taking slow, deliberate steps so as not to break into a sprint. Good thing she'd left her purse in the car. There was no way in hell she was stepping foot back in that house again.

Her parents obviously had nothing else to say to her. She wondered if she was finally officially disowned. It had always seemed so inevitable, it was almost a relief to get it over with. Popping open her car door, she turned her sore, half-blind eyes toward the brightly lit house and saw that Michelle had soundlessly followed her. Pausing half in and half out of her car, Candace just looked at her.

"Well, he's certainly taught you to cuss. Did you sleep with him?" Michelle asked. Somehow she'd known that was the question that was coming, now that they had a moment away from everyone else. There was no malice in her tone whatsoever, and her expression showed nothing more than concern. But there was a flatness in her voice that broke Candace down even more. "Tell me the truth. I won't be mad. I'm worried about you."

She couldn't have lied to Michelle at that moment even if the answer had been yes. "He...stayed with me one night, but it didn't go that far."

Michelle's eyebrows rose. "Really. Well, if that's true, I'm impressed. Candace..." Sighing, Michelle pushed her hair back again, her other hand on her hip. "Listen, sweetie, I realize your experience with men is limited. And that's your business. Just keep in mind, please, that they come and go, especially that one. That'll be the case for probably the next few years of your life, as you get out there more. They might not be there from one day to the next, but your family will. I'd hate to see you drive us all away only to find yourself alone on all sides one day. Don't destroy something permanent for something fleeting."

"At the moment, it seems they're fleeting too. But even if they weren't, I can't see trading what he makes me feel for what they just did. I'll take five minutes with him over a lifetime with them any day. There's no contest. I think I just now came to that realization, but there you go."

Michelle sighed. "Fair enough. Look, I wish things could be different for you. I always have. I'll try to talk to them tonight, but they're pretty unreachable. It didn't work when I was with him, either."

"Did they do something to sabotage you two?"

Her cousin's lips thinned out a bit, tilting up at one corner. "They like to think they bribed me away. But the truth is, Brian and I were already over, and I could sense that. Otherwise, there wouldn't have been anything they could do."

"I see. Don't bother talking to them. You're right, it won't matter. I'll see you later."

Dropping the rest of the way into the car seat, she slammed the door and cranked the ignition. Michelle watched her for a moment before turning to head back in for the remainder of the festivities.

Her cousin had taken it reasonably well. Candace should be relieved that part was over and done with, but she wasn't. Her insides felt shredded. The exhaustion that settled over her wasn't sudden, because she'd been feeling it for days. It was more acute now without the adrenaline rushing through her blood.

Tomorrow, oh, God. Tomorrow. Walking down the aisle to stand next to the woman who'd just belittled her. Walking out beside a guy who might have raped her if no one had bothered to intervene. Not only that, but her parents actually expected her to spend the weekend with him at the lake house? Where she would be fighting off his wandering hands and her mother's matchmaking for two whole days? She doubted his invitation would be *rescinded* for something so insignificant as mauling her. Why, that might be *rude*.

A fresh flood of tears blinded her, and she had to pull over before she'd even gotten to the end of the winding driveway. It was fifteen minutes before the violence of her sobs subsided. By then she hurt all over: her shoulders, her chest, her stomach...especially her stomach. She pulled out onto the road only to ditch it after half a mile to throw open her door and retch. Crying that much had always made her sick.

No one called her cell phone. No one tried to check on her. When she reached her apartment, there were no messages on her machine. Sam would be available if she wanted to talk, but despite her need for someone to care, she didn't really want to interact. Macy was definitely not someone she needed to hear from right now, since she usually sided with the "well meaning" family. Candace snorted as she pulled PJs from a drawer. If Macy loved them so much, and vice versa, it was unfortunate *she* hadn't grown up with them.

Truthfully, there was only one person she needed to hear from tonight. But he wasn't available, hadn't been since that night in his truck two weeks ago. So quickly, she'd found him and lost him again.

As she crawled into bed, she pulled the pillow Brian had slept on over the top of her own and let her tears leak helplessly onto it. Whimpered his name stupidly like a child needing her security blanket.

The damned misery of it was that she was defending a relationship she didn't even have. It would be entirely different if Brian had been here waiting when she got home, if he'd opened his arms and taken her to bed and snuggled her close all night. The shit with her family would have been bearable. Hell, she might not have even cared all that much, it would've been more of the same. If she'd only known he loved her.

She'd brought her cell phone to bed with her, and now she flipped it open, squinting at the sudden brightness of the display in the dark of her room. She rubbed the tip of her thumb over the keypad. A phone number was like the combination to a safe, he'd said, being silly. What in the hell would she find if she cracked this particular one open? If she called him and asked him to come over, told him how much and how desperately she needed him tonight?

He would probably laugh. No telling what he'd been up to lately. What would he even want with her, the naïve virgin, when he could have his pick of women far more experienced and mature? Women who wouldn't almost come all over themselves just because he laid a finger on them. He must think she was truly pathetic.

Snapping her phone closed, she flung it to the floor and flopped on her stomach, begging sleep to come. But sleep was being as pissy as everyone else in her life. She saw every hour on the clock even though she had to look fresh and beautiful like a perfect freaking princess for Deanne's wedding.

By morning, she was ten times as exhausted as the night before. It was only as she shuffled into the kitchen in a stumbling haze that she remembered she was out of coffee.

Today, of all days.

Well, it was a no-brainer. Any other time she might suffer

through. But if she didn't get caffeine inside her body now, they were going to find her out roaming the streets, grabbing people's heads and moaning, "Braaaiins."

Not even bothering to change out of her T-shirt and plaid pajama pants, or fix her sloppy ponytail, she slid on her flip-flops, grabbed her purse and hit the door.

Chapter Thirteen

"Too fucking early, dude. What are we leaving so early for?" Ghost caught his yawn with one hand and hauled the bag of ice he was carrying up on the open tailgate of Brian's truck with the other.

Brian, standing in the bed, grabbed it and gave it a few hard slams against the side to break up the ice before dumping it in the cooler. "Because I want to get there when the gates open."

"When is that?"

"Two."

"Then why the hell are we up at the ass crack of dawn?"

"It's eight-thirty! Stop whining or I'll take your ass back home. It'll be noon by the time we get to Dallas if we leave by nine. That doesn't leave us much time to chill out at Marco's before we go. Crack open those twelve packs."

Grumbling to himself, Ghost ripped open the first and began tossing beer cans to Brian one by one. He shoved them as deep in the ice as they could go. It was shaping up to be a scorcher of a day. Even now, the sun was beating down unmercifully on the grocery store parking lot where they stood. Icy cold beverages were going to be a necessity. But it wasn't all beer, and it damn sure wasn't for the road. He could just imagine getting pulled over with open alcohol containers in the vehicle. His brother would bury him; it was a fight they had all the time. And Evan thought Brian never listened to him.

Ghost grabbed the next in line, a pack of Dr. Pepper, as Brian watched with a smirk.

"I hope you have sunscreen to rub on that head of yours. You look like a cue ball standing out here."

"Fuck you, dude. We're not at work today. I don't have to put up with your stupid bullshit."

Brian laughed and, for the first time in two weeks, felt it was genuine. "Will the UV rays bounce right off? Is that your plan?"

"I swear to God..." The soda cans came more forcefully this time, some of them aimed right at his head. The bastard was quick too. Brian had to duck the last one, and it clattered in the bed of the truck. "Oops, sorry."

"*Watch* it, motherfu—"

"Hey, hey! Don't look, man. But I think that's your little honey sitting over there watching us."

"My wha..." Completely ignoring his order not to look, Brian twisted around to look in the direction Ghost was staring...only to spot Candace's blue Camry sitting on the next aisle a few cars down, facing them. She was sitting in it, and jerked her gaze away when it connected with his. Her door popped open and she jumped out, looking adorably disheveled, and hurried toward the store.

It was just how she'd looked that morning she'd rolled out of bed after tumbling around with him most of the night. Except then she'd been gloriously naked too.

"Shit," Brian grumbled as she disappeared inside. "I did not need to see that." He shot a look at Ghost. "How did you know about her?"

"Starla told me you were sweatin' after some piece who'd come in a couple of weeks ago. It wasn't too hard to figure out which one she was. Never seen you slip your number to a client before."

He wanted to tell him to watch his mouth, that Candace was far more to him than a "piece", but it really was impossible to shut Ghost up and Brian didn't feel like being tortured about her for the rest of the day. "You're one observant bastard, aren't you? So why can't you ever memorize the work schedule so I don't have to call you every night and ask where the hell you are?"

Ghost gave him an exasperated look. He held out both palms as if weighing something in each. "Dude. Work. Women. There's a distinction, see it?"

"Yeah, but you need work to get the women, or else you'll be sitting on your broke ass alone. Keep that in mind."

"Can we go or what?"

"Just a minute."

An alarm was sounding in the back of Brian's mind. Candace had looked...troubled. For appearing to have just rolled out of bed, she also looked as if she hadn't slept in days.

Was she that torn up over him? Or was it something else? Shit. He'd only in the past day or so managed to get his mind off her for more than five minutes. He'd figured it would take her even less time, after the way she'd rebuffed him. But she hadn't looked good.

When she emerged from the store carrying a single sack, he openly scrutinized her and found that it was far worse than he'd initially thought. Even from this distance, he could see how puffy and red-rimmed her eyes were. She could've just had a crying jag in the store, for the way she looked.

Grasping the side of the truck bed, he bounded out and landed lightly on his feet. Ghost made some grumbling, obviously smart-ass comment he didn't catch. He was already headed toward her, never mind that she quickened her pace as if she were going to attempt to run from him. Again. This time, he wasn't letting her get far.

Panic swelling in her chest, Candace strode directly for the sanctuary of her car, but he got there at the same time she did and grabbed her hand as she reached for the door handle. Horrified, she realized she was about five seconds away from total meltdown. His fingers were warm and familiar and so comforting...

"Candace, what's wrong?" he demanded.

Oh, God, and he looked...

She shook her head desperately. Brian took off his wraparound shades and settled them on the bill of his black baseball cap, hitting her with the full force of his dark blue eyes. Out here in the blinding sun, she could see herself reflected in their depths.

"I didn't follow you here," she snapped. "I was out of coffee."

For a moment he looked puzzled, then he chuckled. "Sweetie, that never even entered my mind. But you can follow me any damn place you please, all right?"

She was struggling to contain the impulse to throw herself onto his white sleeveless tee right there in the middle of the busy parking lot. Why did he have to bust out the tattoos today, of all days? They were visible from shoulders to wrists. Beautiful. She wanted those arms around her. She wanted that voice telling her not to worry. But he and his friend appeared to have plans of some sort, and she didn't want to keep him from them. He deserved to go and live his carefree life without worrying about her baggage.

"In fact...follow me now," he said. "Come with us. You look like you could use a getaway."

Her heart stuttered. "W-where?"

"The bunch of us are going to Dallas for a rock festival. I have friends up there we're crashing with. You'd love it, Candace. I know you've never been to anything like that before."

He was the serpent standing there holding out the forbidden fruit to her. Escape. Safety. And dare she even think it? *Fun.*

"And I also know you're mad at me, so look, I won't—"

"I'm not mad at you, Brian."

"Well...there are issues, then. How's that? So this could be just us hanging out for the weekend. No pressure, no worries. I think it would do you some good."

She did too. A world of good. She could be with him, even if she wasn't *with* him. And that actually made sense to her short-circuited brain.

But she had a commitment. She had to be at the church at two. Two *p.m.*, rather. Couldn't forget that. He must have forgotten, but then again, she didn't recall telling him when the wedding was. She doubted he kept up with the Lifestyle section of the newspaper.

And not only did she have to be there at two p.m.—in the *afternoon*, lest she get confused—she had to walk down the aisle with her would-be date rapist. Couldn't forget that, either. But she had decided that no matter what machinations her mother devised, she was *not* going to the lake house for the fun, old-fashioned family get-together. It wasn't happening. She wasn't waking up in the middle of the night to find that freak crawling into her bed. The very thought made her nauseous.

Brian's thumb gently stroked the back of her hand. "Come on. We can get you a ticket, no problem. Come with us."

Her mouth opened. No words would come out. They were too conflicted, jumbling together as her heart and her brain warred back and forth.

"Go home, get your stuff together, and we'll pick you up in twenty minutes or so. Wear something comfortable for today. Once we get there, you'll be on your feet all day long."

He looked so eager and excited for her to go with them. She imagined how her mother and Deanne were going to sneer at her when she walked into the dressing room this afternoon. She imagined Michelle wearing the same cool expression toward her she'd worn last night after her revelation, all traces of warmth gone.

Deanne hadn't wanted her there in the first place. She knew it. Now no one wanted her there at all.

I'll take five minutes with him over a lifetime with them any day.

She'd meant it with all her heart when she'd said it to Michelle. But the next quiet word that came out of her mouth would truly put it to the test.

"Okay."

Riding in Brian's truck toward Dallas when she was supposed to be getting ready to go to the church was probably the most surreal experience of Candace's life. She'd left her cell phone sitting on her kitchen counter, thrown a bag of clothes together so fast she'd probably neglected necessities. And she couldn't stop shaking. At times it was all she could do not to tell Brian to turn around and take her home.

It was too late for that. She was crammed in the backseat of his truck with Starla and Janelle because Ghost had called shotgun and apparently that was a binding resolution. She really didn't mind. This wasn't a date, as Brian had said, just hanging out. Sitting pressed against him for three hours straight might decimate her already frazzled mind. Plus, the girls had wanted her in the back with them. Starla had patted the seat next to her with a big grin and said, "Come on back here with us, sexy."

Ghost had gotten all kinds of excited about the prospects of some girl-on-girl action happening in the backseat, and offered the use of his cell phone to record it. Brian had shaken his head, laughing.

The conversation hadn't stalled since, and she found herself struggling to keep up. It was like wandering into a roomful of strangers who were speaking a foreign language, trying to decipher their gossip and inside jokes. They were probably all the more hilarious for their mystery to her.

"Dude," Ghost proclaimed after about an hour and a half on the road. He dug deep into the duffel bag he'd brought and produced a CD, which he handed to Brian. "Play this."

Brian took it and held it up in front of his face to examine it, but it looked blank from where she was sitting. "The fuck is this, man," he muttered around the sucker in this mouth. She had to giggle at the way he often made questions sound like statements.

"Just play it. You'll like it."

"I'd better or you're walking the rest of the way." He glanced back at Candace. “Ghost favors some unusual shit.”

“Very,” Starla agreed, passing Candace the bag of chips that had been circulating the cab.

As Brian fiddled with the CD, Ghost surprised Candace by turning all the way around in his seat so he could look directly at her. “What’s up with your girl?”

Caught with a mouthful of BBQ Ruffles, she struggled to swallow before she spoke. “Huh?”

“Your girl. The one you came in with the other night.”

“Oh, Macy? What about her?”

“She have a dude?” His dark eyes were intent, almost unnervingly so. He normally seemed so nonchalant. But then, she’d only been in his presence a couple of times.

“Um…not at the moment.”

“Gimme her number.”

She laughed, looking at him incredulously. “I can’t just give you my friend’s number.”

“Why not? She’s your friend, ain’t she?”

“Yeah, that’s why I can’t hand her number out without her permission.”

“What I’m saying is, if she’s your friend, she’ll forgive you. But she doesn’t even have to know where I got it from. I won’t tell her.”

“Who else could you have gotten it from?”

“I’ll say you left your phone sitting in your seat or something and I swiped it and got her number out of it.”

“I didn’t even bring it.”

“Well, *she* doesn’t know that!”

Brian and the girls were laughing. Starla reached up and grabbed Ghost’s shoulder. “Down, boy, turn around now. Stop harassing her.”

Ghost ignored her. “She’s kind of prim and proper, huh.”

“You don’t know the half of it.”

“Oh, shit,” Brian muttered, as if he knew what was coming next. “Dude, turn around. Eyes front.”

"Daaaamn, I *love* girls like that. I love getting them dirrrty."

Candace giggled. "Good luck with that. Look up 'dirty' in the dictionary and it'll say 'Not Macy'."

Starla yelped with laughter, but Ghost only looked pained. "Ah! You're killing me here."

He shook his head and turned back around, grumbling. "I still think you should give me her number."

She was tempted to do it just to get a good laugh out of the situation. This poor guy didn't know what he'd be getting himself into.

Every time Brian had glanced into the backseat on the drive, she'd been smiling. She looked better already, and he had to congratulate himself. But then, his friends could always be counted on to keep the mood festive. Starla and Janelle had made sure she felt welcome without him even having to ask it of them. He'd been afraid Starla's opinion of her had changed after last week. Apparently, that wasn't the case at all.

By the time they pulled up to the curb outside Marco and Kara's house in the suburbs of Dallas, every line of tension in her face had smoothed out. Their plan had been not to call this a date, but God, he wanted to. He wanted to run straight to her side, wrap his arm around her shoulders and introduce her to his friends as *his*. His date, his woman, his girlfriend...hell, whatever title she would allow him to put on her.

He couldn't do that, but there was no denying the magnetism that pulled him toward her as soon as his feet hit the ground. She smiled at him as he came up beside her, and gestured to the sucker stick still in his mouth as she stretched her muscles after the long drive. "New habit?"

"Yeah. Rot my teeth instead of my lungs."

"Ew!"

He laughed, flicking the stick in the back of his truck. Normally he would've thrown it in the gutter, but he didn't want her thinking he was a litterbug.

"When I first saw you pull up at my apartment, I caught

that flash of white in your mouth and I was so afraid you were smoking again."

"I'm doing okay," he murmured as they all walked across the neat green lawn toward the house. "Haven't slipped up yet. Don't worry."

"So, how do you know these people whose house I'm staying at?" She gave a nervous laugh. "I hope they won't mind me tagging along."

"Not at all, they're totally cool. You'll see. They own a parlor here in Dallas. When I want ink, I go to these guys. Marco is my mentor. I did my apprenticeship under him."

"Oh! So they've done all your work?"

"I'm pretty much a showcase for them."

Ghost had overheard. "Yeah, the bastard won't let me touch him."

"Because I can only imagine what you'd put on me," Brian fired back.

The front door to the house opened and Marco's wife flew out, squealing. Janelle and Starla made similar sounds of excitement and rushed forward, crushing her in a hug.

"That's Kara," Brian said at Candace's ear. "I'll introduce you. You'll like her."

The three danced around in a silly merry-go-round hug and finally broke apart, laughing. Kara evaded Ghost's groping as best she could before moving on to Brian and then Candace, surprising him by grabbing her in a hug, too. Candace returned it, beaming.

"Candace, meet Kara." Brian laughed. "Who is not shy in the least."

"I've never met you before," Kara said to her, "but if you're with him then you're all right by me."

"Oh, I'm..." Candace looked at him in alarm, and he gave a little shake of his head to say it was okay. They didn't need to explain themselves to anyone. "It's nice to meet you. I hope you don't mind me coming along."

"Of course not. You guys might be crowded tonight, but we are fully equipped for this sort of thing, trust me. The more the merrier."

"That's if we sleep at all," Ghost said happily.

Kara was still scrutinizing Candace. "Brian, she's adorable! Look at that face. You take good care of him, Candace. Ever since he was a starry-eyed eighteen-year-old kid hanging around our parlor, he's been one of my favorite people."

"Just one of them?" he teased, and she winked at him.

"I'll do my best," Candace assured her, looking overwhelmed.

Kara gave her arm a squeeze and turned to the rest of them. "Marco left with Connor and Tay. Beer run. I'm watching the grill out back, so you guys had better come on in before I burn something down."

"Sw*eet*," Ghost said. "I'm starving."

"Con and Tay made it here already?" Brian asked. "They made good time." His other two workers had ridden separately.

"They said they set the cruise at ninety." Kara rolled her eyes as she led them into the foyer of the house. Brian's hand sought out Candace's and he gave her fingers a squeeze. He really couldn't imagine how she was feeling right now, thrown into the mix with a bunch of strangers the likes of which she'd probably never hung out with before. Kara had sleeves as solid and dense as his own, a nose ring and angelbites. Not to mention everything you *couldn't* see. She was brash and opinionated and, much like him, didn't give a damn what anyone thought. A far cry from the Andrews family, not to mention his own.

Candace probably felt about as comfortable as he did when forced to hang out with his own straight-laced relatives, except she seemed to be having a lot more fun than he did in those situations. Kara grabbed all the girls and headed into the kitchen with them to make drinks. Candace tagged along, complimenting her on the house.

She was just too sweet, too polite. He'd never imagined

falling for someone like her, not in a million years, but if he was honest with himself, he knew that was only because he couldn't have imagined a girl like her falling for *him.*

Chapter Fourteen

Kara was very pretty and even more intimidating. Not that she was unfriendly. She was too cool and too likeable. Surrounded by girls who knew one another and seemed to be best friends, Candace felt she was struggling to keep from blending into the background. She didn't want to let Brian down by not meshing with his friends, but it wasn't just for him. She needed this for herself. To prove to herself that she could function when she wasn't under the protective shadow of her freakishly tyrannical family.

She met Kara's husband and Brian's other two employees when they got back from the liquor store. Marco was tall with long black hair and, as expected, lots of tattoos. He and Brian greeted each other with guy hugs and good-natured insults, but there was no question he was someone Brian had a lot of respect for. The guys headed out into the backyard to take over grilling duties while the girls gathered around the kitchen table.

Candace accepted the beer she was offered, feeling it would've been rude not to do so, but she barely sipped it. Kara wasn't drinking, because apparently she and Marco were trying to get pregnant. The conversation flew fast and furious, skipping from catching up to work to music to Kara's endeavors to conceive.

"So how is the baby-making sex?" Janelle was inquiring. "You would think it would be kind of boring and mechanical, like, 'I'm ovulating! Give it to me *now*!'"

Kara shook her head, laughing. "It's actually not. To me it's even more exciting, to wonder in the middle of it if this could be *the one.* And, girl, it's never boring. I don't think I'll ever get enough of him." Her lips curled as she stared out the window, where the guys were gathered around the grill.

"How long have you been married?" Candace asked.

"Seven years. But we've been together for fifteen. Met in high school."

"Wow."

Kara's attention turned back to her. "How long have you and Brian been dating? It must be a new development because he never mentioned you until he called earlier today to say you were coming."

"Oh, um...actually, we're not really dating. I mean, I wish I could say we were, to be honest, but...it's complicated."

A chorus of voices spoke up at once:

"Girl, he's crazy about you."

"You could totally be with him if you want to be."

"Complicated sucks. Simplify things and go for it."

They all laughed. Candace shrugged and kept her gaze trained on her beer, turning the bottle around and around with her fingers. She was heading in the wrong direction. Things weren't getting simpler; they were only getting more complicated, thanks to her actions today.

It was getting close to one o'clock. Every time she thought about it, a flock of butterflies went wild in her stomach and her heart did a sick flip-flop. What were they going to do when they couldn't find her? This was so against the grain for her. And there was always the possibility that Brian would be angry when he found out what she'd done. What if he hated her for only making things worse? What if it totally ruined the weekend for him? What if he would be disgusted when he learned she was a spineless little mouse who had to run and hide from her problems?

What had she *done*?

She looked around Kara's neat, prettily decorated kitchen and wished she could have something like this. Freedom. A home that was hers. The man she loved and wanted to spend the rest of her life with.

"You've got it bad for him too," Starla observed. She cleared her throat and straightened in her chair. "He probably said something already, but I wanted to tell you myself that I'm sorry I roped him into taking me to the bar the night you were there. It was nothing. He's been helping me through a rough spot with my man. Brian's a great friend, and the whole time we were there, all he did was pine for you, really."

"He did?"

"He was in a funk all night at work. I'm telling you, the man is strung out over you." Starla gave her a look then that led Candace to believe she knew more than she was letting on. "Don't play with his head, okay?" she finished gently.

"That's the last thing I want to do. I... There are some things I'm having to work through right now."

"Let him help," Kara offered. "Don't shut him out."

"I feel like he deserves someone who isn't this soul-sucking emotional burden on him."

"Honey, all he deserves is someone who loves him for who he is. If there's a soul-sucking emotional burden to bear, then so be it. Bear it together."

The three pairs of eyes watching her were kind but inquisitive, as if they were trying to decipher her true intentions with their friend. She could understand. It warmed her heart that he had people who cared about him so much. She'd always considered him sort of a loner type, only to find he had a greater support network than she did.

Kara leaned across the table, her exotic, darkly lined and shadowed eyes intense. "It's worth it in the end. I promise you. Once you wade through all the bullshit and the two of you are all that's left, you'll be glad you took a chance. If you love him."

Oh, God, she was going to cry again. Panicked, she took a long pull at her beer and struggled to stomach the flavor.

Kara had mercy on her and flashed her a wicked grin. "And you have me to thank for talking him into his apadravya. FYI, I accept gifts of chocolate and fine wine."

"Girl, you'd better buy her some Cheval Blanc or something," Janelle muttered under her breath. "I've never had the experience, but I've heard those things are..." She trailed off to give a full-body shudder.

"It hits all the right spots," Kara supplied.

"And hits them over and over and over..." Starla grasped the table edge and tossed her head back in mock ecstasy. Candace felt her cheeks flaring red as the other girls laughed.

Kara's smile dimmed as she noticed Candace hiding behind her beer again. "You like it, don't you?"

Starla interrupted her pretend orgasm to stare at Candace with great interest.

"We, um... I wouldn't know, actually. But I'm sure I will."

"Whoa. I'll be waiting for the phone call to thank me, then. And for the Godiva and Cheval Blanc, of course."

"Did you actually do his piercing?"

"I did. I am a complete professional, don't worry. Hell, ordinarily I wouldn't have even brought it up, but I figured you two were going at it like bunny rabbits already."

Candace startled when the door opened and Brian walked in with a platter of burgers, only to pause when the other three girls dissolved into fits of laughter. "Oh, hell," he said. "I can only imagine what I've interrupted."

Kara had no shame. "We were just discussing the joys of the apadravya. Why don't you enlighten us with the male opinion, Bri?"

He gave a sheepish grin and walked over to the counter. "I'm a good boy and a gentleman. I don't discuss those matters."

"What*ever*." Kara laughed. "Marco said you had plenty to discuss after you put it to use for the first time. You called him raving."

"I have to know," Candace cut in, not particularly wanting to hear about that. "How did he take it when you pierced him?"

"He screamed like a little girl," Kara said.

"The hell I did!"

She sent Candace a wink. "Just kidding. He was one of my silent, stoic ones. Got a pretty good flinch out of him and that was about it. Now tell us how it *really* felt."

He laughed. "Shit. I wanted to scream like a little girl. If I hadn't already had the PA part done, I probably would have screamed, curled up in the corner and cried for my mommy."

"You, sir, are a good man," Janelle said, lifting her drink in his direction. "If only more of you were willing to torture yourselves in the name of getting us off."

"Don't paint me as too much of an altruist," he said, his gaze lingering on Candace. She drew a deep breath, meeting his gaze directly, unflinching. Too often its intensity had chased her own downward. No more. There was nowhere else she needed to look but at him. For a moment, he seemed to lose his train of thought, and she felt a rush of pure feminine triumph. "I get plenty of benefits myself."

In their hometown, among their families, Brian was the offbeat. Here, in this breathtaking crush of colorful bodies, it was her. As they'd entered the main gates and she'd stopped to stare in astonishment, he had chuckled and said, "Welcome to my world."

She'd never seen anything like it before in her life.

She was sore, she was sweating, she was exhausted, she was nearly deaf, and she was having the time of her life. She'd seen every kind of tattoo conceivable (but when she'd made that remark to Brian, he'd replied, "Uh, no. You haven't."). Every hair color that could possibly be imagined and some that couldn't. She'd watched fights break out. She'd witnessed security pile on top of troublemakers, wrestle them to the ground and escort them out. She'd helped someone crowd surf over the top of her head and she thought her finger was broken from the experience. She'd seen two girls making out. Later, one of them had tried to pass her a joint, but Brian had promptly waved it away.

Always, he hovered protectively at her side, shoving

moshers away from her, sending threatening looks to the guys who ogled her or—God forbid—tried to lay a hand on her.

The bands were amazing. She didn't know who half of them were, but electricity filled the air with each new stage set-up as fans anticipated the next set. Music rumbled and thundered over the speakers even between sets as the crowd thinned and loosened a bit, people leaving to get more drinks or food. But when the first bone-rattling riffs of the next band split the air, the crush was back, tightening, frenzied, feverish. There was nothing to do but go with the never-ending flow of bodies as she was pushed and pulled by the crowd.

She would've thought something like this would make her panic. It might have, if not for one startling revelation: she *belonged* here. In this sea of people, she felt actual acceptance. They were all here for one thing: to forget their problems for a while, to let the music become their world. No one knew her or where she'd come from or what she'd done. They were just like her. And all the while, Brian was with her, watching out for her. Every time she looked at him, he was looking back, a little grin lingering on his lips.

Darkness fell. By now, the wedding was over and her family was cursing her name. Once, she'd seen Brian check his cell phone, and her heart had leapt into her throat. What if they called him? Naturally, after last night, they would check with him if she went missing, wouldn't they? Especially Michelle; she surely still had his number.

But he'd simply shut the phone and slid it back into his pocket.

Now, rainclouds were gathering overhead and there was electricity in the air as the crowd awaited Korn's set. Candace's feet and calves ached like crazy and more than once she'd envied the people who had seats, or the girls who were perched on top of their boyfriend's shoulders. She didn't dare ask Brian if she could do that. She'd figured out if you took up that position, you were more or less expected by the crowd to flash your boobs at least once. Not happening.

The lights went out, plunging the stadium in utter

darkness except for the stage, and the roar from the crowd was deafening. Candace joined, but her voice died in her throat as she felt Brian's arms encircle her waist from behind and his lips move next to her ear.

"This place is about to go apeshit," he warned as the crowd surged and propelled them forward. At that moment, she was glad for his arms locked around her. The last thing she wanted was to lose him in the dark.

His shirt was gone. He'd long since stripped it off and shoved half of it in the waistband of his long black shorts. With his damp, naked chest pressed in tight at her back, she wanted to groan in ecstasy...and might have actually done it, since he probably couldn't hear her, anyway. The desire to turn around in his arms and kiss him was overwhelming. She imagined flinging off her own top and letting their bodies slide against each other. But she couldn't very well do either of those things right now, and it was pure torture.

Bass thundered across the sea of people like a storm blowing over the ocean, and the crowd rippled and roared accordingly. She was so short she couldn't see much over the guys in front of her, but she could glimpse the band members as they pounded out the riffs that whipped the audience into ecstasy.

It couldn't be her imagination that Brian was lowering his head a bit, nuzzling his face against her hair. They were getting jostled so much, it was hard to tell. But her breath began to rasp through her lungs. His arms were as impenetrable as steel around her, not allowing for even a centimeter of space between them. She leaned her head back against the solidity of his chest, hoping she wasn't wrong, hoping...

Ohh, yes. He trailed his lips down the side of her face. She closed her eyes and trembled in his embrace. His mouth slid lower, to her throat, and the fingers of one hand danced over the strip of bare flesh at her midriff. The other hand pulled her so close her bottom dug into his groin, where he was hot and hard and straining for her.

He still wanted her. "Want" didn't even begin to cover what

she felt for him. Answering moisture pooled between her legs, and her thighs quaked. She was desperate, aching, oblivious to any and everything else but the need to take him inside her. To give herself to him completely, no more holding back. No more running away.

She cast a quick glance around at the crowd cramming them together—everyone still transfixed by what was happening on the stage—and coaxed his hand higher, letting it slide under her shirt. Even in this tumult of sound, she heard him groan, felt the breath of it against her neck. Once his fingers met the expanse of damp flesh under her shirt, she didn't have to push him anymore. Both hands crept upward until her breasts were fully encased in his big palms, and she tilted her face upward to the sky, only for a cool, solitary rain drop to sting her cheek.

It felt so good, so good, and she almost didn't even care if anyone was watching them. His fingers kneaded gently, soothing the arousal making her breasts feel heavy, and her nipples pebbled against his hands. It amazed her how every part of her responded to him in some way. Her breasts. Between her legs. Her mouth flooding with the taste of desire. Her hands shaking, her knees becoming liquid. Was there any part of her he wasn't master over?

He nudged her head around for a kiss, his lips hot and damp against hers, as bigger raindrops began to sprinkle over them. She couldn't get close enough this way, and it nearly broke something inside her. The rain landed in cold pinpricks on her feverish skin. She needed more of it, or more of him, to douse these flames before they could incinerate her.

Their lips separated, but lingered between light, brushing kisses, the two of them breathing each other's breath. She looked at him, watched the lights from the stage flicker over his expression, in the dark depths of his eyes. There was a whole other world in there, she thought, and it was hers to explore forever if she would stop being so afraid. She was going to try to do that. Starting tonight.

Chapter Fifteen

Candace could feel the cool solidity of Brian's truck fender beneath her ass as he pressed her against it. The sweet, tender burn of his lips across hers, the familiar taste of his mouth...but voices—namely Ghost's—kept cutting through the haze of pleasure enwrapping her.

"Hey, you *did* realize that Korn actually got onstage tonight, right? And they kicked ass? Did you actually fuck out in the audience? That's pretty hot, I guess."

Brian laughed, letting go of her lips but not moving any farther away or looking anywhere else but at her. "Shut up, man." Candace admired him for his ability to still speak. Or even breathe. She closed her eyes and clenched her fists against his chest to keep from running her hands all over him. His skin was warm and still dewy from the rain.

"Leave them alone," Kara scolded, sounding tired. Candace glanced over to see her and Marco in each other's arms as well. Kara's hair was plastered to her face, and Candace could only imagine what her own looked like. "Brian, you guys can have one of the guestrooms to yourselves, you know."

Her heart plunged to the pit of her stomach at those teasing words.

"I ain't sleeping on no floor," Ghost proclaimed loudly. "One of the beds is mine, fuckers."

"You'll sleep where I tell you to sleep." That was Marco, and from the sounds that ensued, the two guys engaged in a friendly scuffle.

It all seemed to be such good fun, but all she could focus on was Brian as he kissed her again. His hands. His lips. His tongue in her mouth. His knee between her legs, pressed hard against her crotch. It was the only thing keeping her from climbing him right here. She was aching so hard it was all she could do not to start thrusting her hips against him.

"Let's figure something out before these two combust," Kara declared, reeling her man back into her arms. "Are we going clubbing or what?" A chorus of yeses went up, but Candace noticed none of them were hers or Brian's. "Bri? I'll give you the keys if you want to head back to the house. It sounds like we're going out."

"Let's go back to your place anyway," Starla said. "I'm gross. I need to change."

Only then did Brian pull away and look at the others, which left his neck exposed for Candace to nibble on. "I think we need to crash somewhere else, actually. Sorry for the change of plans."

"Hey, no problem, totally understandable," Kara said amidst the whooping that followed his statement.

Brian turned back and slid his lips against Candace's ear, whispering, "Is that okay?"

She nodded weakly, feeling how ragged her pulse had grown. Alone with him for the night... Her blood felt thick in her veins, pooling heavily in all the places that were pressed tight against him. Brian's lips slid around her earlobe and tugged gently. Every muscle in her body went rigid. She flattened out her palms and smoothed them over his chest, circling one of his nipple rings with the tip of her middle finger. She knew it would make him groan in her ear, and she wasn't disappointed.

"We've got to get out of here," he growled.

"Yes, please."

Soon after, they were caught in the never-ending line exiting the stadium parking lot, the windows completely fogged. They were alone, the others having been merciful enough to ride with Kara or Tay.

Candace groaned and clutched at him as his lips claimed a patch of skin at the base of her throat and sucked it mercilessly. A moment ago, he'd slammed the truck in Park with a curse and attacked, holding her captive to him in an embrace that had her sprawled across his front seat, one leg thrown over his lap.

She threaded her fingers through his hair, holding him to her. The tickling ache of his suction on her skin was driving her wild, and she tilted her hips desperately, trying to grind against him. He rewarded her by sliding his hand up the leg of her shorts. She nearly died.

His mouth released her, but continued to slide over her damp flesh. "I shouldn't touch you," he said, sounding gruff and unbelievably sexy. "I should leave you so hot that you'll come the second my tongue touches that sweet pussy." Despite his words, he slid his fingers under her panties, the outside edge of his index finger grazing her throbbing clit.

"Oh, God!"

"Fuck, you're soaked." Drawing devastatingly slow circles, he spread the wetness he found through her folds. Outside, rain began pattering against the windows again. She arched against him, so aroused she hurt.

"Please, Brian, faster."

"You don't want to wait?" he whispered, keeping up the same torturous rhythm. "Until we're safe and warm and alone in bed with the whole night ahead? Until I can make you come over and over..."

"Just once, make me come just once, right now."

"Hmm, I'm not convinced..."

She plunged her hand down over his. "If you don't, I'll do it by myself."

He grinned. "The hell you will."

"You have to drive in a few minutes, anyway. You can't stop me."

"You touch yourself in front of me and I'll pull over and have your knees crammed around your ears in a fucking nanosecond. See if I don't."

"Maybe that's what I want," she challenged, his words spiking a thrill in her chest.

"At this point, I don't think it is."

"Please, I'm in pain. It hurts."

"Oh, baby..." Gently, he increased his motion between her legs and she moved her hand, relaxing back against his arm holding her semi-upright. "I'm sorry. I'm in pain, too, I want you so much."

"I'll do anything you want, just—"

"Shh. Let me take care of you."

If the line of cars decided to move right now, she was going to scream. Or she might scream anyway. People kept threading between the stopped vehicles, and Brian must have noticed her following them nervously with her eyes. "They can't see where my hand is," he murmured, working her a little faster with every passing second. She undulated against him, her head falling back.

"I don't think I care too much."

Oh, yes. Yes, yes...

The man knew what he was doing. Just as her thighs tightened, as the pleasure swelled until it dwarfed everything else, he slowed, widening the circumference of his motions and holding her at the precipice until she wanted to cry and beat at his shoulders. "Brian!"

"The cars are moving, baby."

"To hell with the cars!"

"But I have to drive."

"You'd better drive *me* first."

He laughed and quickened again, going after her hard until she exploded against him, the ache wrenching her in two before gradually dissipating to more tolerable levels. Breathless and sighing, she collapsed on the seat.

That had been two weeks in the making, she thought, remembering their very hot interlude outside the bar, when she'd so stupidly run away from him.

He straightened and got behind the wheel, putting the truck in gear with a cat-who-ate-the-canary smile curving those beautiful lips. They moved forward, and she fidgeted and smoothed her hands down her body, still feeling wild and wanton from his touch and the amazing orgasm he'd given her. Her foot—bare because her flip-flop was somewhere on the floor—was in his lap and she used it to graze the massive erection straining his fly.

His head fell back and he groaned. "Jesus."

She wanted to climb up on her knees and suck him right here. It was only fair. Gathering her annihilated strength, she drew up beside him and slid her hand between his legs.

"Baby," he said, one of his hands tightening on the wheel and the other grasping her wandering fingers. "As much as I want that, I don't need to spend myself yet. I want to do it inside you when I'm making you mine for the first time."

She leaned her forehead against his shoulder, trembling.

"If that's okay with you," he finished.

No more running. No more playing. She wanted to be his, if only for tonight, no matter what the future held. "That's definitely okay with me."

With that, she settled next to him, sitting in silence for a while as they inched forward in the line and the wipers intermittently cleared the windshield of the rain drooling down. He reached over and linked his fingers through hers, their hands resting against her bare thigh.

The song playing from his stereo was incredibly sexy, and she could imagine doing lots of naughty things to its rolling beat. "What is this song?"

"It's called 'Bliss', I think, by Syntax."

"I like it." It was appropriate. For once in her life, she'd found that particular state of mind. There would be hell to face later, but right now, she felt at peace. "I'm so glad I came with you. It might sound crazy, since I'm wet and exhausted and can barely hear, but I think it's the most fun I've ever had in my life."

"I'd have been miserable without you."

"You would? Why?"

"My intention was to come here and blow off some steam, but that would have been impossible. Everywhere I looked, I would have seen your face."

She blinked at him, unable to believe he was telling her this. He apparently couldn't believe it either, given that he was staring dead ahead, the glow from the dash lights casting enough illumination to show her the tight set of his jaw. In that moment, so much love for him welled up in her heart that each beat sent an ache through her veins.

Leaning closer, she pressed her lips against his biceps in one gentle kiss, then leaned her cheek into his arm, sliding one hand over his belly.

"Not getting sleepy, I hope," he teased, pulling his arm up so he could put it around her shoulders.

"Tired but wired, I guess."

"I know what you mean," he said. She watched the traffic crawl by and yawned, though sleep was the absolute last thing she wanted to do right now. It was well after midnight. Her family must be going crazy right about now. Every muscle in her body felt twisted out of position. She was wet from head to toe. And all she could think about was getting her hands all over him.

They found a hotel downtown, because he insisted she have something nice. Any roadside chain would've been fine with her, but he'd been relentless in his pursuit. They must've made quite a sight strolling through the lobby after checking in: wet and bedraggled, arm in arm and barely able to keep their hands off each other while they waited for the elevator. Her mother would have fallen out in a dead faint to see her behave in such a way. That was one reason it felt so good.

Once inside their room, she collapsed on the bed and gave a long, bone-weary sigh. "I am exhausted."

"Better build up your strength," he said with a wink as he prowled around and scoped things out. "Want to call room service? It's not too late."

She should be starving, but she didn't think she'd be able to eat a bite. "Hmm, maybe. What I really desperately need at the moment is a shower." Her eyes closed. As excited and nervous as she was, it wouldn't have taken a minute or two for her to fall sound asleep. When she felt weight press down on the mattress, she opened her eyes to find him staring down at her.

"Sounds good to me." He held out one hand. She grasped his forearm and let him haul her up to her feet. Staring into her eyes, he reached forward and slipped his fingers under the hem of her tank top. "Can I take this off?"

Candace bit her lip and nodded, raising her arms overhead while her heart thudded. Gently, he drew off the clinging material, but kept her hands trapped. His gaze roamed down over her breasts, barred from his sight only by a flesh-toned scrap of silk and lace. He brought one hand down to undo the front clasp while she gasped and shuddered. With a touch so light she could scarcely feel it, he spread the garment open, baring her to his warm palm.

"Keep this up and we'll never make it in there," she murmured.

"We will," he assured her.

She smiled. "I'm glad you're so self-controlled."

His caressing hand slid down over her abdomen to fiddle with the button of her shorts. She thought he might have trouble using only one hand, but she shouldn't have underestimated the skill in those fingers. Mere moments later, her shorts dropped around her feet, leaving her in her thong and her unclasped bra, all stretched out for his perusal.

"Beautiful," he murmured.

"I was always afraid you'd find me sort of plain, only having the one tattoo."

He smiled and tugged her hands over his head, settling

them around his neck. "Every artist loves a blank canvas. At least, this one does."

Exhaling in a rush, she pressed herself to him, rejoicing in the feel of her nipples rasping against his shirt. "Do you want me to get more of them?"

"Only if you want more. And only if I do them."

Smoothing the hair back from her forehead, he dropped his lips to hers, his breathing ragged as she opened her mouth to invite the invasion of his tongue. She'd been starving for another taste of him. The slick warmth of his kiss reignited the fire he'd so briefly quenched earlier in the truck, and she clung to him and whimpered in abandon. He smelled of rainwater and the day's heat and musky male, sending her hormones into overdrive.

"I missed you so much," she said between mouthfuls of his dark sweetness. His hands slid down to cup her face and he drew away.

"Don't ever run away from me again." There was no menace about the words; it was more of a plea. But given the possessiveness in his hands, his thumbs tilting up her chin so the darkness in his eyes could burn her deep, she swallowed thickly and trembled.

"What if I do?"

His gaze roamed over her face. "I won't let you get away so easily."

"Promise?"

"Oh, yes."

"Good. I've been a mess. I haven't been able to concentrate in class or—"

"Sweetheart, don't let yourself get all fucked up over me. All you have to do is call, and I'll come running. I was only giving you the space I thought you wanted."

She shook her head adamantly. "I don't want it. I didn't want it then, I only thought…"

"Shhh." He laid a finger against her lips. "It's okay."

She had to tell him what she'd done. She kept forgetting,

kept believing everything had worked out, only to remember...

It was hard to remember anything when he kissed her as he did then. Slow, deep, wet. She was aching, pulsing between her legs with every ragged throb of her heart.

Somehow he managed to back her into the bathroom while stripping off his clothes, only briefly breaking contact with her lips at any time. She did her best to help, tugging and shoving until he was naked. Her thong gave way to one vicious yank from his hand. He shoved the bra off her shoulders, palming both her breasts and jamming her back into the wall with a snarl. She cried out and tried to climb him, sliding one leg up his hip. Needing him to catch it, lift her and...

This was out of hand. His cock was hard and so, so big against her belly, sliding up between their feverish bodies. She knew in theory he would fit inside her, but sweet Jesus, she didn't know how. The bead on the underside grazed her skin, and she couldn't imagine how that was going to feel inside her.

Brian moved one hand to fumble inside the shower stall and crank on the water. Steam billowed, filling the bathroom until he adjusted it to make it tolerable. Then he helped her inside, and she wanted to groan with pleasure as the water fell over her skin in a hot rush. She was already crazed for his touch, but the spray invigorated her even further.

Her nipples had been chafing against him. Now they were soothed by the smooth slickness of his chest. She whimpered, and his answering groan as his tongue slid into her mouth was the most purely male sound she'd ever heard. His arms came up to trap her against the wall, his hips leaning into her so that his cock nestled against her abdomen again. She reached down to grasp it, gave it several loving strokes, but he didn't let her play for long.

His mouth left hers, trailing down her chin and her throat, and she couldn't resist reaching up to touch her lips. They felt bruised. Swollen and aching from his kisses. His mouth roamed over the swell of her breast, the tip of his tongue licking away the water as he kissed a path to her nipple. Candace let her hand flutter down to the top of his dark head as every breath she took pushed the taut crest toward his lips, just where she wanted it.

"God, I can't get enough of you," he murmured, just as the rosy tip disappeared into his mouth and she lost all ability to breathe. His palm came over to cup her other breast, as if he knew its weight had become almost unbearable, and he circled the center gently with his thumb. Beneath his lips, he was doing unspeakable things with his tongue and his teeth, sending little stinging jolts through her only to lick and soothe them away and do it all over again.

Between her legs she was drenched, the wetness slicking her inner thighs having nothing to do with the shower. She struggled to remain upright, and nearly lost that battle entirely when he switched from one nipple to the other. Could she come like this? The pressure couldn't build much more or it would have to break.

His hands came up to steady her hips, which were involuntarily rolling against him. "Easy, baby."

"Brian, I need to..."

"I know what you need."

He'd been bent over to reach her. Now he slid to his knees. *Oh, God.* Her right hand scrabbled for the bar on the wall beside her, seeking some anchor. Her other fingers threaded through his hair. Brian gripped the back of her left knee and hiked her leg over his shoulder, opening her up inches away from his eyes. As if that weren't enough, he used his thumbs to part her labia, leaving her fully exposed, and she sent a cry toward the ceiling and the stars beyond it.

Just as before, she feared she would fly apart the second his lips met her pussy. He didn't allow that to happen. His caresses were too soft, too light to bring her any relief, as he whispered into her recesses how good she tasted, how much he loved seeing her like this. How he couldn't wait to get inside her. To make her his.

When his tongue found her entrance and dove inside, her knees quaked. He had to know she wasn't going to last much longer standing, and it was downright cruel to make her do so.

She wanted to be horizontal, beneath him, consumed by him. He didn't care. He was relentless in arousing her to the breaking point, licking, swirling, pushing his tongue into her.

"I'm going to fall," she whimpered.

"I've got you. You're not going anywhere." She felt the words as heated puffs of air against her wet flesh.

"Brian—"

His lips locked on her clitoris and he sucked mercilessly, wringing a gasp from her that stopped the words dead in her throat. It was an effective silencing strategy. She could no longer speak until he sucked the orgasm out of her, moaning against her and plunging two fingers inside her as she cried out and clamped down on him and writhed back against the wall. Her fingers' desperate hold on the bar was the only thing that kept her standing.

After he'd wrung the last cry from her, he stood and put his hands on her hips, sliding them around to cup her ass and press her against him. It felt so good. She gazed up at him, her eyes heavy lidded. "I love it when you look at me like that," he murmured, his fingers kneading into the plump flesh of her cheeks.

"How am I looking at you?" she managed.

"Like you want to eat me alive, but you don't have a spoon."

She giggled, running her hands over his chest. "That's pretty dead on, I think."

"Yeah? Well, no more holding back," he murmured, leaning forward to plant kisses under the line of her jaw. "I'm yours."

"I'm yours too."

"For real? This delectable ass here is all mine?"

"Mmm. What are you going to do with it?"

"I want to sink my fucking teeth into it, for one thing." She gasped and pushed at him playfully, but of course he didn't budge. It only egged him on. "And spank it red, for another."

"Brian!"

"And other things we don't have to get into yet."

Despite the heat in the shower, she shivered, wondering what he would demand of her as their sexual relationship progressed. It didn't surprise her much to examine her feelings on the matter and realize she would be up for pretty much anything he asked. "As long as you'll be patient with me on some of that stuff."

"I would never ask you to do something you didn't want, sweetie. But you have to speak up and tell me."

"I want you any way I can have you."

"We'll take our time." With both hands, he cupped her neck. And just looked at her, making her feel more cherished than she could ever remember. "Damn, Candace. I can't believe we're here like this."

"I always wanted to be."

After that, she took great pleasure in soaping him down, running her hands all over his hard body and inspecting the details of the designs on his skin. Yes, she definitely needed to thank Kara and Marco for their exquisite work. Some of it seemed to be flowing patterns, but if she followed them carefully she could distinguish other images. Like the green dragon wrapping up one arm and the mermaid and gorgeous blue rose on the other.

If she had to pick a favorite, it was the mermaid. She was incredibly beautiful and serene, sitting on the rocks, with long blond hair flowing over her bare breasts.

"I love this one," she murmured, trailing her fingers over it.

He looked sheepish. "You might not love the meaning behind it."

"Why?"

"Well, mermaids lure sailors to their deaths. She's so alluring, and he gets so desperate to catch her, he dives into the sea and drowns."

"So you got it to remind you to watch out for those pesky mermaids?"

"That, I suppose, and women in general."

She planted her hands on her hips and attempted to glare

at him, but she couldn't help but smile. "Women in general, huh?"

"I never wanted to let myself get derailed, or take my eyes off my goal by chasing after some distraction, or I might never come up for air." He wasn't smiling back. "That's how I've felt lately, Candace. Like I've been drowning. A couple of nights with you and I was going under."

She'd felt the exact same way. "Oh, Brian. I'm not trying to distract you—"

"I know, baby." He tilted his arm in a bit so he could look at the artwork. "She looks like you, too. I never really noticed until after we'd spent the night together. So I thought I was going to be tortured for the rest of my life, having this constant reminder of you on me."

She shook her head fiercely. "I'm here now and I'm not going anywhere unless you want me to."

"Then we're in for a long ride, because I can't imagine ever wanting you to leave me."

A warm, settling peace swelled through her at his words. His eyes were so intense she couldn't look away. Her fingers trailed up to the rose on his biceps. Those eyes were the same vibrant blue as its petals. "What does the blue rose symbolize?"

The corner of his mouth quirked up. "Impossibility. Wanting something you can never have."

"What is it you want?" she whispered.

"The very thing I've found right here."

Stunned, she could only lean forward and rest her forehead against his collarbone, wrapping her arms as tight around him as she could. He went on. "If anyone else asked me that, I'd make up something. I'd never let anyone think I needed...this. But I'd be lying."

"Wait a minute." She lifted her head. "Doesn't that mean those are conflicting symbols, then? Wanting love and warning yourself away from it at the same time?"

"Yeah, well, I'm a conflicted kind of guy."

"Brian?"

"Hmm?"

"Can we go to bed now?"

He chuckled, pulling the hair away from the side of her neck and leaning down to trail kisses up the column to her ear. "Whenever you're ready."

Chapter Sixteen

Brian would say he felt like a teenager again, but hell, he hadn't been this excited about his own first time.

And he didn't deserve her. She could do so much better than him. But he was just the kind of selfish bastard to take advantage of a situation like that, though she had managed to drastically alter the selfish part, and maybe even the bastard part.

Now she was sprawled on the bed for him, her hips rolling in a sexy undulation as his fingers stroked her deep. "Brian, I'm going to…" The words became lost in a long, lilting moan.

"That's it, sweetie." God, he loved to watch her; it was so fucking hot when she came. She threw everything over, gave it all to him. No breathy shudders and sighs with her, it was as if the sensations he evoked in her ripped away all control and left her convulsing.

Her slick passage clamped tightly on his fingers as she tensed and arched and cried out his name, both her hands skimming from her breasts down her stomach to frame her pussy as he worked it through her climax. Those tight muscles were sucking his fingers so deep with every contraction he had to fight his own instincts as he drew them back out. Now that her hands had moved, one pink nipple was inches from his face, quivering with her panting breath. He attacked it with his lips and drew it deep, laving it as her head tossed on the pillow.

It was the second orgasm she'd had since lying down with him, both of them damn near effortless on his part. She wasn't going to get any more open for him. She was ready. Goddamn, but she was so fucking ready.

As the tension fled her and she went boneless under him, he moved away from her, making quick work of rolling on the condom he'd brought to bed. She lay still with her eyes closed, but she was trembling so hard he could see it. He couldn't wait to pull her close and absorb her vibrations.

Settling himself between the open cradle of her thighs, he guided himself to her entrance, nudging into the impossibly tight ring of muscle. Her eyes flew open and she stared up at him, her bottom lip quivering. That lip was too pink, too swollen, too tantalizing. He leaned down and lined it with the very tip of his tongue, drawing it between his lips to nibble it. Against the engorged tip of his cock, he felt her flare open the tiniest bit, the remaining aftershocks of her orgasm reaching for him. It almost sent him over the edge.

"Can I have it, baby?" he whispered.

She gave the briefest of nods, which caused her mouth to slide over his. "Yours."

"Mine." He gathered strength in his hips, slid forward against her resistance. It gave, and her fingernails dug into his shoulders as her eyes fell closed again. "No, open them, Candace, let me see you."

She did, and like some kind of psychic vampire he fed on those emotions flashing through her gaze. Pain, fear, love, determination, astonishment, surrender...oh, God, the sweetness, the rapture...

"Fuuuck," he groaned, pulling back. The first hot, swollen inch of her had fisted him so tight he lost his breath. He'd been worried about her, but what a hell of a debacle this would be if *he* couldn't go on.

"Don't stop," she begged, moving her hips, seeking to rejoin him. "You aren't hurting me." If only she knew how much she was hurting *him*. That soft, wet oblivion opened to him again and he sank forward, a groan tearing from his lungs, and she took his entire crown, engulfing his barbell so that he felt the tug all the way through his shaft and up his spine. She gasped as it slipped inside, caressing her upper and lower walls. Caught in her tight squeeze, he struggled to maintain control, to not go too deep too soon.

Her thighs went tight on his hips, the strong muscles hindering his advancement. “Spread your legs wider, let me go,” he said, staring into her beautiful eyes. She did, only to clamp them hard again when he pushed. “Is it starting to hurt, baby?”

“I…”

“Talk to me, so I can make it better.” And get his mind off his own desire to plunge wildly into her.

“Overwhelming,” she breathed. He withdrew, holding his cock and gently teasing her clit with his lower bead until her face muscles went lax with pleasure.

“Ohh,” she moaned, her legs falling open again.

“Better?”

She nodded. “But I want you back inside me.”

Fuck, he loved this woman. His cock glided down through her slick petals and slid almost effortlessly into her pussy again. So, so wet. She was just finding it difficult to stretch around the broadest part of him. “I want that too, baby, so much.”

He kissed her, slow and soothing, picking up a quick, barely-there rhythm with his hips. Too much of this and he was going to blow his top way too soon, but it was the only thing he knew to do to help her. “Relax for me, take me deep. You said you want me there.”

“Oh, yes…”

Sweat broke out across his shoulders as he increased his force by tiny increments. “Think about getting the tattoo, how it stung, how you didn’t know if you could do it at first, and how beautiful it was afterward.”

“That turned me on so much. I was afraid you could tell.” Her voice was strained, but he loved that she was trying so hard.

“I could.” He gave a little shove deeper, wrenching a gasp from her and an answering groan from him. “All I could think about was ripping off my gloves and stripping you down right there."

"I wanted you to."

"I'm here now, baby. Right here. I want you just as much as I did then."

"Brian, please, I need you. Just...just do it."

"You don't need me to be rough this time." His rocking motions were carrying him deeper even as the orgasm built up in his shaft, drawing his balls up tight. His heart was like a jackhammer in his chest. He needed to pull out and catch his breath before he embarrassed himself, but he was deep enough that the long drag out of her body might be his trigger. So he stopped, braced up on his arms, panting and trying not to look at her. Another trigger might be the sight of her loveliness pinned beneath him, all spread out and open to him.

Who was he kidding? *She* was his trigger. He was loaded and ready to fire at the first hint of pressure where she was concerned.

She whimpered and shifted impatiently under him, and he quickly pressed a hand flat to her stomach. "Don't move."

She was so damn obedient, she actually listened. He let his thumb wander down to her clit, stroking the stiff bud and feeling her internal muscles clench around him reflexively. "Shit, Candace."

"I can't help it, you do this to me. I need you. I lo—" She broke off, and he did look at her then, silently begging her to complete that thought. *Please, please...* But she only licked her lips and skimmed her hands over his biceps.

Maybe she'd only been about to say she loved how he made her feel, or she loved being with him, or she loved puppy dogs. Fuck. There was no way a girl like her should be falling for a guy like him. But that didn't stop him from wanting her to. God, how he wanted her to.

He moved his hand and lowered himself over her, wrapping his arms around her and pulling her close to his body. "Grab me and hold on tight."

Her soft arms snaked around him and her legs locked around his waist. He blew out his breath and pushed. Her gorgeous mouth opened as her body did, yielding, allowing him deeper. Her head tilted back on the pillow, exposing the graceful column of her throat, and he couldn't resist sinking his teeth into the side. She shuddered, and he was dimly aware that her fingernails dug into his back harder with every luscious inch of her that he gained. He stopped his motions, pulled out in one delectable slide, pushed all the way in to the hilt.

"Oh, God," he groaned, more of a prayer than a curse. She was paradise. Fucking nirvana. What breath he had was wrenched from his lungs. That hot sheath wrapped so tight around him, muscles stretched and quivering around his girth as she held him in her depths...

Candace ran her tongue over her lips, her blue eyes staring ravenously up at him despite the tears streaking her cheeks. Shit. She was about to eat him alive and request seconds. He knew it.

"You did it," he murmured, managing a weak smile for her. He brushed at a droplet shining at the outside corner of her eye. "Are you okay?"

"Yes. I'm more than okay."

"Now tell me what you want me to do."

"Move," she said, sounding desperate. She made a little rocking motion with her hips.

"What happened to getting dirty?"

"Fuck me," she all but snarled at him.

"That's my girl." Slowly, he withdrew, watching her face intently. She sighed, her eyes rolling back as her lids fell closed. When he was just about to slip out of her tight channel, instincts broke through and he shoved back in, fierce and deep.

She moaned, her knees lifting at his sides. "Please, please, please..."

"Like that?" he whispered, doing it again. Filling her up quick and hard, dragging out slow. A rosy glow was spreading up her cheeks, and she arched her breasts against him so that the hard peaks of her nipples grazed his chest as he moved. "Or how about this?" Rolling his hips rhythmically, he set a slow, fluid pace.

"Mmm, that's...ohhh, Brian."

Gauging her breathy moans, he found her sweet spot. Whenever his bead brushed it, she gasped and shuddered and clutched at him, so sensitive. Giving her time to get used to the sensation, he gradually decreased his movements until he was working that spot back and forth, until her sighing, staccato groans were musical with her pleasure.

"You're the sweetest fucking thing I've ever seen," he rasped, hearing how savage he sounded. He'd always been prone to letting crazy shit tumble out of his mouth during sex, things he sometimes didn't even remember later, and he almost dreaded what she might tear loose from his soul without his permission.

Her tongue swept over her plump lips, leaving them glistening. Her arms tightened around him. She whimpered his name. More tears squeezed out from between her closed eyelids.

"I can't wait to watch you come this time. Oh, my God. You're going to take me with you when you do. I wish we didn't have anything between us, I wish I could fill you up."

Her brow furrowed hard, lines appearing between her delicate eyebrows. The muscles in her thighs went rock hard. He knew it was coming, could feel it in the way her slick heat contracted around him. Her groans formed into words: his name, curses, deities. He abandoned his rhythm, gave her one long, hard stroke and sent her flying.

It was no effort to let go and join her. His release had been poised in his shaft from the moment he'd breached her. In sweet relief and a rush that made the room spin, he drove her through her climax and flooded the condom tip, sorry that he couldn't let it loose inside her, couldn't leave her with a part of himself this time. That urge had never been so desperate before.

Shaking all over, he collapsed over her, careful not to crush her with his weight. She felt so fragile beneath him. Burying his face in her damp, sweet-smelling hair, he breathed her in and simply basked in the afterglow. Her grip on him was still as fierce as it had been during the throes of her orgasm, and she muffled her little sobbing sounds by pressing her mouth tight to his neck.

"All right, baby doll?" he whispered, lifting a bit so he could find her lips with his own. He didn't want her to suppress those sounds. He wanted to drink them up. She sighed as he kissed her, her warm, minty breath playing across his mouth, and she settled to stillness in his arms as if his kiss alone had soothed her.

He didn't know what to do with this much love being thrown at him. He wasn't used to it. Sex to him had always been about two people getting off on each other. This was a whole new world.

Yeah, he was a sap, and he didn't give a fuck anymore.

Only reluctantly did he withdraw from her, turning away to dispose of the condom. Her blood streaked it, and he froze. He, who was supposed to be an expert at talking people through painful procedures endured for the greater good, was momentarily rattled.

What if he'd hurt her more than she let on? It wasn't any surprise to see the bloody remnants of her innocence on him, but he still felt like a slimy bastard. He'd gotten rough in the end. She might bring out the animal in him, but he could've at least tried to keep the fucking beast caged until she was more accustomed to this. She deserved to hear everything he had to tell her.

He left the bed and came back with a damp washcloth, his thoughts in turmoil. Candace lay with her eyes closed as he snapped off the lamp and crawled back under the covers with her, loving her intake of breath when he gently slid the washcloth between her legs. "Better?"

She turned her face into his shoulder, the shyness in the gesture inciting a whirlwind of fierce protection in him. "Mm-hmm."

"I love you," he murmured. There was no stopping it. He might as well have commanded the wind not to blow, such had been the need to not hold back anything from her at that moment. "I think I always have."

As far back as he could remember, he'd never uttered those words to a woman. He couldn't even recall the last time he'd said them to his mother. And here they'd fallen out of his mouth and he didn't even have the throes of ecstasy as an excuse.

Well, maybe he did. He was still in them.

"I love you too," she said, simple as that.

There was no doubt in his mind about her sincerity, even if she hadn't been able to say it earlier. Her heart, her vulnerability, her fear...all of it had been right there in her eyes. She could break him down with a single look.

He stroked her hair back from her forehead with his free hand, propped up on his elbow. "I am so sorry I hurt you. All the way back to when we first met, I am sorry for *anything* I ever said or did that might have caused you even a moment's displeasure."

"Brian, you haven't done anyth—"

"No, I have. Even being with Michelle when I should have been with you all along."

"Don't apologize for that. She liked you a lot. You liked her too."

"She didn't brighten the whole room for me when she walked in the door. She didn't make my whole day better just by smiling at me, or make me ask myself what she would think of me when I said or did something shitty to somebody. She wasn't the one who made me want to get off my ass and do more, be a better person. Only you've ever done that, sunshine."

Even in the darkness, he knew she smiled. "I missed hearing you call me that. I had no idea you felt that way about me."

"I am out-of-my-head crazy about you."

They fell silent as she nipped little kisses across his chest. He contemplated dozing until her voice drifted through the pleasurable haze in his mind.

"Brian... I have to tell you something."

Oh. Shit. The way her voice had darkened from its sweet coo didn't bode well. If she was about to trot out some line about how she had feelings for him, but this had just been about sex or getting back at the parental units or whatever-the-fuck else, he might as well take a sledgehammer to his own skull right now and get it over with. "What?"

"Deanne's wedding was today."

Of all the things he'd expected her to say, that wasn't it. "Weren't you supposed to be in that or something?"

"I was supposed to, yes. I left last night after the rehearsal dinner, and didn't tell anyone where I was going. And then I saw you this morning, and...here I am."

Christ, she should have said something. He never would have—

Exactly. If she'd told him she couldn't go with him, they would still be right where they were before. He wouldn't have wanted that for all the world. "No one has any idea where you are?"

She shook her head, looking miserable.

"No wonder Michelle called me twice today."

Candace stiffened in his arms. "She did?"

"Yeah, at the concert. I let it go to voicemail both times, and I never bothered checking the messages."

"Don't check them, please. I don't want to know what's going on. I don't want to ruin this." She sighed. "I hope you aren't mad at me."

"Why would I be mad?"

"Because I was afraid you might have been thinking that everything was fine and people knew I'd come here with you and were okay with it. But as usual, it's not fine at all. I'm going to try to keep you out of it as best I can, but when I get back I'm going to be facing—"

"Don't you dare keep me out of it. I want to be right there at your side when you go home. I want them all to know where you've been."

"And I was afraid you might think I was a wimp for running away from my problems instead of facing them. Brian, I couldn't. Deanne paired me with that guy I told you about, the one who cornered me at the party. Mom even invited him to our lake house this weekend. I ended up in a huge argument with everyone. So, wimpy or not, I ran. I couldn't take any more."

"I get it, sweetheart." His vision was washed with a red haze at the thought of that douche bag trying to get his hands up her skirt all weekend long. *Hell*, no. That shit was over with, as of this moment. She was his, and no one hurt what was his. "I don't want you to worry about it. I'll be there, and I'm not going anywhere. We'll stay gone however long you want, in fact."

"I have to get back tomorrow. I have finals starting Monday."

"Shouldn't you be studying?"

"I'll be okay. And I know there are other options out there for me, so I don't give a damn what they think or do anymore. But I'm so used to them taking care of everything. I'm scared."

"It's scary for anyone. You just buckle down and get through it. But in your case, I'd wager it's mostly their fault for sheltering you so damn much." He gently stroked her face with his thumb. "All locked up high in your tower. I want to rescue you."

"Like a knight in a fairy tale?" Her voice was quivering, and he wondered why. Here he was trying to be all white-knight dashing for her...

"Yeah, sweetie. Just like that." He kept soothing her, rubbing her back, tracing the line of her nose with the barest brush of his lips until he felt her relax.

"That's what I've always dreamed of. What I've always wanted."

"Well, that's good. You've got it now."

"But what I've realized lately is that as much as I've fantasized about the fairytale, and wanted it to be you, what's become most important to me is getting to a point where I'm able to save myself."

He probably had no business being proud of anyone. It sounded condescending, and he was certainly in no position for that. The emotion that swelled in his chest for her was more like reverence. If she would keep him around so he could watch her spread her wings and fly, it would be enough. But he wanted to be right by her side. "I'm there in whatever capacity you need me. Savior or cheerleader, whatever. I'm flexible."

"God, I love you," she whispered, tilting her head so that she captured his mouth with hers.

Let tomorrow take care of itself, he thought. She might have left a clusterfuck waiting back home, but tonight, they only had each other. And her lips were so sweet against his, he could have eaten her alive.

In fact, that sounded like a damn good idea.

Chapter Seventeen

His friends were going to take one look at her and *know,* but Candace didn't mind. In fact, it gave her a wicked little thrill.

Every time she moved, she felt him. He'd left a raw, aching fullness between her legs that kept her on the verge of arousal even when he wasn't anywhere near her. Whenever she sat, she found it hard to resist grinding her hips in tiny circles to drive the sensation deeper, to send aftershocks through her body.

The faint pink mark of possession he'd left on her neck when they'd been waiting in line after the concert was plainly visible when she was wearing this tank top. She loved that it was there...even if her mom would have called her a trashy whore. The thought made her chuckle, though it was grim.

There was the music to face today.

She didn't want to go. She could've lived forever in that hotel room with him, if it meant never having to face the world again. With his arms around her, she had the only thing she needed.

They stopped for breakfast and lingered over coffee, putting off the inevitable as long as possible. Her stomach felt jittery as she watched him, finding pleasure in even the most mundane things like his lips closing around his fork and the way he held his coffee mug. She would probably never get over her fascination with his mouth and his hands. Both were such efficient instruments at driving her wild.

Back at Kara's, the crew was apparently still asleep. Brian

said they'd probably only just gone to bed. Kara answered his insistent knocking with a big yawn, wearing a huge T-shirt and her hair an unruly mess. "Hey, guys. You look way too bright-eyed. Coffee?"

"Just had some, but I can always use more," he said. They stepped in, and Candace had to laugh at the carnage of bodies and blankets and air mattresses strewn throughout the spacious living room.

"Yeah, we had a few more people come over last night," Kara said, following her gaze as they walked toward the kitchen. She wasn't bothering to keep her voice down. Given the snores, those guys could have slept through an earthquake. "Probably a good thing you two went elsewhere if you wanted privacy. Our neighbors are going to lynch us someday."

"Sorry to get you up, but we need to round up my guys and get back home." His hand stroked up and down Candace's back. "She has finals starting tomorrow and I want to make sure she studies."

"I told you I'd be fine," she protested, giving him a pinch on the butt.

Kara was watching them with a knowing smile as she pulled mugs down out of the cabinet. "Awww. You guys."

"By the way," Candace said to her, "thank you. A million times." The memory of the way it had felt when he stroked her depths with those beads still drove shudders through her.

Brian looked at her suspiciously as Kara laughed. "You're welcome a million times. And I was joking yesterday. All I require as thanks is that you come with him whenever he visits us. We'd like to get to know you better."

"Deal," she said.

"I won't let you corrupt her," Brian said with mock warning. "That's my job."

It took forever to get the others roused, and then a heated argument ensued over who was going with Brian and who was staying to get some more sleep and riding back later with Connor and Tay. Since space was limited in Connor's car, at least a couple of them were going to have to go with Brian.

"I'm never riding with anyone else again. I'll find my own damn way," Ghost complained. "Dragging my ass out of bed two days in a row..." He grumbled on into incoherence.

"Good," Brian said, cutting him off. "All I know to tell you guys is to draw straws. And anyone scheduled to work tonight better have their asses there on time."

A chorus of groans went up. "Shit, that's me," Starla said. "I'd better ride with you, then. Oh, Brian, I almost forgot." She tugged her shirt up a bit, separating it from the waistband of her shorts to reveal a funny little happy face drawn on her midriff. "I got Jonathan Davis's autograph! He was doing a DJ set at the club we went to after the concert. Can you ink it on when we get back?"

Brian grinned. "Cool. Sure thing."

"Why can't I?" Ghost asked.

Starla dropped her shirt and rolled her eyes. "Because I'd rather not be molested throughout the process."

The closer they got to home, the tenser Candace grew. It was back to reality. Yesterday it'd been easy to pretend today wouldn't come. Now it was in her face.

Brian kept a firm grip on her hand as he drove. At least she had him beside her now, and she wasn't defending this all for nothing. He was hers, and she was his, and nothing her family could say or do would change that at this point. But it was going to get ugly. Really ugly.

"What do you want to do?" he asked after everyone was dropped off and they were alone in his truck. "Do you want to come home with me?"

She blinked at him. "Really?"

"Sure. You can stay with me as long as you want."

That would be a dream come true. And it might actually have to happen before it was all said and done, but for now, she couldn't ask that of him. It would only be more running. She had to try to get through this on her own.

"I would love that. Honestly. But...I need to face them right now."

He gave her fingers a squeeze. "Then I'll stay with you until you confront them. That's an order. I'm not leaving you to go through it alone. I'd scheduled myself to work later, but you can hang out at the parlor with me."

His tone brooked no argument, so she sighed and nodded. "Okay."

Her apartment was silent as they entered it, as she expected, but it felt strange. Like the silence after the apocalypse. She didn't know what she'd expected to find, but for some reason it was disturbing to walk into the normalcy of it now that the world had changed. It should've been trashed, or the electricity cut off, or the locks changed or something.

Brian shut the door behind them as she stood staring at everything, everything that wasn't hers. Her gaze alighted on her cell phone sitting on the counter, but she was afraid to pick it up to see how many missed calls and outraged voicemails and text messages she had.

"Oh, God," she whispered, feeling unsteady.

He was right there, guiding her toward the couch. "Sit down. It's all right." She dropped onto the cushion and he sat beside her, facing her. "Don't let yourself get all worked up. You don't even have to do anything today. Take some time before you agree to see them, let everyone cool off."

"Cooled off isn't really a state my parents ever get to." She sighed. "It's okay, Brian, I'm fine. I did what I did, I have to take the heat. I mostly hate that you're going to be around to see this, but at the same time I'm glad you're here."

"Don't you even worry about it." He grinned. "You probably don't know this, but in a verbal sparring match, my mom would make Sylvia Andrews look like a Chihuahua yapping at a mastiff. And you don't grow up with someone like her without learning to hold your own."

She relaxed against him, snuggling into his chest when his arms went around her. "Tell me about your mom. I've never met her."

"What to say about Mom. Well, she's highly opinionated, she can kick my ass one minute and be fiercely protective of me the next, and she's famous for reverting to Italian when pissed off. But she hates my tattoos."

"Are you close to her?"

He was silent for a moment. "I don't see her nearly often enough. It's complicated. But...yeah, my mom is pretty cool."

"Do you think she'll like me?"

"I think she'll be crazy about you. How could she not?"

"Well, my own parents hate me, so it stands to reason someone else's could, too, I guess."

"They don't hate you, baby. They can't possibly. Anyone should be proud to have you as a daughter. That isn't to say I know what the fuck their problem is, but it can't be that they hate you, not in a million years."

She could have argued with him, but she was too exhausted. He would see what she was talking about shortly, the open disdain and disappointment in her mother's eyes whenever she looked at her. Candace had begun to detect it shortly after high school, but now there was no questioning it.

She was tired of doing that, anyway. Tired of trying to figure out what it was about her that disgusted her mother so. She didn't want to think about anything else. And having Brian alone in her apartment was too much temptation.

It amazed him when she lifted her face from his chest and crawled over in his lap, straddling him and lowering her mouth to his. But as usual, it was insta-erection where she was concerned. He groaned into the sweet cavern of her mouth, sweeping his tongue inside to taste more of her.

"You know that night you came over?" she asked between warm, melty kisses.

"Nah, I have no idea what you're talking about."

She giggled and circled the tip of his nose with her own. "I was standing in the kitchen, looking in here at you...and I had this very fantasy. Maybe a *little* different, but it was you sitting right here on my couch, me sitting on top of you. Only I was naked."

Holy shit. He was already throbbing against her center, which he could imagine was hot and wet beneath her shorts and panties. His hands swept under her shirt and lifted. "I think we can fulfill that one."

Quickly, she jumped up and shed her shorts, returning to him in her bra and panties. A few more tugs and she was braless as well, sitting astride him with those mouthwatering, pearly pink nipples at almost the perfect level with his mouth. He tasted each one of them in turn, giving them flicks with his tongue, finally capturing them in his hands. The sounds she made as he kneaded gently were delectable, helpless and enough to drive a man wild. Her fingers came up over his, and her head rolled back on her shoulders.

"Take your hair down," he whispered, watching as one slender arm lifted and she pulled the scrunchie out of her hair, so that it fell in one luxurious shudder of gold waves about her slender throat. Some of the tendrils reached his hands. He wanted to ball it up in his fist. Wanted to push her down and shove himself deep into her mouth. There were a thousand things he wanted to do to her. But above all else he wanted to be inside the tight heat of her pussy again. That had been the most incredible thing he'd ever felt in his life.

She was already working on it, attacking his fly until she had him sprung loose and into her gentle hands. He sank into the cushion and let his head roll on the back of the couch while she stroked him. "Oh, God."

"I want it," she murmured, the simplicity of the statement sending another surge of arousal up his shaft as she lifted herself high on her knees and held his cock in position to impale herself.

"Sure you're up to this?" he whispered, knowing the answer but needing to be sure.

"Oh, yes," she breathed.

"Good girl."

He reached out and tugged the crotch of her panties to the

side, biting back a moan at how damp the fabric was. Given that, he had to touch her there, had to get some of it on his fingers, had to feel how hot she was. Otherwise the shock of her hitting his cock might cause him to erupt on the spot.

She paused to let him play, her thighs trembling. She felt so good, so swollen, so wanton. He loved that she needed him so much. When he couldn't touch her another moment without losing his mind, he jerked her into position and kept her panties wrenched to the side as she eased herself down over him. Her little white teeth sank into that lovely, trembling lower lip as she did so, and he wanted to growl from the very sight of it.

This time, her body drew him right into her tight, wet heat, deeper, drinking him in. There weren't words for it. Rivers of sensation shot up his shaft, pulling every muscle in his body to the breaking point. Candace moaned, wrapping her arms around him as he locked tight into her body.

He smeared his lips down her throat. "I love that. All wrapped up in you." Grasping her ass cheeks in his palms—he wanted to weep, having an ass like hers in his hands—he slowly lifted her until he teased only the shallow depths of her pussy. Candace wiggled and bit his neck, rolling her hips in circles until he couldn't stand it anymore and lowered her on him again. She threw her head back and gasped, that molten gold hair flipping back behind her shoulders. Just as he was marveling at how wet she was on his dick, her moisture flowing down around him, coating him...

"I didn't give you time to put anything on," she whispered.

Shit! He couldn't believe he'd forgotten. It hadn't even crossed his mind, and he was a stickler for protection. When it came to unwanted microbes, he was no less careless with his body than he was with his parlor, and you could eat off the floor in that place.

Even more unsettling was his lack of panic over the situation. In fact, he only wanted more of her, harder, faster, until he exploded inside her with no barriers between them.

That would be crazy at this point. He gritted his teeth in

agony and forced himself to ease her up so he could dig in his back pocket for his wallet. Her mewl of frustration was almost enough to derail him from the clumsy endeavor of opening the little packet he extracted. "Trust me, baby, you feel so fucking good, it's not like I want to stop." The words tumbled out in a rush.

She leaned over to whisper in his ear, punctuating each word with a seductive nibble. "Hurry up, or I'll start without you." Then she treated him to the sight of her fingers trailing lightly down her belly, toward her pussy.

Dammit! Didn't she know what that did to him? He growled, unable to get the damn latex on and unfurled fast enough, remembering how hot and wet and tight she'd been around him. Just as her fingertips disappeared between her legs, eliciting a moan from her lips, he seized her waist and yanked her up over him again. Settled her damp heat over the turgid head of his cock. Nearly died as she allowed herself to sink, swallowing him inch by inch.

"Do you love me?" she panted, taking him deeper, deeper.

Ordinarily, this would not have been the ideal time for a girl to ask him that question. In the heat of the moment, he would have gladly walked on his elbows for the rest of his life for this feeling. But he could honestly say now, with her, the answer he gave was the absolute truth. "Beyond all reason."

"You'll be with me no matter what?"

"You'd have to beat me away."

"I don't want to think anymore. I just want to know you're mine and nothing else matters."

"This is all that matters." Digging his fingers into her ass, he showed her the rhythm and then turned her loose, watching as she moved on him. Her breasts swayed in front of his eyes and he reached up to cup them, rolling them in his palms so that her nipples stabbed into his hands.

She searched for the angle she wanted and found it, leaning back with her hands on his knees. When that wasn't enough to anchor her, he grasped her forearms and she locked her hands around his in return, using his strength to keep herself from falling as she went after her own pleasure with a fervor that left him devastated. It was everything he'd felt last night to the *n*th power, her hot passage gripping him with such sweet need, he couldn't breathe for it. Couldn't think, except about her.

His release welled in his shaft, swelling him even larger inside her. This was going to be over way too fast, but they had all night. And tomorrow night. And forever, if she'd have him. The disconnect between his mind and his body wouldn't allow for him to have any control whatsoever.

Thankfully, as with all the other areas in his life, she was right there with him. She clenched up around him and cried out as the surge overtook him and it was final: he wasn't going anywhere. She was his, and he was in this for the long haul. Marriage, kids, little league, ballet recitals, soccer practice, grandkids, the whole bit. He jerked her close to him and cursed as she contracted around him, milking him for more and getting it. He knew he was a goner. And it was okay. It was all good.

It was more than good. It was the best damn feeling he'd ever known, as if all the wrinkles in his life were being smoothed out at once.

"Ohhhh, God," she sighed as she came down from her own heights, melting like butter over him. Her thighs released their vise grip on his hips, and the biting crescents of her fingernails unclenched from his shoulders. He nuzzled under her chin and absorbed her post-apocalyptic shudders, smiling at the sound of her teeth chattering near his ear.

Gently, he lifted her so he could pull out, watching her expression slacken as the bead of his barbell slid over her sensitive, inflamed tissues. She settled back down and draped herself over him.

"Sorry about earlier," he said. "I never forget. Everyone would go apeshit if you got pregnant."

"I truly, honestly don't give a damn anymore."

"I think I'm rubbing off on you in a bad way."

"Unless there's a major monkey wrench in my cycle or something, we should be in the clear."

"Just so you know, I'm clean. I get myself checked every few months because of the job. I haven't been with anyone since the last time." He stroked her hair, urging her to lift her head so he could stare deep into her eyes. He wanted her to believe what he was about to tell her without a doubt. "I meant what I said, sweetie. I'm not going anywhere no matter what happens."

"Brian, I know," she whispered, frowning at him as if there shouldn't have been any question. "I've never doubted you. I'll see about getting on birth control as soon as I can so we won't have to worry about it so much."

He lifted her knuckles to his lips and brushed them gently. "You will?"

"I don't want anything between us."

"Me, either. Although you do realize, BC was a big, fat fail for my brother and his wife. As evidenced by baby Alex."

"Yikes. That's scary."

"I suppose we can always double up when I'm feeling particularly virile."

She burst out laughing. He loved that sound so much. It was clear as wind chimes, capable of turning even the stormiest of days into warm blue skies. "You mean there are actually days when you don't?"

"Not really. Scratch that. I'm always pretty fucking virile."

Chapter Eighteen

The knock on the door came early that evening.

It actually wasn't a knock. A half-dozen fists could've been pummeling the surface outside. Candace and Brian jerked awake on the couch, where they'd dozed off wrapped in each other's arms.

"Shit," she whispered. Thank goodness her curtains were shut tight, or someone might have seen them through the window. She jumped off him and threw on her clothes while he went into the bathroom. She was still standing there, chewing her knuckle, when he emerged a couple of minutes later.

"You okay?" he asked, eyeing her suspiciously.

She gave a nervous laugh. "No, but I'll manage."

"Do you need me?"

"Always, but stay here for now, okay?"

He nodded as she turned and headed for the door. She probably looked a fright: hair a mess, clothing disheveled from hours on the road...and she probably smelled of sex.

A hysterical laugh bubbled up, but she didn't let it go. She also didn't bother to peek out and see who she was about to confront. Taking a deep breath, she snatched the door open.

She must have had a hell of a look on her face, because her mother's carefully honed glare turned to surprise in an instant. Candace let her own gaze sweep down her mother's figure with all of the disdain she'd suffered over the last few years. "What?"

"After what you've done, you have the nerve to ask me

what?" Sylvia turned toward the parking lot behind her and motioned for someone. Great. More people to make her feel like scum of the earth.

"What do you mean what I've done? Maybe I got sick. Maybe I went for a drive and had car trouble."

"Nonsense. You could have called. We called *you*, we came by, we checked everywhere we knew to check. We even called the police."

"What bothered you more, Mom, that you were worried about me or that I skipped out on the wedding of the year?"

"Now that I know you're okay, what bothers me most is your irresponsibility. I have no idea what's gotten into you."

I do, she wanted to say. *He's around six-two, heavily tattooed and fucks like a god.*

"You're always saying I should make better decisions. Yesterday morning I was presented with an option, and I made the best decision for *me*. Not for you, or Deanne, or anyone else. I'm done being so selfless. I'm sticking with selfish for a while."

As her voice trailed away, she shifted uncomfortably when she saw who was coming up the walk toward them. Jameson and Michelle. Dammit. She had to fight not to step back and slam the door.

"Candace, is he here?" Michelle asked quietly.

She nodded, and Jameson surged toward the door. Fury flashing through her, Candace shoved viciously at his chest before he could get past her. "You calm down, James, and don't you dare come in my house starting anything with him."

Brian must have heard the commotion, because he came up behind her and yanked the door all the way open. "You got a fucking problem with me, James?"

Jameson, ever the type to go off half-cocked until things started to get serious, seemed to shrink a bit. "I've got a problem with you screwing my sister, yeah."

"I suggest you get the fuck over it."

Sylvia backed away from the stare-down, but Michelle and Candace insinuated themselves between James and Brian as best they could. Both the guys had their feathers ruffled, but she would lay bets on Brian any day of the week. He was the only one between the two who had absolutely no fear in his glare, though that worried her. A lot. “Brian, it’s not worth you getting in trouble,” Candace murmured, her hand planted on his chest.

James exploded. “What the hell is wrong with you, Candy? Siding with this piece of trash over me? I’m not worth *him* getting in trouble?”

“That’s not what I said! You need to get out of here. This doesn’t have one damn thing to do with you.”

“It has to do with all of us,” Sylvia interjected. She was staring at Brian as if he was something she’d found on the bottom of her shoe. “And I don’t have to go anywhere. I think you forget whose name is on this lease, Candace.”

“Yeah?” Brian asked, shifting that burning intensity to Sylvia, who took a step backward as if he was going to physically assault her. “There’s no one’s name on my lease except mine. You keep this up, and there’ll be another one. This shit stops right here. I don’t give a damn who you call.”

Michelle just looked at him. “I have one question,” she said quietly, and he turned to her, his expression softening. “Is Candace the one you were talking about the other night?”

Candace’s frown deepened. When had the two of them talked? About *her*?

He nodded. “She is.”

As if some decision had been reached in her mind, Michelle took Jameson’s arm and pulled him back. “James, come on. It’s all right.”

“The hell it is,” he thundered.

Michelle looked imploringly at her aunt. “Aunt Syl, you’ve seen that she’s fine, now you’ve got to let her live her life. If he’s who she wants, that’s her decision, not yours. If you don’t let her go, you’re going to lose her forever. He loves her, and he’ll take care of her.”

But Sylvia Andrews was ever the ice queen, and the fires of

hell probably wouldn't even melt a drop from her. "I *refuse*," she all but hissed at Brian, "to stand by while you move in on my daughter."

He slid his hand over Candace's shoulder. "I'm already in, and there's nothing you can do about that."

Candace put her arm around his waist. "Mom, I love you, and I realize I acted irresponsibly. I wish it hadn't come to that. But you can either accept us, or you can do your worst. I don't care. Cancel my lease, I'll move in with him. Cut off my tuition, I'll get a job until I can get some student loans and finish on my own. I have half a mind to do that, anyway, because I'm tired of depending on you if this is what my life is going to be like. You have no power here anymore. I know that drives you crazy, but all I can tell you is to get yourself in therapy or something, because like he said, it ends here. Right now."

Sylvia's expression steadily fell during her harangue. James's only became more outraged, and he stared at her much the same way her mother had looked at Brian. "My God, Candace, what have you lowered yourself to? You would turn your back on all of us so you can be his whore—"

The movement beside her was so sudden she blinked and almost missed it. One moment Brian's arm was around her shoulders, the next he'd lunged forward. One loud, painful crack later, Jameson dropped to the ground, blood gushing from his nose. Immediately, she knew any headway she might have made had just been destroyed.

Oblivious to Michelle and Candace grabbing at his arms, Brian bent over and with both hands jerked James up by his collar. "If you even dare to *think* the word whore again where she's concerned, I'll hang your nuts as knockers on her fucking front door, you got me?" Throwing him back down, Brian straightened and looked at Candace, barely leashed fury seething in his dark eyes. "If they won't leave, I have a simple solution. We'll get the hell out of here."

"Oh, you don't have to worry," Sylvia said, staring down at her son, who was rolling over so he could get to his feet. Candace could swear there was disappointment in her expression. "We're leaving, before you can assault someone else." That wintry gaze lifted to Candace's face. "You see what you're getting, don't you? How long do you think it'll be before it's you lying on the floor with a bloody nose?"

Even Michelle rolled her eyes at that comment. "Aunt Syl, that's freaking ridiculous, and you know it. If I were the physical sort, I'd kick James while he's down." She stepped over him and brushed past Candace and Brian as she entered the apartment. "You guys come talk to me."

Brian followed her, but Candace lingered at the door. "Mom, I..." Her voice trailed off, but Sylvia lifted a quelling hand anyway.

"I don't want to hear it. You do what you feel you have to do, Candace. I don't care anymore, either."

"That's not what I want. I don't want you to *not care*. I just want you to see how you've hurt me, especially about this. He means everything to me. Maybe we'll stay together forever, and you know what? Maybe we won't. Right now that's not the point. The point is, he's my choice. The risk is solely on my shoulders."

Jameson got unsteadily to his feet and walked away without a word, his hands cupped to catch the blood still pouring from his nose. He didn't stop or reply, even when Candace asked if he needed a towel. Sylvia turned without further comment and followed him. Just before Candace shut the door, she heard her mother warn him that he'd better not bleed all over her leather seats.

She found Michelle and Brian sitting at the kitchen table, Michelle staring at nothing in particular, Brian brooding. He kept flexing the hand he'd used to punch Jameson. Candace went straight to the freezer and got some ice for him to put on it, wrapping it in a thin dishtowel.

"Well, that actually went over a little worse than expected," she proclaimed, dropping into a chair with them. Brian let her take his hand and settle the ice on his knuckles. "I didn't count on actual bloodshed."

"Yeah. Sorry about decking your brother," he muttered.

"Hell of a way to make a good impression, huh?"

"It's all right." She sighed, stroking his forearm. Deep inside, it made her proud that her man was strong and fearless enough to defend her physically, if it came to that. And that he cared enough.

Proud, hell. If it wouldn't be entirely inappropriate, she'd be grinning like a fiend.

Poor Jameson. He'd run off at the mouth to the wrong person. Despite everything, she loved her big brother, but she'd always known his day was coming.

Michelle's lips quirked. "I take it my ride left."

"Sorry. I'll take you home. So how much does Deanne hate me?"

She seemed to debate it for a moment. "Deanne was...weird. At first I could see the steam rising, and I thought we were going to have a major meltdown they'd hear all the way up to the space shuttle, but then it was as if a calm came over her and she didn't really care anymore. She was so ready to walk down the aisle and get the whole thing over with. She stuck Becky back in the wedding."

Candace laughed. "Tattoo and all?"

"Yep. She didn't have much choice, unless she wanted a lone groomsmen during the recessional. She made her try to cover her tattoo with gobs of foundation, though."

Brian scoffed and Candace sent him a smile. "I'd have told her to fuck off," he said.

"Yes, I'm aware," Michelle said, rolling her eyes fondly.

"So...when did you two talk?"

Brian opened his mouth, but Michelle beat him to the punch. "I called him. It was after we all went to lunch, and we'd been talking about tattoos. I really just wanted to check in on him. I had no idea about you guys."

"But you said you talked about me?"

Brian shook his head. "She asked if I was seeing someone. I told her about you without really saying it was you."

"And what he told me is how I know he's serious." She

smiled at him, a little sadly. "You take care of her. You'll have me to answer to if you don't."

"Don't worry. She won't ever be picking herself up off the floor with a broken nose," he said bitterly. Candace felt terrible that her mother had insinuated that about him. It was just a taste of what she dealt with on a daily basis. Maybe now he understood.

"Hey, congratulations, that punch was a beauty," Michelle said. "And Aunt Syl's face was priceless."

"Why, thank you."

"I pretty much missed the whole thing," Candace said.

Michelle looked at her. "And *you*. I think I like this new side he's brought out in you. Before all of this, I'd never seen you stand up to them."

"For all the good it did me. I'm just worried about the repercussions."

Michelle gave her a worried frown. "Honestly, I am too."

Brian looked Candace in the eyes, his own serious and troubled. He put his uninjured hand over hers, where she was still holding the ice over his sore knuckles. "Baby, I need to get to work. You're still more than welcome to come with me. In fact, I wish you would. I don't want you being alone right now."

"It's not like they're going to come back and hurt me or something—"

"I still want you with me. Maybe take your mind off things for a while."

"Are you sure you'll be able to work with your hand this way?"

He pulled it from under the ice and wiggled his fingers. "It's not that bad." Sending her a wicked grin, he chuckled. "I guess I should've had enough presence of mind to give him a left hook, though."

Watching him that night, Candace was afraid he was hurting more than he let on. But if that was the case, he suffered through without a single complaint.

After a while she retreated to Brian's office, called Sam—Macy was inexplicably absent tonight—then spent the rest of the time poring over her notes for her psych final tomorrow. All of his employees were fun and gracious, but she hadn't wanted to hover out there with them. She didn't want to get in their way, or make them uncomfortable. How did they feel about the boss's girlfriend hanging around watching them work?

And she supposed she really was his girlfriend. The thought was almost too astounding to entertain.

"You okay?" he asked from the doorway. She shifted her gaze to him, resisting the urge to lick her lips at the sight of him leaning against the frame. So tall, so gorgeous, with his normally intense eyes gentle as he looked at her. No telling how long he'd been standing there, watching her. He looked comfortable.

"I'm fine. Are you?"

Brian nodded, stepping in and dropping into the chair beside the door. "It's pretty slow out there. Sundays usually are. I told them we could go ahead and shut down. I think they're still tired and hung over from last night."

"Aw. Nice boss," she teased.

He grinned. "I'd love to go home and boss you around a little bit."

"*Really.* Well, I regret to inform you that you aren't the boss of me, Mr. Ross."

Smoothing his hand down his goatee, he gave her a long appraisal that made her insanely curious as to what was going on behind those eyes. "What if I was?"

"Huh?"

He shrugged. "I was just thinking how good you look sitting in here, and you mentioned getting a job to your mother. I could use someone to handle the business side of things so I can be out front most of the time. It would be perfect, because you could work around your class schedule."

"That sounds ideal, but...have you really thought that through?"

"No, not really. It was just an idea. I know what you're going to say, though, and you're probably right."

"It would complicate things. Not that I have any doubts about you at all, but it's so early. If we didn't work out, God forbid, what would happen?"

"I would never do you wrong like that, Candace. Even if we didn't work out, you could stay until you found something else, if you felt you had to quit. I wouldn't screw you over with your job. And I trust you wouldn't screw me over, either."

"Depends on what you did, I guess," she joked.

He laughed. "Hey, now, why does it have to be me who messes up?"

"And I don't know that you could afford me."

Something melted in his gaze, in his expression, and her heart softened. Any more of that and the mushy organ wouldn't be of much use to her. "Now, that might be a legitimate concern," he said. "I don't know if I can afford you now, but I'm damn sure gonna break the bank trying."

She was hoping to not have one more reason to love him, because he was enticing her to leave everything she'd ever known and insinuate herself fully into his life. It was thrilling and terrifying, and if there could only be *one thing* to make her want to hang on to her former self, she thought maybe she could resist his all-consuming allure.

But, no. He took her home to his apartment, and she found she even loved where he lived. Her community was silent and dull, mostly parents and working professionals who wanted it quiet at all times. She rarely saw any of her neighbors—except for the ones who kept her entertained most nights with the sounds of their sexual escapades, of course; it seemed she was always running into them. Usually she was too embarrassed to look them in the eyes.

They hadn't been at Brian's apartment twenty minutes when some of his neighbors stopped by to invite them to a get-together in the courtyard by the pool. Brian declined, but she liked the whole atmosphere of the place: laid-back, easy-going fun. She'd lay bets no one here was going to snap your head off if you wanted to play your music a little loud one night. Even now, the muffled sounds of the party could be heard below.

Brian's place was neat and sparse, a typical bachelor pad, she imagined. Not that she had been in any of those. He had the essential furniture and lots of toys: HD flat, X-Box, Wii, awesome computer set-up, a massive stereo system.

Several pieces of abstract artwork covered his walls, along with some bizarre surrealist pieces that looked like they could've been done by H. R. Giger. It wasn't until she peeked in one of the two bedrooms and saw his makeshift art studio and the work on the easel that she realized most of the art on the walls—here and at his parlor—must be his. The same style, despite the nuances.

He looked so modest when she told him how much she loved it. And when she asked if he could paint something for her, he wordlessly took her hand and led her back in the room.

"Something I did a few days ago," he said, riffling through several canvases stacked against one wall. "I just...had to."

What he pulled out then made her lose her breath. It was *her.* Her face, laughing with her chin in her hands, sketched out with charcoal in a way she could only describe as...loving. Meticulous. She found herself glancing around the room to see if he had a picture of her somewhere that she wasn't aware of.

"It looks so much like me. It's...beautiful. I mean, it's a beautiful drawing, not that I'm beautiful—"

"Stop that. You are beautiful."

"You did this a few days ago?"

"Yeah."

While they hadn't been speaking. He'd drawn it and then hidden it from his sight. Trying to exorcise her from his mind? She brought trembling fingers to her lips. "And...you didn't have a picture of me for reference?"

"This is how you looked at me once when I was still with Michelle, when I said something undoubtedly stupid I can't even remember now. I just know the way you laughed at me stuck in my head and I couldn't get it out. Your face is so clear in my mind, Candace, I could sketch it in my sleep."

"Please don't hide this away anymore," she said, hearing how tiny her voice sounded and hating it. Her eyes were burning.

"I won't. I haven't been home since seeing you yesterday morning, and everything that's happened in between... I'll hang it over my bed, if you don't have any problems with that. Initially I was going to paint it, but I think I like it just like this."

"It's perfect. I don't care if it's in the bathroom. It needs to be on display."

He burst out laughing. "Come on, help me put it up. I hate trying to hang shit without someone there telling me if it's straight or not."

What started as a playful endeavor ended with them on his bed in the quiet dark afterward, the moonlight falling across them in slats as it shone through the blinds. He stole her breath away, loving her so slowly and gently she was a quivering mess of helpless adoration for him. For every move he made, every breath he took as he was deep inside her body, she fell further. He was almost troublingly silent; the only sounds in the room were her sighs and moans and the sounds of their joining, the shuddering of his breath.

"Brian," she whispered, turning her face toward the window as he trailed his warm lips down her throat. Outside she could see the pale orb of the moon through the blinds, could hear the party still going on down below. His hand swept under the back of her knee, pulling her leg high on his hip so that he could go deeper in one long, slow thrust that left her gasping.

"What is it, sunshine," he whispered back.

Tears leaked from her eyes, trickling down through her hair spread out on his pillow. "I'm so scared."

"Don't be. I'm here. It's all going to be okay. Don't run away from me. Don't shut me out."

"I'm scared because I'm losing myself and I *can't* shut you out."

"That's a good thing, sweetheart. That's good. Oh, God, Candace..."

Was it good that she was so stripped bare for him? He held more power to hurt her than anyone else in her life right now.

His movements were becoming more disorganized, lost to passion, his breathing more ragged. She half-heartedly tried to fight the sensations building around his possession of her, not wanting to give him any more, needing to hang on to something of herself, but it was no use. The more she fought, the more she lost, until she was drowning with him in fierce, dark waves of ecstasy.

He groaned and throbbed inside her, once, twice, buried so deep she could hardly breathe. Despite being sore and sensitive from the past couple of days, she couldn't resist him, couldn't deny him when he wanted her. Everything about this encounter had been tender and comforting, as if he realized she needed that from him right now. It had only gutted her all the more.

"You feel so good," he murmured, holding her close as she shivered through aftershocks. "Don't be afraid anymore. We're done with that."

Wrapping her arms tight around him, she buried her face in his shoulder, pressing against his warmth. "I feel safe with you, safe from everything *except* you. If I make one wrong move, I can lose this. Lose my shelter. This isn't how I wanted to save myself."

He lifted his head, but she couldn't see much of his expression. His hand was exquisitely gentle as it smoothed the hair back from her forehead. "I don't know why you think you have to do everything with no help from anyone," he said softly. "You have people who love you. Lean on us. All of us. You don't have to be alone. You're not."

"I've only ever leaned on someone, and look where it's gotten me."

"Don't let them destroy the trust you have. Don't let them taint what you feel for me. I couldn't stand that, for us to be so close to having it all, only to lose it because of them. You would only be letting them win."

Those might have been the magic words. Above all else, she couldn't let them win, not this time. They'd won almost every battle so far in her life, and even the ones they'd lost, they still tortured her over. She'd fought way too hard for him to *ever* give up.

For the second night in a row, she fell asleep in his arms, and she didn't think she could ever go back to being alone in bed. When her mother's harsh voice echoed in her dreams all night, he was there. When she heard his voice, saw his face in her mind, only to wake up to a split second's terror that their time together had been nothing but a dream, he was there.

When sunlight replaced the moonlight channeling into the room, and she figured she wasn't going to wring another moment's sleep from her feverish, overworked mind, she tunneled beneath the covers, intent on giving him a *really* good morning.

Chapter Nineteen

If only they could market an alarm clock like *this*.

Brian was already in the middle of a fairly PG-rated dream about her, but it turned X-rated in a heartbeat the moment her warm tongue slid over his cock. His eyes flew open and he reached under the covers to grasp her hair, thanking God above she was really with him.

She didn't show him any mercy, getting him up and going down with none of the timidity she'd had the first time. His piercing didn't even faze her. She took it all with a fervor that had his abdominal muscles contracting with the sudden rush of blood to his cock.

She groaned as he swelled in her mouth, the vibrations of it skittering up his shaft. His head pressed back into the pillow as he lifted his hips, instinctively trying to push deeper, but she raised her head to evade him. Her hand wrapped around his base and stroked, using the moisture she'd already left to ease her motions, and he was in heaven.

"Oh, God, Candace. Try to take it deeper, baby. Oh, s*hit.*"

She did, and he felt his tip graze the back of her throat. So hot, so wet, so fucking good. He tore at the covers desperately, needing to see her, needing to watch her swallow him down. Her gaze flickered up at him, fiery blue, and he nearly passed out from the eroticism of those sweet eyes looking at him with such ferocity. With a tenderness he didn't know he possessed at this point, he stroked her face one time before collapsing onto the bed and losing himself in the heat of her lips wrapped around him, the suction, the sweetness.

At some point he dimly heard his phone ring, but it wasn't as if he could be bothered to deal with anything else at the moment. She had him pinned and helpless as a bird in the clutches of a hungry cat.

The building pressure reached a fever pitch and welled up in his shaft. A torrent of curses fell from his lips. The tip of Candace's tongue was a stiff little instrument of torment, pressing hard into the underside of his cock as her mouth rode the length, and he lost his last grip on control almost before he had time to warn her.

She paid no heed, letting him erupt in her mouth as his every muscle pulled tight enough to rip away from the bone and he fisted both hands in her hair, careful not to shove her down. After the past two days, he should've been spent, but he kept finding more to give her, until she took the last and only reluctantly stilled her stroking hand.

The way she pulled back and licked her lips then killed him. If he hadn't been utterly annihilated, he'd have had her on her back in an instant.

She crawled from the bed as he lay panting. He'd somehow managed to turn half sideways on the mattress, and he spent the next few minutes drifting and gathering his strength back, staring up at the sketch he'd done of her. When she came back and cleaned him up with a towel, he surprised her by grasping her and throwing her down, her thighs spread around his hips.

"I love you, baby," he said, pinning her hands down. Her lips parted as his gaze traveled down to her naked breasts and caressed each one in turn. "I want to taste every inch of you."

Her words were little more than a whimper, and goddamn, did that ever turn him on. "Brian, I want that too, but I have my final and—"

"Shh. I know. So I'll taste every inch of you tonight. Right now, I'm going to taste those inches that make you cry out my name."

Sliding his hands up her thighs, he pushed them farther apart and moved down the length of her body, breathing warm air over her pussy before he let her feel the touch of his lips. Her muscles pulled taut under his hands and he tightened his grip on her in response, keeping her spread beautifully open the way he wanted. Her pink flesh glistened in the sunlight pouring into his room, and he kissed her there as deeply as he would her mouth, lips caressing, tongue gently swirling. When her hands flew down and scrabbled for something to grab, he released her thighs and laced his fingers through hers.

"Ohhh, Brian..."

She was getting close already, delectable pink flushing a deep rose. He dipped his tongue as far as it would go into her, seeking a taste of her tangy female essence. When she was as slick as he could get her, he raised up, seeing that the pretty blush had also stolen into her cheeks and splotched her chest. Releasing one of her hands, he slipped one finger inside her. Then another. She tossed her head and moaned. Blowing out a breath, he eased in a third, wiggling them deeper inside her and feeling her hand clamp down on his as her brow furrowed.

Oh, *fuck*. She was so tight on his fingers he could hardly move them. But *she* was moving, barely rocking her hips, trying to help him go deeper. He leaned down, fluttering his tongue over her clit until she went liquid around him and he could ease through her better. His cock was aching for attention again, but this time was all about her.

But, holy hell, when her fingers crept over her own breast and teased the nipple into a stiff peak, he almost broke that vow to himself. Something in his eyes as he watched her must have scared her, because the next time her gaze alighted on his, her own eyes widened and she drew a sharp intake of breath.

"Come, baby, before I lose my mind and fuck you raw." For his own sanity, he drew her between his teeth, sucking her clit with gentle pulls he wouldn't stop until she exploded. She was so wet his fingers were coated with her juices, and the sudden, added rush of moisture as she moaned didn't help his ragged mindset. Jesus Christ, she was hot, and she was his, *only* his. He'd never been one to get caught up in obsessing over a girl's former lovers, but knowing he was the only one to go where he was right now...

The only one to ever make her tighten up, shudder and sob. Her pussy rippled along his fingers and her thighs spread even wider, allowing him to plunder her depths. He took advantage, searching for the spot, hoping he could get deep enough with his fingers to find it. Abandoning one, he plunged back in and barely grazed the tiny rough patch among all her softness. Her hips wrenched off the bed. He manipulated it ruthlessly, sucked her hard, and she flew over the edge.

The cries she emitted were musical, and he wished he could be everywhere at once because he'd love to drink them up, kiss her into a frenzy. Hell, he'd love to flip her over, haul her ass into the air, and fill her up. He could only stay right where he was, watching over her mound as her head tossed and her breasts heaved and her body formed a lovely arch. It was enough to make a motherfucker weep.

The tension bled from her, and he knew she needed him to hold her, to still the tremors. He moved up, carefully settling his weight over her as he slid his arms under her. She wrapped him up in her embrace and sighed.

"Was that good, baby?" he murmured, kissing her throat.

"That was better than good. This is getting...out of control."

"In a good way, right?"

"I hope so."

Troubled by her words, he chose not to reply. If they got into all that again, he might end up keeping her here all day trying to talk her down from the ledge. Only she had the power to pull herself back from it, to trust him. But he didn't like how fucking helpless he felt standing there watching her teeter back and forth.

While she showered, he put on coffee and turned on the TV and scrounged for something to make for breakfast. He wasn't big on that particular meal; he usually woke up too late for it. But she must be starving, and the nearest grocery store was only right around the corner. He scribbled out a note to her and grabbed his keys and cell phone.

Flipping the latter open, he saw that Starla had been the one to call him earlier. Weird. It wasn't even ten yet. She'd left voicemail, which he called to check while strolling toward his truck in the mild spring morning.

The voice on the message didn't sound like his friend at all. It was halting, with a trembling edge of panic. "Brian. You need to come to Dermamania, now. Someone...someone tore the hell out of it."

Stopping dead in his tracks, he nearly dropped the phone. His blood froze up in his veins.

How bad is it? How bad, Starla, fucking tell me now.

"All the front windows are broken...it doesn't look like anything was taken, they just trashed the place. Flat screens busted...oh, Brian, I want to cry. You've got to come now."

She hung up. His legs were already eating up the distance back into his apartment, where Candace had just stepped out of the shower wrapped in a big black towel. She met him with a big smile that melted soon as she got a good look at his face.

"Someone has vandalized my goddamn parlor. I've got to go."

"I'm coming with you. Give me two minutes."

Unable to stand pacing around his apartment for fear *he* would vandalize something while he waited for her, he went outside where the most damage he could do was tear a few bushes out of the ground. Just as he was contemplating it, Candace ran out of his door and down the flight of steps, her hair damp and bouncing on her shoulders. Wordlessly, they climbed in his truck. It was a struggle not to lay rubber in the lot, and he managed not to run any red lights, though it was tough.

Shit, shit, shit. It had to be Jameson Andrews. Only he hadn't thought that little pussy had it in him to pull this off. Or even seek out thugs to do it for him.

Then again, this was exactly the kind of chicken shit thing he would do. He couldn't best Brian physically, so go after one of the things he loved the most.

Beside him, Candace was sitting tense and upright, her fingers twisting her purse strap in her lap. He wondered if she was having the same thoughts he was.

"Could your brother have done this?" he asked harshly.

Her head turned toward him. He could see her in his peripheral vision. "I don't know, Brian."

"What do you mean, you don't know? You know him better than I do. Is he capable of this, or not?"

Her arms raised, and looking at her, he saw she was rubbing her temples. "James has a bad temper. Yes, I can see him doing something like this. It doesn't mean he did."

"Yeah? Well whoever did it didn't steal anything. They weren't after money or equipment. They trashed the shit out of the place. It was done out of rage."

She made a quiet sound. She was crying. "I'm so sorry."

"Jesus fu— It's *not your fault.* But I do hope to hell you won't miss him too much, because I'm going to kill that slimy little shit when I get my hands on him."

The instant he turned onto his beloved parlor's street, he saw the police cars. Sickness churned in his gut. It was like approaching a car wreck, fully aware he was about to see something he didn't want to see, but he couldn't look away regardless. Candace's hands went to her mouth.

"Oh, God," he muttered, pulling up to the curb and all but tumbling out of the truck. There was nothing but a gaping maw where the windows used to be, surrounded by yellow caution tape. Starla and Janelle were outside in the parking lot, talking to police officers. They were both crying. More officers were milling about inside the building, where it looked as if someone had turned loose a tornado and let it wreak havoc.

His vision went far beyond crimson. It went a hot, hellish black. This wasn't real, this couldn't be fucking happening…

Gentle hands slid over his shoulders, but he stepped away from them. Starla had seen him and was running toward him, her cowboy boots clattering on the asphalt. He caught her before she could slam into him, holding her by the arms.

"Do they know anything?"

She shook her head, agitating more tears into spilling. "They're going to the other businesses around here, asking questions, but they don't have any leads yet. They want to talk to you."

Of course no one had seen anything. Their town was the type to put out the lights and pull up the covers by eleven or so, and after the businesses were closed, there was really no reason for anyone to travel this street unless they were up to no good.

He needed to call Evan.

The police officers were efficient and took down his information, and he was more than happy to tell them about all the new enemies he'd made. But unless the cops could hand him Andrews's ass on a silver platter at this very moment, they were pretty much useless in his eyes. And that wasn't happening. Not only had no one seen anything, but so many people came and went through the parlor all day that fingerprinting was pretty much out of the question.

He felt so fucking powerless, his mind such a muddle, he might as well have been an invalid. Once the cops were done with him, all he could do was stand and stare into what was left of his sanctuary, where glass now covered the floor, his art and posters were ripped off the walls, chairs strewn, padded tables ripped and gutted. It looked like his insides felt. Candace stood with the girls, giving him his space.

And why wouldn't she? He'd just thrown her hands off him as if she'd done this or something. As if she were the one responsible, even after he'd told her she wasn't.

"Brian."

He turned around at the familiar voice, one he usually wasn't too fond of hearing but the very one he wanted right now. It was all he could do not to pitch himself into his brother's arms as Evan walked up beside him, his features grim as he took in the damage. "I heard it on the scanner this morning. I'm sorry, man."

Brian shoved his hands back through his hair. "What the fuck do I do, Evan?"

He blew out his breath. "Nothing now. Wait. I'm sorry I don't have better news to tell you."

"God*damn* it."

Evan put a hand on his arm, glancing back at Candace. "I need to talk to you about something else. Come over here."

He went around the corner of the building with Evan, his mind adrift in such misery that at first he didn't even wonder what his brother might have to say. Once Evan turned to him with his brow creased and his mouth set in a tight line, he felt a tingle of unease. Maybe seeing him out here wasn't such a good thing, after all.

"I got a call from a friend at the police department this morning. Jameson Andrews has filed an assault charge against you. You need to go in and give your statement."

The nightmarish haze in his thoughts turned into a vicious black hole, consuming everything. "Lousy lowlife son of a motherf—"

Evan cut in, his voice firm, as Brian walked furious circles trying to contain the urge to slam his fist into the brick wall and pretend it was Jameson's face. "*If you don't go in*, Brian, there'll be a warrant issued for your arrest."

"I can't leave, man, I gotta—"

"Look, I realize you're worried about your place and getting it cleaned up, but there's nothing else you can do here right now and I don't want to see you hauled off in handcuffs. Candace doesn't need to see it, either. You need to go and get this taken care of. All right? Brian? Look at me."

"That bastard most likely *did this*, and now..." Brian stopped pacing, took a breath and tried to calm down. Finally he lifted his head and looked Evan in the eyes. "All right. What am I looking at?"

"It depends. It's a class A misdemeanor, and we don't prosecute those, the county attorney does. It could all get dropped, or you could be looking at a stint on probation. Probably not any jail time, although it's possible."

"That's fucking *marvelous*."

"Like I said, that's unlikely, especially if you're cooperative. That's why I'm telling you to get your ass to the station now."

"Do I need my lawyer?"

"Are you fighting it?"

"I don't guess. I only did it in front of three other people."

"You can call him if you want, but it'll probably be the same outcome either way. Do you want me to go with you? I can't do much except wait outside for you."

For some reason, he needed that. Even if Evan wasn't in any position to help, he'd feel better knowing he was around.

Pride didn't go down very easily, and it tasted like shit when it did. "Yeah, if you don't mind. I guess I can tell Candace I have to go in because of this." He gestured to his parlor. "But I don't want to lie to her."

"Probably best you don't. Does she have somewhere to go?"

"She came with me, and I don't want her going home by herself."

Evan reached forward and put his arm around his shoulders. "Come on, then, and let's figure something out."

Candace bit her lip as the men came back from the side of the building. She'd heard raised voices, but she hadn't been able to make out the words. Both of them were wearing identical expressions, but then she'd just realized that if you took Brian, cleaned him up and stuck him in a suit and Ferragamos, you'd have Evan. The resemblance was striking.

And now, they both resembled carved granite statues. Brian motioned for her, and she left the group of his friends and employees she'd been huddled with. Her heart hadn't quit its frantic pounding since he'd first told her what happened, and it tripled at the look on his face.

"Your brother has filed charges on me," he said sharply.

"Oh, my God, Brian."

"I have to go to the police department before they cart my ass off to jail, and you have a final, so—"

She tried to understand that he was extremely upset, but his tone wounded her. "If someone can take me home, I'll be fine."

"I don't want you to go home."

"I'm not going to have a nervous breakdown if I have two hours by myself," she snapped. "My family isn't going to kidnap me and ship me off to a convent. I'll catch a ride home with Starla or someone, and I'll be okay."

"All right, fine," he said, starting to turn away toward Evan's truck. "I'll call you after I'm done."

"Maybe you shouldn't bother."

He froze, looking back at her. "What?"

"I'll wait for you," Evan muttered to him before walking away so they could talk.

Candace waited until he was out of earshot before she dared open her mouth. "It's obvious what's going on here. You'll hardly look at me, you're barking at me like I wronged you somehow, and I get it. It's fine. If you'd never gotten mixed up with me, you'd still have your parlor, and you wouldn't be going to the police station right now. I'm just—"

"Goddamn it, Candace, don't do this right now. Not now. I can't hear this from you on top of everything else." The expression on his face would be in her nightmares tonight. "Excuse me for having my livelihood trashed all to hell and a shiny new criminal record out of the deal. I've got enough shit to deal with, don't you think?"

"No one said you had to hit Jameson. I never asked you to do that. But at the same time, I didn't have to run off on Deanne's wedding and piss everyone off. It's no more your fault than mine, Brian, but maybe this isn't the best thing for us right now."

He was still stuck on her statement about Jameson. "I wasn't about to stand there and listen to him talk about you that way."

"Fair enough, but that was your decision. I told you to let me handle things. And now, I'm asking you to let me handle this." She wanted to weaken at the look on his face, but she had to stand her ground this time. "You take your time getting everything back on track. It looks like you have a lot of work ahead of you. Let me try to smooth things over with my family. Maybe once everything is settled, we can try again, if we're inclined."

"*No*," he said, and she felt her heart shatter at the sudden pleading in his voice. His hand came up as if he meant to touch her face, but he caught himself. She really wished he hadn't. One touch and maybe she would forget all this, forget what she had to do. "I'm sorry my head is fucked up right now, all right? I'm sorry if I made you feel like I blame you. I don't, I swear. Can we talk about this when we're more rational?"

She gave him a sad smile. "I'm perfectly rational right now. If you were, too, you'd realize that I'm right. It isn't just about what they're going to put me through. It's what they're going to put you through too."

"I'm a big boy. It might not look like it right this minute, but I can take it. I think you forget where I came from. I think they do, too."

"I don't know if *I* can take it."

"So you're giving up. You're going to live under their rule for the rest of your life. Marry whatever buttoned-down yuppie they throw your way and pop out a half-dozen kids."

"And what do *you* have envisioned for the future?" she snapped. "I want to finish school and have a career. I *would* like to have a family someday. You probably think that sounds like a life of hell—"

"You're pigeonholing me, and I don't fucking like it. I'm doing what I love right now. Every day, I get to create works of art and help people express themselves. I watch their faces light up when they see how their new ink came out, and I see their eyes well up when it's something that means the world to them. I never need to do anything else. I don't want to." He stabbed a finger toward the building. "*That's* my fucking future, Candace, right there. Anyone who's going to be a part of my life has to realize that."

"And they're trying to destroy it because of me. Don't you see?"

"Listen, I have to go. But I *will* call you later, and you'll answer, and we'll talk about this."

"It's just going to make things harder—"

"I told you I wouldn't let you get away from me the next time you run. I meant it." His gaze continued to bore into hers, even as he walked away to Evan's truck and popped open the door. "I meant it, Candace."

She watched them pull away, feeling lost and alone and...a million other things, none of them good. Starla—who along with every cop milling around the place must've heard every word they'd flung at each other—came up and put an arm around her shoulders. "Come on, I'll take you home."

The ride was tense, Starla's makeup-less face showing all the devastation she was feeling. Candace told her where to go and then didn't know what else to say. After hearing everything that was said just now, maybe Starla blamed her too.

It wasn't until they pulled in to the parking lot that she spoke. "Don't leave him like this. He needs you, even if he can't admit it. Brian is moody. Things get to him. If you leave him right now, it'll kill him."

"It might kill *me* if I stay. This weekend has been..." She drew a breath. "It's been beautiful and amazing and the scariest thing that's ever happened to me in my entire life."

Starla's brown eyes searched her face intently. "You're in love for the first time. Of course it's scary. But you don't run away from it. Now is when you stand together and push through."

"My family is going to try to make his life hell. It looks like they're already starting to do it. He doesn't need me."

"Then if I were you, I'd give them hell right back."

Chapter Twenty

Brian stared out Evan's truck window, glaring at the world. They'd just left the police department, where he'd sat and written out everything that transpired at Candace's apartment yesterday. He wasn't too concerned with what was going to happen with all that. It was aggravating, but nothing compared to what was left of his parlor.

Or what was left of his relationship with her.

The police had been interested in the fact that his place had been vandalized the very night of the fight. Jameson obviously wasn't smart at all. It was just a matter of finding someone who could place the bastard at the scene, or proof that he'd been there.

"You all right over there?" Evan asked.

"No. Pull over at the next convenience store. I need cigarettes. As soon as I get some, I'm gonna light up five of 'em simultaneously, and inhale those fuckers."

"Had you quit or something?"

He paused, considering telling him he only hadn't smoked one yet today, because he honestly didn't think he was going to get through this day without nicotine. But the truth tumbled out on its own. That was happening a lot lately. "Yeah."

"Then I'm not pulling over. Hang in there, man." Evan chuckled. "No wonder you clocked Jameson. You must be climbing the walls."

"That didn't have anything to do with why I put that asshole's lights out."

"All right. Tell me the story."

Brian glared over at Evan. "Are you my brother or my prosecutor right now?"

"I'm always your brother, you hotheaded little shit. But you need to exercise better judgment."

"Really. Let me ask you something, *brother*. What would you have done if, the day you and Kelsey got back from Hawaii that first time, she had a brother who got in her face and called her a whore right in front of you?"

Evan blew out a whistle. "Damn. I watched her ex-husband call her a bitch the day she caught him and Courtney together. No—he told her to quit acting like a bitch. I lunged, but he jumped back and the girls got between us. Kelsey was in my face yelling at me not to throw everything away over him, because he wasn't worth it. I thought it totally would be just to feel the bastard's jaw connect with my fist *one time*."

"It did feel pretty damn good. Not so much now, though." He flexed his fingers, wincing as pain flared through knuckles that were still sore. "You had a hell of a lot more to lose than I did, though."

"Sounds like you've got plenty to lose," Evan said pointedly. "Don't mess things up with her by acting like a lunatic. If you want to win her family over, decking her brother isn't the way to go about it."

"To hell with her brother. And her family."

"Okay, how about this, then. I don't think it's a good idea to nearly break your drawing hand on a piece of trash like Jameson Andrews."

"My hand is fine," he snapped.

"They're going to come at you any way they can. I don't think I can get you out of this one."

"I haven't asked you to, and don't do me any favors. I'll suffer the consequences and like it, as long as it's for her." His brother digested that in silence for a while, staring straight ahead at the road. Brian watched him, thinking of a thousand things he wished he'd never done, never said. "Does it freak you out being a dad?"

Evan laughed. "You're all over the map today, boy."

"Does it?"

"It makes me feel about a million different things. Mostly insanely happy, but freaked out is definitely in there somewhere... Wait. *Shit*, Brian. Tell me Candace isn't pregnant."

He shrugged. "Anything's possible."

"Do you love this girl?" It wasn't a gentle question. It held all the promise that if Brian gave the wrong answer, Evan was going to pull over and throw him out of the truck.

"I'm fucking crazy about her."

"Fucking crazy I've gathered. But I asked if you *love* her. I asked if you'll say the words. I'm talking true, enduring, unconditional, hold-her-hair-while-she's-puking-from-morning-sickness love."

"Hell, yes, I'll say the words! I love her. I told her I love her. I'll hold any frigging thing she wants me to."

"Well, you damn sure didn't talk to her like you loved her earlier. I thought about emasculating you right there in front of everyone."

"You didn't hang around long enough to see me grovel. And I appreciate your restraint. I feel emasculated enough as it is." He reached up and rubbed his face hard. "But I do love her."

"She's a sweet girl. Don't screw up anymore, Brian. And don't get her pregnant, please? For God's sake? You are not ready for that level of commitment and respons—"

"Don't give me your shit, man, it's not as if I'm trying to. You weren't either, if I recall."

Evan grinned. "Kelsey says we're so in love we can't help but bond even at the molecular level."

"You're not going to be one of those couples who has nineteen kids, are you?"

"Nah. We definitely want at least one more, maybe two, but not right away. Alex is a handful."

"You know, as I was sitting in the police department earlier,

I had a thought."

"Uh-oh."

"At this point, if it weren't for Candace, I would have no problem moving away with you and Kelsey. Starting over somewhere else...yeah, it sounds pretty awesome right about now. You were right. But now she's in the picture, and..." He trailed off, frustrated at his own inability to express in words what he was feeling: that no matter what she said to him, or what she did, he wasn't going anywhere. He could keep his word on that, at least.

"You'll get things up and going again, don't worry. Shut down for a couple of weeks or so, get everything functional and you'll be fine. While you were in giving your statement, I called to have your front windows replaced. They're going to get to it as fast as they can, so at least everything will be protected from the elements."

"Thanks, man. For everything. And I'm sorry about all— Shit. I'm just sorry."

Evan glanced at him, then clapped him on the shoulder. "Don't mention it."

Brian drew a deep breath, trying to clear out all the gnawing emotion. "Does Dad know?"

"Yeah, I called him too. He'll help out any way he can. We all will."

"You guys have given me too much already. I'm starting all over again."

"Now you're just being dramatic. Your insurance should cover criminal mischief."

"That's great and all, but I still feel like I'm rebuilding the place practically from the ground up, and I want that piece of crap to pay for it, because he can. This was personal, and I want it taken out of his ass."

"Regardless, we can't sit around and wait for that to happen. I know you're pissed, but keep your head on straight." When Brian didn't reply, Evan went on. "Everyone is really proud of you, whether you see it or not. And we're all outraged about this. The damage is definitely in the felony range. If Jameson Andrews did this, they won't let me work the case but I'll have a damn good time watching his ass get nailed for every penny."

They turned onto Dermamania's street, and Brian's stomach pitched in sick dismay as the eyesore it now was swung into view. *Dramatic, my ass,* he thought. Somehow, after being away for a few hours, it looked even worse than before. "You and me both."

Candace took the week to concentrate on her finals and unwind from the wild events of the prior weekend. Once that was over and done with—and she somehow passed all her courses—she welcomed the lazy days of summer break. She didn't plan on having too many of them; she spent most of her time poring over want ads and turning in job applications. Even if it was something part time she could fit around her class schedule this fall, having that tiny bit of independence could only be helpful to the soul.

And thank God, she got her period. When it was a day late, she'd nearly panicked, thinking that one moment of forgetfulness might've had far more serious repercussions than she'd imagined possible. It might feel awesome and romantic in the moment to think about Brian's baby growing in her belly, but for twenty-four long hours she'd done nothing but bite her nails and wonder what on God's green earth she'd do with a kid at this point. Yeah, she'd definitely been scared straight on that one. She'd gone straight to her doctor and gotten on the Pill.

Whenever Brian called, she answered, like he'd said she would. But surprisingly, he didn't push her. He talked about how Dermamania V2, as he called it, was coming along. She could tell how excited he was to be reopening soon. He and his employees and Evan had been working every day cleaning up the place. Kara and Marco had come down to lend him any equipment he needed until he got his own. Candace was disappointed she didn't get a chance to see them, but she was determined to stay away for now.

It didn't take a rocket scientist to figure out his strategy. His way of chasing her was giving her the space she'd demanded. It was working better than any flowers, gifts, candy or stalking techniques he could ever have employed, because she missed him like crazy.

She wanted to run to him, and knew she couldn't. Not yet. There were so many reasons: for herself, for her family where things were slowly getting back to normal. For the fragile relationship with her parents, who seemed to be looking at her in a new light. Despite everything, she found she needed and wanted their support. In the beginning it had been much like walking on eggshells, but now she and her mother had been getting along better than she could ever remember since she was a kid. Seeing Brian again so soon might only tear it all down again.

And then there was her brother to deal with.

Jameson was an entirely different story. He'd sported two black eyes for days. She visited her parents quite often, and he was always there, as if he was hiding out. He might as well move back home, for the way he lingered. It was one more thing that added to her suspicion.

He was scared. A ringing phone or a knock at the door could make him jump out of his skin. But damn if she could get him to crack, no matter how many knowing smiles she sent his way. Her very existence had become all about torturing him.

"It's only a matter of time before they catch the guy," she told him ominously one night at dinner when her mom and dad left the room for a moment.

And the next evening: "The investigation is moving right along. Evan says they're closing in."

"Who cares," he would growl every time.

And she'd return with some variation of, "Doesn't it bother you that vandals are running loose through town? Although it's funny they haven't hit any other businesses, don't you think? Just Brian's. I wonder why."

There were times he would get up and leave the room.

He was so freaking guilty. And there was nothing she could do about it...except make his life hell, as Starla had said.

Nothing she could do about it...until one very shocking phone call.

Macy sounded funny from the moment Candace answered. It was extremely odd for her to ask how things were going with Brian, but it was one of her first questions.

"They're...okay," Candace told her. "We're just talking, letting things cool off. I think all I needed was to step back and catch my breath. Now I've caught it, and everything is clear, and I don't feel right without him."

For some reason, that made Macy dissolve into tears. "I'm so sorry."

Dumbfounded, Candace muted the volume on her TV and sat up straight on her couch. "Mace, what's the matter?"

"I've got something to tell you," she sobbed. "You're going to hate me."

What in the *hell?* Candace spent the next two minutes trying to calm her friend down, assuring her there was nothing she could do to make Candace hate her. Although, given the girl's reaction, that still remained to be seen.

"I was at Dermamania the night it was vandalized. I saw Jameson's SUV drive by once, really slow. The only reason I even noticed it is because it looked so much like his, and I wondered if it was him and what he would be doing there. When I left later on, it was parked in a lot a couple of blocks down. I thought surely I was mistaken. But now, after what happened between him and Brian..."

Candace's pulse was pounding in her ears. Seeing his car go by...was that enough? Dammit, she wished she had Evan's phone number. "Why were you there, Macy?"

Dead silence on the other end for at least ten seconds. "I met Ghost there late that night."

Ho. Lee. *Shit.* "Ghost? How did that happen? I never gave him your number."

"Did he ask for it?"

"Yeah, on the way to Dallas. I thought there wasn't any way you could be interested."

"We ran into each other at the sushi bar. It was the evening you guys got back from the concert. We talked, and he got my number. He called after he got off that night and asked me to meet him there."

"Macy, I don't know which has shocked me more..."

"I know, okay? I didn't want to get Jameson in trouble, and I was scared. But it was him, and it's not fair that he's getting away with it. I haven't talked to Ghost about this at all."

"He must have not seen anything, or Brian would have been all over it. Where were you?"

"We were sitting in the parking lot in my car. I figure James was waiting for us to leave, but at the time I didn't think anything of it. I didn't know what had gone down between James and Brian and I had no idea he was about to trash the place, you know?"

Candace remembered she hadn't talked to Macy that night. Macy really hadn't known to look for anything suspicious. "I would ask what you were *doing* in your car, but obviously not much if you noticed my brother driving by."

"It did not go there," Macy said adamantly. "We just talked."

"Uh-huh, and are you still *talking*?"

"Talking. Yeah. That's all."

"I can't even imagine carrying on a serious conversation with that guy, but whatever."

"There's something about him..."

"Hey, you don't have to explain. I'm not going to torture you over your decisions like you did me."

"I'm so sorry," Macy wailed.

"I'll tell you what. If you'll go tell this to the police, all will be forgiven. I'll go with you, if you want. James was angry and lashing out, and he's my brother, but you didn't see Brian and how heartbroken he was. James owes him, big time. Maybe I can talk Brian into not pressing charges if James pays him for the damage. Maybe an I'll-drop-mine-if-you'll-drop-yours deal."

"I would feel so much better if he did that."

"I can't promise it, and that's up to him. But no matter what, Macy, you have to follow through."

Macy sniveled. "I know."

"In fact...do you want to go and talk to him now?"

"Not particularly." Candace could definitely understand that. The thought of seeing him set off flocks of what felt like hummingbird wings in her own belly. "He'll hate me too for not coming forward sooner. It's been almost three weeks, but it's been eating me up."

"I'm pretty sure he'll be so happy to finally get some closure that he won't even mind all that much."

Chapter Twenty-one

Candace hadn't realized the parlor was open already. When she and Macy pulled in, it looked good as new, and upon entering the only difference she could see was the flat screen TVs hadn't been replaced yet.

Janelle greeted them with a big smile, coming forward to give Candace a hug. Ghost looked up from the tattoo he was working on and met Macy's stare with a lascivious grin. Candace couldn't resist giving her a hidden nudge with her elbow. Love was indeed a strange thing.

She didn't see Brian anywhere, but his truck was parked outside.

"Is he here?" she asked Janelle quietly.

"In his office. I daresay it would be fine for you to go on back." She winked at her.

Taking a deep breath, she tore Macy away from the object of her desire and steered her toward the back.

Brian looked up from his laptop as they entered, and the yearning that filled his expression when he saw her was all she needed to know how hellish these past weeks had been on him. It was a fight to keep the burn of tears out of her eyes. He rose out of his chair as if pulled by puppet strings and crossed the room to wrap her in his arms. "God, it's good to lay eyes on you," he murmured, his lips near her ear.

The familiar warmth and solidity of his body was something she didn't want to release. Ever. She buried her face in his shirt and inhaled his scent as deep into her lungs as she could. "I miss you."

"I just...fuck, I don't know what to say. I didn't expect to see you."

Candace glanced at Macy, who was biting her lip in apprehension. "I'll be glad to talk, but right now, Macy needs to tell you something."

Brian looked at the other girl as if he'd forgotten her presence. "Oh, hey, Macy."

"Hi. Um...I'm just going to blurt this out."

He gave a perplexed chuckle. "All right."

"I can place Jameson at the scene the night this place was trashed. I was in the parking lot. I saw him drive by, and he also parked a little ways up the street."

"Holy sh— Are you sure?" He looked as if he wanted to grab her in a bear hug and twirl her around. Candace noticed she left out the details of why she'd been here, and he was beyond questioning it.

"As far as seeing a face, or a license plate number, no. But it was a black SUV with a sticker on the back windshield, right where his Baylor sticker is."

"Son of a bitch." Then he winced, glancing at Candace. "Sorry, I know that's your brother."

"You don't have to apologize."

"I need to call Evan." He turned and headed for the phone, but stopped dead in his tracks when Candace placed a hand on his arm.

"I need to ask you something, Brian. I understand you're angry. And I have no idea if this will work or not, but I thought we should approach you first. If Jameson would agree to drop his charges against you and pay you for all of the damages, would you not press charges against him?" For a second, disbelief filled his expression, and she rushed on before she could lose him. "It would do nothing but help our situation. You'd both get out of trouble, you'd get compensated, and...it might help relations between us and my family."

His brows dipped low over his eyes. "Yeah, and what about

that? Are you saying I'm out of the picture if I don't go along?"

She swallowed and shook her head. "No, I'm not. I'll understand if you need to do this. It'll hurt watching you tear each other apart, because the fact remains they're a major part of my life, but so are you. I can't turn my back on either of you. I need you to all coexist without driving me to drinking, and this is the only way to make that a possibility. Like I said, I haven't talked to Jameson and I don't even know if he'd be susceptible. But if he's confronted and told his ass is about to go down, I think he'd do just about anything to get out of it. He's scared to death."

"Good," Brian grumbled. "But you don't seem to realize how hard it's going to be for me to let this go. I've been through hell these past three weeks, Candace. We're all still exhausted from getting the place open again. Accepting payment for my troubles and turning my back...it's going to feel like he's buying us off, when what he needs is to suffer like we have. It's not just me. It's all of them out there too."

"I understand," she said quietly, thinking that she loved him more at that moment than she ever had before. He was so sincere and devoted to them. There was no question in her mind he would be that way with her, too, if she would let him. "I'm not trying to push you. I was just throwing an idea out there."

"I'll do whatever you need me to," Macy said to him. "I feel awful about this."

Brian frowned at her. "Wait a second. What were you doing here?"

"Can I plead the Fifth on that? For now, at least? I wasn't vandalizing anything, honest."

Candace grinned. "Yeah, except maybe for Gh— *Ow*!"

He couldn't believe she was here. Any second now, he expected to wake up with his face smashed to his keyboard, having finally succumbed to exhaustion. But so far it hadn't happened. She was here and she'd just told him news he'd been waiting to hear for weeks.

And she was asking him not to do anything with it.

He couldn't make a decision about that now, because it wasn't only his to make. As he'd told her, it was about all his artists who'd busted their asses for weeks helping him get this place cleaned up, who hadn't deserted him to find other jobs. It was even about his brother, who'd argued cases all day long and then shown up here in the evenings, taking time away from his wife and son to roll up his sleeves and get dirty with them. It was about Kara and Marco, whose equipment he was still using for the time being. There hadn't been time to get his own yet, but he would be taking care of that in the next few days.

But on the flip side, it was also about Candace, whom he'd realized he loved more than his own soul. It was about giving her what she needed to be happy and stable and to balance the scales in her life.

Macy had left them alone. Candace sat in the extra chair in the office while he perched on the corner of his desk, letting his gaze roam over her. Shimmering blond hair, catching the overhead light in every strand. Downturned blue eyes, as if she was too shy to meet his gaze now that they were alone with their intimate memories of each other.

He cataloged every detail of her, from the slightly accelerated rise and fall of her shoulders as she breathed to the pulse jumping so, so faintly in her throat. He wanted to put his mouth there, feel it throb against his tongue. Feel it race as he touched her.

Without a conscious thought to do so, he went down on his knees in front of her, grasping both her hands. If she wouldn't look up at him, she could look down at him.

Her tiny, surprised intake of breath caught in the air between them. He lifted her knuckles to his lips, aching so hard to touch some part of her. "Being away from you has been...hell. I could wax poetic and tell you it's been like being torn away from my own soul, or missing a shard of my heart, but in the end it's been absolute torment. I'm missing all those things if I'm not with you."

"I love you so much," she whispered. "So many times I've

wanted to break down and run to you, but I've been doing well. I'm afraid...afraid to—"

"I realize it's important to you to try to make your own way. I'm so sorry if I jeopardized that and scared you off. That was never my intent. You tried to tell me, but I kept on bullying you, telling you it would be okay, when you weren't okay. I know you've never felt this way before, and I shouldn't have pushed for so much so fast. I should've given you plenty of time to get used to me. I'm fully aware I can be an unendurable bastard sometimes. People make sure to remind me of it pretty much on a daily basis."

"You're a good guy, Brian. The people who know you best know that."

"Not good enough for you. But I've pretty much made peace with that fact."

"Well, that's good. Too much angst gets tiresome after a while."

"I'll try to remember that," he said, wanting to laugh but unable to force the sound out. Her face held him mesmerized, he was so intent upon reading her emotions. And again, he didn't want to push. He needed an answer from her, something concrete, or hell, even a *hint* of what the future she foresaw might hold. If she wasn't ready to give it, he was simply screwed.

"I just don't know right now."

What don't you know? Tell me and I can make it right. Those were the words that crowded up in his throat, but if he spoke them, she would only bolt, grab her friend, and leave him again. This was requiring a delicate touch he didn't have. Naturally, he only wanted to break something.

She went on, her voice high and cracking with emotion. "I can't be the reason you're punching people out and my brother is running around committing felonies. I can't go on hurting people because this *wildness* you make me feel is so irresistible that I would forsake them all to be with you. I can't be in the middle of this anymore. I don't want to be the cause of all this strife. I won't be."

There was such fierceness in her eyes that he knew trying to persuade her to give him another chance would be a lost cause. She was broken, but she was determined.

"Please don't look at me like that," she said.

"How am I looking?"

"Like your heart is breaking."

"It is, sunshine."

"Brian, don't!" Her face dropped into her hands, and she took a long breath. He reached over and pushed the door closed in case anyone ventured back their way, then simply sat, watching her and stroking her knee. Afraid if he opened his mouth, he might shatter the fragile mood.

Suddenly, she pitched herself forward, wrapping her arms around his neck as amazement swept through him. He held her, breathing in her scent as if it were the antidote to a poison in his veins. Her lips trailed gently over his cheek, seeking his own, finding them, melting into them. Warm, whisper-soft and searching. So fucking sweet. Every sense he possessed exploded, the surge of arousal practically supernatural as he resisted every urge to throw her down and get inside her. Her hands sank into his hair, her body slid forward to join him on the floor.

"Oh my God," he rasped, trying to catch his breath around her hungry, fevered kisses. She whimpered and shuddered against him, pulling him closer as if she was trying to crawl through him. Her tongue teased its way past his teeth, her mysterious, delicate flavor flooding his mouth. He plundered hers in return, desperate for more of it. He didn't think this thirst for her would ever be quenched, but he was damn sure dying to attempt it.

That's why it took every atom of his self-control to reach up and seize her wrists and push her back.

She stared at him as if he'd just left a blade stuck in her heart, wounded astonishment churning in her blue eyes.

"No," he whispered. "Not with all this uncertainty between us." That delectable bottom lip trembled. "Trust me, it's the hardest thing I've ever done in my entire life. But for your sake, for ours, I'm going to do what you asked me to do. I'll lie here on the floor and hold you all night, if you need me to. But if I touch you any more than that, I'll lose my mind."

She blinked at him, a sort of wounded bravado filling her expression. What the hell did he do now? He'd never felt so completely and pathetically helpless before, not even when he'd pulled up to see his place of business trashed to hell. As Evan had told him then, the only thing to do was wait. Wait on her to figure things out. There were scant few virtues God had seen fit to bless him with, and patience was probably the least of them.

What alternative was there to waiting? Turning his back? Not likely. Not on her. Anyone else and he might've shown her the door and breathed a sigh of relief once she'd used it.

But the thought that he might bide his time only to have her decide in the end she couldn't be with him...that thought made his heart seize up in a tight, burning knot.

"I could have you, Candace. I could come barging back into your life and you wouldn't try to stop me. Even if you did, I could break down your defenses. I could've taken you right here on the floor, and you wouldn't have said no. I could push and seduce and boss my way in. What kills me is that if I did that, you'd be mine. Every natural impulse I possess is screaming at me to do all those things, just to have you. So I've got my instincts in a chokehold right now, trying to keep from acting on them because it would only put us back in the same situation we were in before, and you don't want that."

She looked at him, her cheek resting on her drawn-up knee. It was another image that would haunt him until he had to exorcise it through his art or explode. He went on. "I don't know what better way to tell you I love you and I'm serious, other than explaining how out of character you've got me acting. You can ask my brother about that. I'm sure he'd be glad to give you an earful. All I can talk about is you, even to him. To all of them out there. They don't know what to do with me. No one wants me around anymore. The portrait I drew of you is still over my bed, I can't stand to look at it, but I can't make myself take it down. I'm a mess over you."

"You always sound like you're coping pretty well on the phone."

"Don't be fooled. I have to maintain at least some shred of dignity. It's all a front for you."

A pained expression flickered over her features, and she crossed her arms over her knees, turning her face into the safe haven they made. "I'm a mess too. I need and want you to barge back in just as much as it's in your nature to do that. And you're right, I wouldn't stop you, if only because I don't have that much strength now, but we would only end up right back here. So the fact that you're holding back means more to me than you could possibly realize. Thank you, Brian."

He'd poured his fucking heart out and she'd thanked him. Sweet baby Jesus, this only kept getting worse.

He rested his head back against the desk behind them, staring straight up into the overhead lighting until he went half blind. "I should get back out there," he said quietly. "I'll leave with you in a heartbeat if you ask me to, but otherwise—"

Candace scrambled up as if she'd been waiting for a chance, any chance, to flee. "I'm sorry, I didn't mean to keep you from work."

"It's fine. I'm glad you came by."

"Will you let me know what you decide about my brother?"

He got to his feet beside her, unable to resist reaching out and framing her face with his hands. Her gaze had followed him all the way up, and they were standing so close together her head tilted back as she looked at him. Her eyes were tinged red, her dark lashes spiky, her lips still swollen from the pressure of his kiss. The silk of her hair and the warm satin of her skin mingled underneath his hands.

This wasn't right. She was *his*, dammit. She'd filled in all the missing pieces in his life. If she jerked them out now, he would collapse, parts of him scattered so far and wide he might never gather them back together again.

"I will," he said, struggling to push the words past the lump in his throat. Past the need to throw her over his shoulder and run out the back door, hold her captive at his place until she finally cracked and swore to be his for the rest of their lives.

Her hands slid over his own and pulled them away, holding briefly before letting go. The loss of her warmth sucked the air from his lungs. “No matter what happens,” she said, “I love you. Just know that if I can’t be with you, it was because I loved you so much I couldn’t burden you with my issues.”

“Baby, they’re not that big of a deal,” he insisted. “When it comes to how I feel about you, they’re nothing. They don’t even play in.”

“Like they didn’t play in three weeks ago?”

“We’ve got him nailed. He won’t strike at me again. None of them will.”

She emitted a humorless laugh. “You don’t know them very well.”

No, he didn’t, he thought with a sigh. As he walked her out to the front so she could get her friend and leave, his mind raced desperately, trying to zero in on a plan. He had to do *something*, for God’s sake. He’d gotten through most of his life sitting on his ass, letting wounds fester, not giving a damn. But he couldn’t do that now. Not this time.

It was the sight of her walking out the door, and the agony that ensued after she was gone, that hatched the thought. It was the pity in everyone’s eyes that caused it to take hold and burn.

Most likely, he was insane. Hell, he was probably shit-all stupid to even consider it.

She’d said he didn’t know her family very well. Maybe the only answer was for him to get better acquainted.

Kelsey and Evan sat in their robes with him at the end of their dining table, both of them wearing matching expressions of concern. Kelsey had just put a cup of coffee in front of him, but he didn’t want them to see how much his hand was shaking if he lifted it. He’d woken them up but there wasn’t any other place he knew to go. They'd been talking his situation to death for a half hour now.

"Brian, when I said I couldn't wait for the right girl to get her hands on you, this isn't what I had in mind," Kelsey said.

He grunted something that resembled a laugh. "The next time you say something like that, I'm not leaving my house for a year."

Evan propped his head on his fist, looking as if one slip might leave him snoring on the tabletop. "This is all up to you, and I'm beside you no matter what. If you can settle this *to your satisfaction* without having to put Candace and Macy and everyone through the wringer, then I say go for it. But if you can't, then take the bastard to the mattresses. You were the victim here. Talk to him and see what he's open to. There's no harm in it. Just don't kick his ass again, whatever you do."

"Oh, man, that'll be tough. Remembering what he said about her, and knowing that it's all their fault her head is all screwed up and—"

Evan perked up, frowning at him. "Whoa, there. I think there's another influence at work messing with her head. I'm playing devil's advocate here for a second, but they probably think the exact same thing about you. That their sweet, innocent Candace would still be sweet and innocent if that unscrupulous Ross boy hadn't corrupted her. From what you've told us, she's changed right in front of them, practically overnight. They're panicking."

"She needed to change, though. She needed to—"

"I'm inclined to agree, but who are you to say what she needs? You've got to stop that," Kelsey said gently, putting a hand on his arm. "I can tell you from past experience, women don't like it, and it's not going to do her any good to go from being on their leash to being on yours. And even if she did need to make some changes, that doesn't mean you should expect them to let her go so easily. You have to be understanding of their side of it, or you're never going to get anywhere with them."

"True," Evan said. "You have to predict and examine and

understand every argument the other side is going to throw at you. It's not about being the one who's right. It's about showing them why they're wrong, and in your case, it's not even that black and white. But that's how you win."

Brian gave in and nursed his coffee, craving some revitalization. Evan was watching him carefully. Kelsey glanced at her husband, looking troubled, before turning back to Brian.

"What you need is sleep, honey, not caffeine. Why don't you stay here tonight? I don't want you out driving in the shape you're in."

"Not like I'm drunk," he muttered.

"Maybe not on alcohol."

"I think you should stay too," Evan said. "In the morning when we're all rested, we'll figure this out."

Baby Alex took that moment to cry out from his crib in their bedroom. Kelsey laughed as she got up from the table. "When *you're* rested, anyway," she said to Brian. "No rest for us."

"I couldn't sleep if I wanted to. I can stay up with him, if you guys are tired." Both of them stared in astonishment. "What? Just give him his bottle and sit watching metal videos with him until he goes back to sleep, right? How hard can it be?"

"Oh, dear God," Evan groaned. "You really have no idea."

Chapter Twenty-two

"Candy, I really think it would do you good to get out for a while. You haven't been over in days. Won't you at least consider it? No one's asking you to marry him."

Candace listened to her mom go on and on about some guy they wanted her to meet at dinner tonight and resisted the urge to facepalm. And to cry while doing it. She'd shed enough tears after seeing Brian the other night that she should still be dehydrated. Macy had held her for damn near an hour in her car after that episode while she made herself sick on sobs. Then Sam had joined them at her apartment and they'd all ended up tearful messes for one reason or another. Crazy. Their cycles must be synced or something.

But thank God for her friends. She would be totally lost without them.

"I'm not ready, Mom." And if there was still a chance with Brian—someday—how could she jeopardize it by even meeting this person her mom was going on about?

It didn't really matter, her mind returned. It wasn't as if she could ever feel that way about anyone else again. She was ruined.

"All I'm asking you to do is come to dinner," Sylvia said. "No harm in that, is there? He's just a guest. It's not a set-up."

"I might come to dinner, but it's not to meet him. And you'd better not give him that impression, or I swear I'll leave." It was getting easier and easier to stand up to her mother on these matters.

"Fine," Sylvia said. "I'm glad you're coming."

She was so not up to this. The prospect of finding someone new to date did not even register on her map, but she didn't even feel like socializing, especially with a stranger. Going through the same old conversation, answering the same old mundane questions: "What's your major? How much longer do you have? What do you want to be when you grow up?"

The thought was nearly unbearable. She'd had a promising job interview with the town newspaper today—maybe she'd change her major again to journalism, really freak the parents out—and while exciting, it had drained her. She wanted to lounge in front of the TV in her PJs the rest of the evening, but she'd been doing way too much of that lately.

Pulling up a couple of hours later to her parents' house in an impressive area of town known as the Heights—where Brian's mom and dad also lived—she was tempted to drive on around the circular driveway and go back home. There was no unfamiliar vehicle parked anywhere in sight, so maybe the guy wasn't coming. Whoever he was. She hadn't even thought to ask, to see if she might know him, but then that was how little she cared.

She hadn't put much effort in her physical appearance, wearing her hair down over a simple peach blouse and black slacks, but her mom didn't even lift an eyebrow as she bustled her in cheerfully.

The woman certainly seemed sure of herself over this one. It only made Candace more determined to fight all the harder. Whoever she ended up with, it could *not* be someone her parents chose. Even if she liked that person tremendously, she thought, there was no way she could give them the satisfaction over that. Maybe she was being irrational, but she didn't care. One thing she could never forgive them for was their interference with her and Brian. Her love life was off limits, the one area she couldn't let them control.

"I don't think he's coming," she commented rather smugly as they were seated at the dining table. Ha! Trying to set her up with a no-show. He'd probably stand her up if they ever made a date. Which they wouldn't.

"Oh, he isn't going to be here until seven," her mother said.

Candace checked her watch. It was ten till. Her dad sipped from his wine glass and smiled at her. Phillip Andrews cracking a smile *just because* was the equivalent of hearing a chorus of angels singing from heaven, or something. It just didn't happen.

Candace returned it and then frowned as she brought her own glass to her lips. The doorbell chimed. Despite herself, she jumped. Everyone was acting too frigging weird.

"I'll get it," Sylvia declared, jumping up from her seat and gliding smoothly from the room.

"What's with her?" Candace asked her dad, leaning toward him and keeping her voice low.

Phillip made every effort to look as if he didn't know what she was talking about. It was pretty pathetic. "How do you mean?"

"I mean, I don't think I've seen her this chipper in—"

Her voice simply failed, along with much of her vital functions—heart stopping, breath seizing up, brainwaves crashing—as a low male laugh sounded from the foyer. But its incredible sexiness wasn't the only reason she nearly expired right there in her chair, still staring wide-eyed at her dad who was now grinning like a fool.

It was because she *recognized* that laugh. Because she'd heard it so many times. In her dreams. In his arms.

With a sound akin to a sob, she rose out of her seat, pulled toward that voice by a force as natural and irresistible as the gravity that kept her feet on the ground. Never mind the fact that she felt as if clouds were beneath her every step.

She flew around the end of the dining table as he came in—*him*, Brian, he was here, in her *parents'* house!—and went straight into his arms without checking her speed. He caught her as surely as she'd known he would, arms tight and protective around her, promising with the strength of their hold to never let her go again. One hand sank into her hair, fisting it, holding her head against his chest.

And she wanted to laugh, because he was dressed much as she'd seen him that first night in his parlor when she'd lamented that he probably had a date later. Covered nearly from neck to feet, missing his visible piercings. Although she'd lay bets her favorite one was still in place, and the naughty thought sent a burning flush up her cheeks.

She didn't open her eyes until she was quite sure she'd gotten a handle on all the emotions that threatened to fly out of her. Her parents had settled back at the table.

"You're welcome to go and talk, if you want, and join us later," Sylvia said.

"Thank you," Candace said to them, without letting go of him. "Thank you so much."

Her mom made a shooing gesture as if all the mushiness was getting to her, so Candace grabbed Brian's hand and led him through the house to the back door.

There was a little pond with a fishing pier and gazebo out on the property, and it was such a clear, gorgeous evening, warm and musical with the sounds of early summer. The moon had just begun its ascent into the heavens, casting its wavering reflection across the gently rippling water. He laughed again as she all but dragged him out toward it, her fingers linked through his.

"Slow down, sweetheart, you're about to launch into space."

"I am! How in the world did this happen?"

Their steps rang off the wooden planks, and he waited until they reached the gazebo out over the water before answering. She sat on one of the benches and pulled him down beside her, so they were only surrounded by the sounds of lapping water and the lull of the crickets. "I came over to see them a couple of nights ago. Them and your brother."

"I'm…I'm amazed…and so incredibly happy, but are you *insane*?"

The vivid colors of twilight were reflected in his eyes. "Over you? Absolutely." He took both her hands in his. "Is this okay? I didn't want to do anything to push you."

"This is more than okay, Brian. This is...miraculous."

The relief in his features tugged at her heartstrings. He must've been so worried this move might put her off. "Good. The way you were looking at me at first, I didn't know if it was happiness to see me, or 'Hello, psycho alert!'"

"So that part when I flew straight into your arms didn't clue you in a bit?"

"It was all in slow motion. It took you a year to get to me, don't you know?"

"How on earth did you win them over?"

He cocked one eyebrow at her. "What, are you saying I can't be charming when I have to be?"

"No one who's ever been on their bad side has managed to do it yet."

"It's doubtful anyone on their bad side had the power to send their son to jail, but didn't out of the goodness of his heart."

She wanted to hug him again. "So you and Jameson worked it out?"

"Make no mistake, he still pretty much hates my guts. But we talked, and he fessed up. It's all worked out, and everyone is happy." He smirked. "And free of criminal records."

"And my parents were just so glad you didn't prosecute...?"

He stroked her hair. "They were tough to take, but I convinced them how much I love you. It wasn't hard. I can't seem to talk about you without my voice cracking." His hand sank deeper in her hair, and he brought his other up so he was gently holding her face. "I told them I was sorry the incident with Jameson had to happen, but not sorry I did it, because I will always defend you."

She trembled, unable to look anywhere but at him, not having any reason to look anywhere else.

"Plus," he said, "I think they were impressed with how hard we worked to re-open. Showed everyone I'm not such a slacker, after all, I guess."

"No one thought that—"

"Yes, they did. It's sort of the rep I've had since high school. But, Candace, we're going to take it slow this time, okay? So you don't get scared again. There's no rush...unless you want there to be. You call the shots. I just want to know that I'll see your face at least once every day. That's my one requirement. I need my sunshine."

"I think we can manage that," she said. She stroked his ringless eyebrow meaningfully. "But tell me this isn't permanent."

"*Hell* no. Are you kidding? I thought it might be important to show you that I'll try to fit in your world as best I can. You do so well at fitting into mine."

"Good. Because the piercings?" She leaned closer, putting her lips so close to his ear she knew the breath of her words tickled it. "They get me hot."

"Fuck," he groaned. "Keep that up and I'll pierce myself shut."

"Well, don't do that. I like you the way you are."

His lips smoothed over her forehead. "Yeah?"

"Oh, yes. And if you don't kiss me soon..."

"Mm. What are you going to do?"

"I have no idea, but it won't be pretty."

"Everything about you is pretty." As gentle as the breeze, his lips skimmed down her nose and landed simply, beautifully, on her own. His thumbs stroked her cheeks as she opened to him, wishing they didn't have to go back in there, wishing they could go straight home so she could love him all night long. But they had that to look forward to.

As they walked toward the house hand-in-hand, he sighed. "I hope this doesn't turn out like *Meet the Parents* on steroids." Candace cracked up laughing as he went on. "Your folks don't have an urn containing mortal remains anywhere near the dining area, do they? Can I ask your dad if I can milk him?"

"Brian!" She smacked him, getting hysterical now.

"Maybe I'll go out on the roof to sneak a smoke and damn

near burn the house down."

"You haven't started smoking again, have you?!"

"Well damn, you've only put me through the wringer these past few weeks. Can you blame me? Don't you still love me?"

"I'll love you no matter what," she said sincerely.

He dropped a kiss on the top of her head. "I'm joking, I haven't had a single drag, and I gotta say, if I made it through this without lighting up, I've got it kicked. Hey! I babysat the other night."

He looked so excited and proud about that, she wanted to eat him up. "You did!"

"Yep. My little nephew. I got puked on, peed on and fussed at, but I also got smiled at a lot too. That was cool. I think he likes me."

"Aww, that's sweet. We should keep him one night and let Evan and Kelsey go on a date."

"I'm making strides and all, but I don't think they trust me enough yet for that."

"Maybe they'll trust me."

"I don't know. I'm not so sure I do."

She looked up at him incredulously. "What?"

"You came over here thinking you were meeting up with some other dude."

Mouth dropping, she stopped in her tracks. "I did not! I came over here for dinner with my parents, that's it. Believe me, they're constantly foisting guys on me in one situation or another, it's not anything new. I just ignore it as best I can."

Brian caught her by her chin and put his lips close to her ear. Anticipation shivered through her, her arms going around him by instinct. "I'm kidding, sweetie. But I can tell you now, those days are over."

Oh, thank God for that. She certainly wasn't going to bemoan their passing.

Chapter Twenty-three

"Ohmigod, ohmigod, ohmigod..."

"Candace, relax."

"I can't!"

"Breathe, honey."

"Screw your breathing. I'm doing nothing *but* breathing."

"It's too much. Slow and deep, in through your nose, out through your mouth. You're going to be fine."

She tried to obey, but ended up covering her face with her hands as Brian moved into position over her. "No. Get away."

"You wanted this. You asked for it. You're gonna get it."

"I can't change my mind?"

With a fond expression that looked more than a little exasperated, he glanced down at her. "Is that what you want? To get up from here knowing you let fear win out?"

She shook her head, whimpering.

"It's going to be so fuckin' hot. You'll love it and you'll want me to do more."

Hearing him talk like that as he loomed over her started a melting in her belly. She couldn't resist reaching out and touching his arm, trailing her hand up his elbow and under the sleeve of his dark blue T-shirt. Memories of last night shivered through her mind. "I always want more."

"God, ain't that the truth." His Latex-covered hands put the clamp on her belly button.

"Ohmigod, ohmigod..."

He gave an abrupt, harsh "Shh."

"Hold my hand!"

"I can't, I need both of mine. But I can get you the pussyball, if you want it."

"The *what*?!"

The laughter that burst out of him sent shivers through her despite everything.

"Get Starla," she snapped. "*She'll* hold my hand, and not give me any lip about it." He rolled his eyes. She snorted and muttered, "Pussyball. Whatever."

With a snicker, he turned his head toward the door and hollered for the other girl. Then he gave a sad shake of his head. "Fraidy cat."

"You hush."

He leaned over and gave her a brief, sweet kiss that had her going up in flames there on the table, even as it soothed her ragged nerves. "I'd hold your hand if I could."

"I know," she whispered back, just as a loud "ahem" sounded from the door.

"Am I needed?" Starla asked. She'd dyed her whole head hot pink. Candace loved it, but she'd never have the guts to do anything like that.

"Hold my hand, please. In fact, hold both of them."

Laughing, she moved to Candace's other side and took both her hands into her warm ones. "Don't be scared. He's good and he's quick. The guy who did mine seemed to take for-freaking-ever."

"Great."

"I'm going to tell you to take a deep breath, and let it out," he said. "When you do, I'll push it through." She didn't want to look down at what he was doing, she just felt him moving the clamps on her belly button. And damn if she didn't want to arch up into his hands, but she couldn't very well do that now. Maybe she shouldn't have requested Starla's assistance, after all. Suddenly, all movement paused.

"Ready?" he asked.

"No."

"Deep breath."

Oh, God. She took the plunge and drew it in, knowing there was no way out now. She could hold it until she was blue in the face, but eventually, she'd have to let go.

"Let it go, baby." The warmth and humor and love in his voice were what did it, reminding her that she trusted him absolutely. And letting go was the very thing he represented in her life. She didn't even pause; she let the air rush from her lungs, gave it all to him. It was more of a sigh.

A sharp, precise agony flared at the site where his hands were, and was gone as quickly as it had come. "Oh," she breathed, glad it had only lasted an instant. Brief as it was, it left her shaken, a bizarre languor washing through her. It wasn't unlike the moments after he'd given her a particularly strong orgasm, when she collapsed in utter bliss and exhaustion.

"She barely flinched," Starla said proudly, letting go of her hands and patting her shoulder.

Brian was still intent upon his work, threading her jewelry through the piercing. She had to grit her teeth a few times during the process, but he was quick and, before she knew it, it was all over. "There. See, you came out on the other side. Are you okay?"

She closed her eyes and smiled. "Wasn't so bad."

"You can lie there for a few minutes, if you want. I'll get you something to drink." He stripped off his gloves and trashed them. "Thanks, Star."

"Sure thing. Congratulations, Candace. It's beautiful."

"Thank you."

The two went out, and she lifted her head to look down at the shiny silver sun winking from her belly button. It *was* beautiful. That he'd put it there for her made it even more so. A second later, he came back in with drinks and helped her sit up on the table before popping the tab on one and handing it to her.

"I love it," she told him. "Thank you."

He smiled. "Now, about aftercare."

"Uh-oh."

"I'm just saying. If the lucky guy happens to come along in the next few weeks, you need to be creative. Because other people's sweat is bad, bad, bad."

She put her arms around him, drawing him in and spreading her knees apart so he could have room. "Ooh, I think I like the sound of the being creative part." His lips dipped in to taste hers. Once. Twice. His hands went to her hips, then slid under her baby tee.

"Can't be creative in here, though," he warned. "I'm a stickler for sanitation, and well, you know."

"Later?" she whispered, nibbling his ear.

His hands stroked down to her bare thighs, fingertips teasing around the hem of her shorts. "You don't even have to ask."

"Brian, your mom is on the phone."

Damn. Why didn't he have a client under his needle right now? Then he wouldn't feel bad about rejecting the call.

"Throw it here," he said, finishing up sending Candace a dirty text message in reply to the equally dirty one she'd just sent him.

"Are you sexting again?" Janelle demanded. "Cut it out. Go home and do the real thing. We've got this." She gave the phone an underhanded toss in his direction.

"Thanks for bellowing that out with my *mother* on the line," he muttered, lifting it to his ear. "Hey, Mom."

If there was one thing that could be said about Gianna Ross, she was to the point. "Why have you been holding out on me?"

Oh, crap. He gave a nervous laugh. "Which part?"

"Who is the blonde I saw leaving your apartment the other morning?"

He made a *tsk* sound. "Spying on me. For shame."

"Absolutely not. I was driving past on my way to town. I thought I might've been mistaken, but I'm pretty sure I wasn't. She came out of your door."

"You weren't. She's my girlfriend."

She gasped in excitement. "A girlfriend! Never heard you commit to calling one a girlfriend. Don't make me ask again who she is."

"I figured you knew. Evan knows, and I was always under the assumption that you two share a brain."

"Ah. It's no surprise that I can't count on you to tell me anything, but now he's *really* going to get it."

He grinned, and now that he stopped to think about it, was kind of looking forward to how happy his mother was going to be when she learned who he was seeing. "It's Candace Andrews."

She was silent for a moment. "Oh, Brian. *Candace Andrews*?"

What the fuck? She should've lapsed into paroxysms of joy to hear he'd fallen for someone so sweet and nice and just generally good for him. What the hell was wrong with all these people? "Don't tell me I'm going to hear it from you, now. What's wrong with her?"

"Nothing at all. I don't know her well, but she seems lovely. It's the thought of dealing with her *mother* through the wedding and the births and the birthday parties that worries me."

A few months ago, those words would have made him choke. Now they seemed like inevitable truths. But still. "Don't you think you're getting ahead of yourself?"

"No, not at all. Mainly because I know your dad so well."

"What does that have to do with anything?"

"You probably don't want to hear it, but you are so much like him that it scares me. Sometimes it takes you a while to find a purpose, but once you do, you're unstoppable. Just like him. I knew when it finally happened for you, it would be forever. You wouldn't let it be any other way. It's your nature.

How do you think he convinced me to move halfway around the world to be with him? The man has powers of persuasion."

"Yeah, well. You need to behave yourself around her mother. I've already assaulted one member of the family. I can't have you assaulting another."

"Who on earth did you assault?"

"Her brother. It's a long story. But it's all okay now."

"Well, that's good. But I don't get physical, dear. If she rubs me wrong, I'll simply ask her how her tryst with the new tennis instructor at the country club is going."

Brian had been strolling toward his office in the back to continue this conversation. At her words, he stopped dead in his tracks. "*Really.*"

"Oh, yes. So you keep that useful tidbit of information handy. Never know when you might need it."

"So we're resorting to blackmail now?" He laughed. "You're slightly evil. Maybe I should've called you way back at the start of all this."

His mom sighed. "Yes, you should have. Maybe you'll keep that in mind from now on."

"I'll try."

"Good. Now when are you bringing her over to meet us? You realize you're not off the hook, just because your brother gave me a grandbaby. They're moving away. So we need to rush this along."

He had to suppress a shudder, thinking about how close he had come to losing her. "Trust me, Mom, the last thing we need to do is rush."

Later that night, after letting himself in to his apartment, he found her already in his bed with the covers pulled up. Ordinarily she would wait up for him until whatever time he walked in the door from work, but lately she'd been trying to get her schedule back on track. School was starting up for her soon, and she had a few early morning classes.

They both kept their own places, but in the couple of months they'd been together—finally, truly *together*—he thought he could count on one hand the number of nights they'd spent apart. On those nights, he'd found he didn't sleep well no matter how tired he was. Without her tucked against him, he was restless. She'd become a very grounding, calming force in his life. The eye to his hurricane.

He showered and slipped into bed, drawing her close, though he didn't want to wake her. Oh, he did a little, just to see what sort of mischief they could get up to, but she needed her sleep.

She mumbled sweetly and nestled against him, her backside snuggling against his groin. Of course, it responded accordingly. "Hi."

He leaned over and placed a kiss beneath her ear. "Hi, yourself."

"I got sleepy." The sexy, drowsy purr of her voice didn't bode well for his leaving her alone and letting her sleep.

"It's okay." He slid his fingertips very gently over the area of her navel. "How is it?"

"A little sore, but good. I love it."

"I told you."

"I know you did."

"Maybe you'll learn to listen to me someday," he teased, and she gave his arm around her a playful smack.

"It's like everything else in my life, I guess," she said after a moment. "Even with you. I worry and I stress and I freak out over everything. But once I let go and get through it...it's beautiful."

"I'll always do what I can to make sure it's beautiful in the end, sunshine. No matter what it is we have to get through." He chckled. "And on that note, my parents want to meet you this weekend."

She responded with that girly giggle that never failed to summon every iota of testosterone in his body and send it raging. "Oh, no. We're not starting all over, are we? What if they hate me?"

"I'm really concerned that they might. I guess I'll just have to let you go if—"

He burst out laughing as she twisted in his arms and shoved him onto his back, rising up to straddle his hips. "You deserve to be punished for that one. Severely."

"Do your worst, baby. *Please.*"

She stared down at him, her pretty eyes twinkling in the dim light. "Give me a minute while I decide your punishment. It must be slow and torturous." She ran her hands down his arms, leaning over to follow one of them with her mouth. Shit, he loved that his ink drove her so wild. It made him want to get more. And here he'd thought he was done.

She drew away, lifting so she could look at him. "Your family seems a lot cooler than mine. We should totally blow their minds. Maybe I ought to dye my hair purple, just for that occasion."

He grinned like a fool. With each passing day, she proved more and more she was a girl after his own heart. She loved horror movies. She loved his music. His body art. She'd even get down and dirty in a mosh pit with him.

But beyond all that superficial, surface stuff, she challenged him, she drove him, she opened his eyes to everything that was beautiful in the world, everything he'd always overlooked before.

Why God had seen fit to smile upon him in such a way, Brian would never know.

Candace leaned down to nibble his shoulder, and against the softness of her coconut-scented hair, he smiled. "And there's always that Mohawk I've been considering..."

About the Author

If Cherrie Lynn's parents are to be believed, she's been writing since before she can remember. Through her formative years, her stories evolved from epic graphic novels about dragons and unicorns to middle school angst-inspired teen soap operas. Once she discovered her mom's romance novels, she finally found her place.

She adores electronic gadgets, heavy metal, gaming, and horror movies. You can often find her traveling far and wide to catch her favorite rock acts live, but she's much too fragile to go near a mosh pit.

Cherrie lives in Texas with her husband and two kids. She loves hearing from readers, so drop her a line at cherrie@cherrielynn.com or visit her at www.cherrielynn.com.

CPSIA information can be obtained at www.ICGtesting.com
Printed in the USA
LVOW11s0255021214

416608LV00001B/92/P

9 781609 280802